TREADING WATER

TREADING WATER

Claire Collison

This edition published in Great Britain in 2005 by
Polygon, an imprint of Birlinn Ltd
West Newington House
10 Newington Road
Edinburgh
EH9 1QS

www.birlinn.co.uk

ISBN 1 904598 41 2

British Library Cataloguing-in-Publication Data
A catalogue record for this book is available
on request from the British Library

Typeset by Hewer Text Ltd, Edinburgh

For Ginni

Acknowledgements

Huge thanks to:
Everyone at the Dundee Book Prize and Polygon,
for letting me get a foot in the door.
Judith Murray, for her advice and encouragement.
Rob, for the weekly meets; Piers, for his generosity;
Sarah, for being a great reader; Patrick, for keeping the faith;
and my friends and family, who know parts of this story,
for their continued love, support and indulgence.

What Have You Lost?

I dreamed I was eating a giant marshmallow. When I woke up my pillow was gone.

Tommy Cooper

What have you lost?
I have lost my innocence
I have lost my figure
I have lost my appetite
I have lost my confidence
I have lost my keys
I have lost my sense of perspective
I have lost my sense of smell.

It wasn't the first time Alison had played this as she swam up and down the pool at the Brixton Rec. The chlorine stinging her eyes, she changed course to avoid the lap Nazi who pounded towards her, and made herself do a final length of crawl, her least favourite stroke.

I have lost my memory
I have lost my temper
I have lost my favourite earrings
I have lost my sense of humour
I have lost consciousness
I have lost a bet
I have lost my cat

Thick blue nylon rope divided the pool into thirds. The lane nearest the changing rooms was 'fast' and the middle lane was 'slow'. Arrows directed you to swim clockwise. The third lane had no instructions. Alison always swam in the third lane. The truth was that although she enjoyed the freedom of being able to stop mid-lap and just float or tread water for a while, she would be hard pushed to classify herself as fast or slow. It depended. She held onto the edge of the pool, looking out of the window, across the railway track with its clumsy bronze statues of people waiting for trains that never arrived. Beyond the platform, rooftops slung with washing lines. Pegs like ossified birds swung to and fro.

In the gym above the pool, people on treadmills walked nowhere. The 'No Petting, No Dive Bombing' poster displayed on the wall was – amazingly – the same one that Alison remembered from her childhood. Before, it had been funny in the way that it was so blatantly disregarded. Now it was merely anachronistic in a place that seemed to have already shaken off any associations with fun. You swim to de-stress; you work out to live longer. Swimming had changed in her lifetime, Alison thought. She remembered a painting she'd seen at the Tate: a swimming pool full of turquoise, chlorinated noise. Above all, it was the noise of the painting that she remembered; that din of the baths.

The floor was slimy when she heaved herself out, and she imagined verruca viruses breeding in the warmth and wetness, as inviting as agar jelly in a Petri dish. She padded back to the changing room and retrieved her stuff from the locker. As she headed to the showers, she thought about that cat.

On her way to the Rec, she'd seen a poster for a lost cat. A pathetic black-and-white A4 photocopy that had got soggy in the rain, the words were written in loopy seventies bubble writing filled in with scribbled Biro. Underneath was a photograph the size of a large stamp. Alison had studied it. The black-and-white cat looked supercilious, the kind who would lash out. Alison disliked cats, but nevertheless she had to congratulate herself on this little show of resilience. Time was when that would have reduced her to floods. That's the thing with grief; it unhinges your judgement. You find yourself no longer exercising the discretion of where, when, and how you emote. It decides.

What have you lost?
I have lost my sense of decorum
I have lost my mother.

Rescue Remedy

Beth's List
If I had to describe Jo as a building, it would be a beach bar
Alison would be a post office
Hannah a town hall

Hannah's List
If I had to describe Beth as a building, it would be a wisteria-covered summerhouse
Alison would be a tree house

Alison's List
If I had to describe Hannah as an animal, it would be a gazelle
Beth would be a lioness
Jo a squirrel
I would be a dog

Beth's funeral took place on a sunny day outside her home in Andalucía. Her friends and family arrived with flowers which were placed around her coffin in the shape of a heart. Her sister broke down as she read a passage from *Little Women*. Her best friend had consumed an entire bottle of Rescue Remedy and read clearly, with a deputy head's authority.

Alison was one of the pallbearers who carried her away to the sound of Bob Marley's 'No Woman No Cry', as Beth had requested. Alison's friend, a DJ, was in charge of the ghetto blaster. He had to switch the tape off abruptly before the next song, Gloria Gaynor's 'I Will Survive'.

3

Fishy

'Mummy, do fish die if you touch them?'

Hannah looked up from the sink. She had a matter of seconds to read Jo's expression. Her daughter was a study in nonchalance, from her refusal to make eye contact as she fixed her stare on a postcard pinned to the fridge door, to the way she twisted the corner of a tea towel as if she didn't trust her hands. All this fitted with the indifference of her voice, betrayed by only the tiniest catch, which Hannah knew meant she was bluffing.

Those fish. They were to blame for the macaroni-cheese-encrusted Pyrex she was scouring right now. Since their arrival, the connection between fish and food had been made. Irrevocably. Cause and effect had kicked in, and she and Jacques had to face the fact that they had unwittingly reared a little vegetarian.

Hannah put down her Brillo pad. 'Why?' she asked. 'Did you touch them?'

'No-o.'

That telltale catch again. Why did these life-changing moments just drop on you like this? One of the reasons – indeed some (Hannah) might say the only reason – for keeping a fish was to introduce your child gently to the concept of mortality: you get fish; you love fish; fish dies. It is buried in the garden under a couple of wooden ice-lolly sticks fashioned into a cross. In the early days, you leave a little posy of flowers in a jam jar on the grave each morning before school. Time is a great healer, and fish owners have short memories. Gradually, things return to normal. Finally the day

5

arrives when you come across the goldfish bowl in the garage next to a half-empty bottle of white spirit, and customise it into a space helmet for one of your dolls without even flinching. You have now been initiated. Gained without too much pain. That's what's supposed to happen.

Hannah scowled into the suds. The problem was she wanted the first time to be perfect. That sounded ridiculous. But Molly's card had been marked from the start. The two fish had been bought from the Brighton Asda only a week earlier. Hannah was old enough both to marvel and to despair at the concept of buying anything from fish to barbecue briquettes under one roof. They had been selected from the tank by Jo, fished out by a young lad with rotten skin, and transferred into a plastic bag. For fifteen pounds you got the whole kit: bowl, gravel and a little brown plastic bridge which out of water looked like a fake turd. The spotty boy had shown Jo how much of the food to sprinkle on the water. 'But not too much,' he said, pinching the mixture between finger and thumb, 'or they'll eat an' eat until they pop.' The full responsibility of having a pet was revealing itself to Jo, and she rose to the challenge, listening intently and absorbing all the new information.

The question of their gender was never really discussed; they were fish with girls' names rather than girl fish. Molly and Polly. Molly, the smaller of the pair, had been lack-lustre from the start, and as soon as they were home Polly, with a healthy survivor's instinct, had proceeded to butt her bowl-mate, who did nothing to protect herself. The spectacle was brutal, and made more so by the distorting fish-eye lens of the glass bowl, warping the action that swilled above the pink gravel floor of their fight pit. Jo watched this gruesome display like some reality television show, transfixed as Polly mercilessly pursued the sickly Molly through the shipwreck bridge, buffeting her up against the glass.

And now Jo was blaming herself. This wasn't going the way

Hannah had planned. Not at all. She wiped her hands on the tea towel that Jo still held, and sat down.

'Well, if you were a fish, can you imagine what a blooming great finger would look like?'

Jo tried to smile, but it was the Brave Soldier face, which could turn on a sixpence to tears.

Hannah tried again. 'I don't think it's a good idea to touch them, but it wouldn't make them die, sweetheart.'

Jo looked unconvinced and Hannah was mad at herself. Why couldn't she tell her the truth: the fish would die, but not through anyone's fault.

4

Donkey's Tail

The phone rang: 'May I speak to Mrs Vine?'

Alison flinched at the Mrs, but didn't correct her.

'Speaking.'

'Good morning! I'm calling you from American Life.'

For a moment, Alison thought it might be work. *Life* magazine? A commission? 'Yes?'

'Here at American Life, we're trying to raise awareness of female cancer.'

Alison said nothing.

The woman continued. She had a trace of an accent. Scottish.

'As I'm sure you're aware, female cancer in the under-fifties is on the increase. Are you under fifty, Mrs Vine?'

'Yes.' She didn't hear what the woman went on to say, but felt an old exhaustion as she interrupted her. 'Are you trying to sell me insurance?' she asked.

'Er, yes.'

'No, thank you.'

'OK. Thanks. Goodbye.'

Alison switched off her laptop. She'd been pushing the same sentence around the screen for the past half hour, like the last forkful of food on a plate. Ever since the phone call. She looked out of the window and noticed the geraniums on the ledge. They were parched. That was enough of an excuse. She found the watering can, filled it from the shower-hose in the bathroom and carried it outside, leaving a trail of drips along the corridor.

Like Mickey Rooney and Judy Garland, she'd decided that instead of waiting for the country cottage she should embrace the small strip of balcony on the first floor of her nineteen-thirties flat in Brixton, and just get on with it – put the show on right here. In truth, she knew she'd hate to live in English countryside: the prettier the place, the uglier the people. Hannah and Jacques had settled on Brighton, but she needed a bit of grit. Brixton by the sea would be nice, maybe Barcelona. But for now it was love the one you're with, and it felt good to settle into something. Not much grew easily, but the honeysuckle was progressing on its journey round the front door, and the jasmine was leafy, even if short on flowers. Nasturtiums were effortless, though prone to caterpillars, and the lily of the valley, a present from Hannah, had multiplied to fill an old coalscuttle.

A single length of donkey's tail dangled over the edge of a six-inch pot. Alison carefully poured in water. 'American Life, bollocks,' she muttered as the water seeped into the saucer. This was the cutting she'd wrapped in damp cotton wool and laid carefully in a Tupperware box to bring back from Spain, where they cascaded like dreadlocks from planters attached to the whitewashed walls. Beth would regularly snap off a length if anyone admired them, offering vague instructions: just stick it in some soil, it's no trouble, it should take easily. They were green-grape green with the same matt bloom; minty green ropes of juicy beads that she could propagate with no effort at all. She could grow things so easily. Tumours as well, it transpired.

Opening the A3 folder, Alison pulls out Beth's X-rays. Pegged on consultants' walls, they have been disseminated; used as illustration and justification. Internal landscapes of bone and blood. She finds the mammogram and holds it up to the light.

Left breast, right breast.

She can see through the X-ray, through her living-room window and out into the garden. The leaves on the far tree that smells of buckwheat when it rains are swaying on a breeze; swaying through the filaments of matter, the motes of dust and the smeared windowpane. She picks up the scissors and separates left from right, then turns the two pieces round. Using a long strip of Sellotape, she joins them together again, a hemisphere. A moon. A planet of milk and blood and love and tissue.

5

Mother-of-Pearl

Hannah's toes peeped out from the lavender-scented water, and she manipulated the tap with them to add more hot. The dexterity of her feet had always been a source of pride to her. Under the water's surface, her legs looked mottled. She bent her knees as she sank down, her body squeaking against the enamel. With her head submerged, she let out measured breath through pursed lips, whistling a chain of small bubbles. This was what you were meant to do if you had a panic attack. Not that she was. This, or blow into a paper bag. The water tugged at her hair as she lifted her head again. She reached for the bar of soap. It sat on a mother-of-pearl shell in a pool of its own slippy juices. Hannah had been given the shell when she was Jo's age.

It had taken two stories and a cassette of nursery rhymes to get Jo to sleep tonight, as she lay squashed into the space between her dolls. Hannah remembered what it was like being in bed before dark on late summer evenings; the noises from the garden heard through the open bedroom window. As she was conjuring up those sounds, she heard a key in the lock downstairs. Jacques. She knew both his habits and the layout of their home so well that she could tell exactly where he was and what he was doing. It was a skill that still spooked him. She heard him put down his stuff on a chair, enter the kitchen and look in the bread bin. He cut himself two slices of the loaf she'd bought that morning. After rummaging in the fridge and making a sandwich, he looked through the post that had arrived after he had left, and turned on the television, flicking through the channels while eating his sandwich. He switched it off, put his plate in the sink, and climbed the stairs. He pushed open the door to Jo's room and looked in on his daughter. After a moment he pulled the door almost to – just as Jo insisted it must be.

'D'you think she could fit a few more dolls in there with her?'

He sat on the edge of the bath at the tap end, clasping Hannah's ankle. She placed her free foot over his hand, anchoring him.

'Tell you what, that bastard fish is going to break her heart.'

In the hall, Hannah and Jacques had their faces pressed against the glass bowl. Molly was unravelling in front of their eyes. Bits of white-flecked scales seemed to be coming loose. Her mouth opened and closed; slack, unfocused. Polly looked positively sleek in comparison; she kissed her reflection, nibbling the food balanced on the water's surface, pulling it down through the membrane that divided the elements. Jacques rubbed the small of Hannah's back.

'I remember when I first came to England. I was round at someone's house, and they invited me outside to show me the goldfish pond. I went into the garden expecting to see something extraordinary, something magnificent and royal: golden fish! They were just ordinary orange fish.'

'What are they called in French?'

'Orange fish.'

'You must have felt terribly cheated.' Hannah shuddered. 'I don't think I can watch much more of this.'

Molly sheltered under the bridge, Polly circling her. Hannah was loath to lumber the fish with human characteristics – all that Disney crap – but it was difficult not to. Bullying is a human thing: fish just do what fish have to do. She knew this, but it made for ugly viewing. She walked through to the kitchen and Jacques followed.

'Would it be wrong to replace it with a Molly Mark Two?' As she spoke, Hannah was conscious that Molly had become 'it'. She felt cowardly, but pulled herself together. It was a stupid, dud fish. She continued, 'You could pick it up from Asda tomorrow; switch them over by the time Jo gets home. She'd never know.' Jacques said nothing. He studied Hannah. 'I know it's pathetic, and I promise, when they die a natural death after a reasonable time, we'll do the burial and mourning stuff, but not yet.'

He was silent because there was too much to say. This distress at a sick fish was something that could be remedied. The layers of grief that could unravel and leave her as raw as sushi would be less easy. They were complicit in this.

'I finish at four,' he said. 'You'll have to keep her occupied till I can switch them.'

6

Dorothy

The 'Back to School!' posters were already plastered across the windows of Woolworth's. Alison saw them from upstairs on the 159 bus as it crawled along Brixton High Street. They still made her queasy. And the marketing always started weeks before the holidays were due to end, like some miserable parent saying, 'This holiday lark is all very well, but . . .' She felt a pang of sympathy for Jo, even though as far as she was aware Jo loved school, and she made a mental note to send her something. Not a furry pencil case or a Barbie lunch box or anything like that; something completely un-school. She wondered what.

Between the bus stops across the road, she could see a woman holding a young boy in position on the kerb as he peed into a drain. So much easier with boys. Beth used to hold her expertly in a floating squat, legs akimbo, never a splash on her shoes. Or if they were caught short on a journey (and they always were) she would open the front and back doors on the verge side, creating a private cubicle for her or Hannah.

Years later in Spain, she and Beth had been reeling back from some party. A Fourth of July celebration serving only cava and peanuts, everyone dressed in red, white and blue. Awful. Alison had got so plastered she'd told the assembled company, 'Yo soy Dorothy Lamour.' Escaping, staggering down steep Moorish streets, they'd found an alley where they both squatted down to pee.

'Watch out, mine's coming towards you.'

A warm yellow stream trickling past Alison, negotiating little pebbles and bits of grit, finding the tributary of her own stream, forming a piss river.

When they went to the far beach at Manacar, Alison always knew when Beth was having a wee. She'd sit in the shallow water, where the waves reached. Her hands at her sides, making arcs in the sand, or examining with extreme interest some pebble or shell, the sublime smile of concentration and affected nonchalance.

At the hospital they would do their music hall number, their Flanagan and Allen routine, walking from bed to bathroom. Beth holding onto her shoulders as Alison wheeled the drip, their steps in time, both humming 'Underneath the Arches'. Later still, the sound of heavy rainfall on the plastic skylight had exactly mimicked the sound of urine on bedpan. They had both remarked on the fact.

7

Brown Bread

The supermarket was fluorescent bright. Scanning the contents of the aquarium, the realisation washed over Jacques that he had very little idea of what Molly looked like. Relativity suddenly became something very practical and particular: he knew the one fish only in relation to the other. All around him, people were pushing trolleys, choosing one type of cereal over another without any doubt or anxiety. An instrumental version of 'Your Cheatin' Heart' was playing in the background. Jacques blinked hard, mesmerised by the air bubbles streaming through the tank; the wispy, shimmering marmalade creatures darting past his eyes. He was convinced that whatever choice he made would be wrong. Why did people consider keeping fish to be a calming activity? Concentrate. Think. All he could say for sure was that Molly was smaller than Polly, paler than Polly, and had darker eye markings than Polly. He pointed to the fish that least resembled Polly.

The man serving him scooped a ladle of water from the tank to add to the displaced fish, like adding brine to an order of olives at the deli counter. He knotted the polythene bag and handed it to Jacques. Second Molly sloshed about like a prize at the funfair, without the fun or the fair.

'Don't forget, it'll need a good half-hour in the bag before you stick it in with any others.'

Damn. How could he forget? He'd never known. And he'd certainly not allowed for the extra time.

Hannah was on her way to collect Jo from a friend's when he called.

'What do you mean, "acclimatise"?'

'That's what you have to do, apparently. The water temperatures need to match.'

'OK, we'll hang around here.'

'Hannah?'

'What?'

'What should I do with First Molly?'

'Oh God, I don't know. Look, I've got to go. See you at five.'

She hung up. Holding the plastic bag carefully, he slipped the phone back in his pocket. A kid in a baseball cap watched him as he stepped from the bus.

Double-locking the front door, he checked the time. Twenty past four. He placed the bag gently in the empty sink, opened the kitchen drawer and rummaged through the cutlery. The silver tea strainer with its own stand that he'd bought in a second-hand shop when he still lived in Paris. He wasn't sure what had made him buy it, still less why he'd packed it when he moved in with Hannah. Perhaps, he considered, because it had been some kind of sign that he was destined to live in this country of tea drinkers. He found it and ran through to the hall. Molly was not well, but nor was she dead. Jacques rolled up his sleeve and scooped her out with the tea strainer. She offered little resistance. Cupping his left hand underneath to catch the drips, he charged up the stairs. Kneeling over the toilet, he flipped the fish into the water in the white porcelain bowl. He flushed the chain, praying that she would disappear. She did. He ran back down to the kitchen, picked up the bag and walked to the hall, squashing the entire thing into the neck of the bowl. The water level rose, sloshing over the sides. When he returned with a cloth, Polly had come over to investigate. Second Molly looked like a boil-in-the-bag kipper, and First Molly was brown bread dead.

There was just enough time for a shower. Jacques stood with his eyes closed, letting the water hammer on his neck. He felt an intense

17

sadness. It was to do with the hurry: there had been no time to say goodbye. He thought about all the goodbyes he'd ever said. And those he hadn't. This is what happens, he realised as the water washed over him; each new loss, no matter how tiny and inconsequential, is added to the pile. Loss is cumulative as well as specific, and we accrue grief.

Five to five. Jacques undid the bag and pulled the polythene out of the bowl. He had just unlocked the front door and washed his hands when he heard Hannah's car. Jo made straight for the bowl. Hannah walked through to the kitchen and Jacques gave her a thumbs-up. She smiled and walked over to him. As they kissed, there was a shriek from the hall. They ran through.

'What is it?'

'Look!'

Jo was shiny-eyed. They all peered into the bowl. Second Molly swooped up from the bridge and circled Polly; paler, darker-eyed, and twice her size.

8

Sump

'Did Jo suspect foul play?'

'Hannah's not sure. They just said Molly had been eating up all her food and it had made her big and strong – or strig and bong, as we used to say.'

Alison and Bill were standing in a wedge of space, a cartoon cheese portion of space reversed out of a hip-high lake of glossy black oil in a gallery in Swiss Cottage. The oil filled the rest of the room, starkly level against the white walls. Two sheets of aluminium joined in a point were all that separated them from it. The stench filled their nostrils, industrial and sour. The rafters above them reflected in the molten lead surface, quivering with refracted light.

'Have you and Hannah decided on a date to do the ashes?' Bill asked.

'Not exactly.'

Alison watched as a filament of dandelion clock danced on the air just above the oil's surface. Bill was one of the few people she didn't mind asking the question that had been hanging over this past year and a half. When was she going to move on? That was what most people meant by it. But she knew Bill wasn't asking like that, and that he could cope with her answer.

She had learned that the world separated into the bereaved and the not. Bill was in that club whose membership is as clearly defined to those belonging to it as any secret society – a mere nod, a weary look, a thin smile proof enough. When Alison had first found herself about to become a member, she had wanted to shout in public places, 'Do you not realise? Has it not occurred to you that your parents will die?' She wanted to tell people who sat obliviously, drinking coffee, 'You will be orphaned and you will not be ready. Not ever.' Why had she not known this before? But she had quickly realised that closing one's eyes, covering one's ears and humming, in the hope that the whole thorny issue will somehow disappear, is part of it: it is only revealed on a need-to-know basis. For the survival of the species, she supposed. She tried to recall exactly when she could contemplate starting a sentence which didn't contain the words 'dead' and 'mother'. She pitied and loved her friends who had stuck by her through that. But even they had their limits, and she worried they would suffer bereavement fatigue. The fact of the matter was she couldn't move on until Hannah was ready. They had to do this together. Alison was stuck. She was sick of talking about it. She knew she could lean on Bill, only sometimes it was nice not to. Knowing she could was enough.

They filed out of the installation, relieved to be in the airy space of the main gallery, and stood in front of a large colour photograph. It showed a flabby woman in a grubby slip. She was slumped forward, studying the surface of a table. On it was a spew of jigsaw-puzzle pieces. Dislocated. Alison squirmed. They moved along, pausing to see the various characters inhabiting a room somewhere they'd never been and were unlikely ever to go. They walked through the gallery, not commenting on the photographs, but each glad of the other's presence.

'I can't stand jigsaws,' Alison said, breaking the silence.

'Me neither.'

The pub was their favourite kind: seedy and unfucked-about-with. Although it was still mid-afternoon, there were a fair number of drinkers at the wooden tables. Shafts of pure light poured through the windows almost religiously, cutting through the smog of cigarette smoke, and making Alison feel wicked.

'I should be working,' she announced to Bill.

'What are you up to?'

'A spot of porn.'

'How fabulously post-fem of you.'

'Actually, porn's a bit strong. It's more erotica, I suppose.'

'What's the definition? Erotica uses a feather, pornography the whole chicken.'

Alison snorted Guinness. 'Definitely feathers, then. How about you? What should you be doing?'

Bill was art correspondent for a London listings magazine.

'Writing up the Whiteread. Have you seen it yet?'

'No; is it any good?'

'I think so. She started making her best stuff after her dad died, did you know?'

'No.'

Bill poured the remnants of Guinness froth into his mouth and licked his lips.

'When I was at college, we did this exercise in life drawing, looking at negative spaces.'

'Sounds a bit hippy; like negative vibes?'

'No, not like negative vibes.'

Alison smiled. She could wind Bill up so easily when he got serious about art. She opened a packet of cheese and onion crisps, split the bag and sat back, pouring a handful into her mouth.

Bill scowled at her. 'Basically,' he said, 'instead of looking at the form, you look at the spaces it makes. Whiteread does that. She'll mould the inside of a hot-water bottle, or cast the space under a bed. They're really simple and beautiful.'

'Sorry to be thick, but what did her dad's death have to do with it?'

'They're negative spaces; they're what's missing.'

9

Passion

This is like being inside a huge breast, Alison thought as she lay back on the picnic rug in the Albert Hall; a single, Amazon's breast. Above her, the nipple of the dome was just visible. Beneath was a curious array of white platelets suspended on a system of rigging, for the acoustics, she presumed. They looked like flying saucers in a B movie. The place was such a hotch-potch of the ornate and the practical. The fat bunch of electrical cables running the circumference of the gallery behind the dry-blood red of the railings; the chintzy light fittings on the veined marble pillars. If this is a breast, we are in the areola.

She and Bill had queued for two hours to prom it for the *St Matthew Passion*. Not just because it was such a bargain; she much preferred the atmosphere up in the gods. All around them, people were getting ready; settling down against the pillars with books and embroidery, or unpacking picnics. Bill had already opened a couple of tubs of olives and now he opened the Chablis with his portable corkscrew and poured it into two stainless-steel tumblers. Alison propped herself up to take one from him.

'Cheers, my dear,' she whispered, clinking metal against metal.

In fact, she thought, there was an inverse relationship between how much you paid and how good a time you had. The most expensive seats were the most miserable – the corporate entertainment boxes for people who bought compilations called things like *Smooth Classics for Rough Days*. Alison wondered if there would be a follow-up, *Rough Classics for Smooth Days*. The really depressing thing was, there probably would.

The audience grew quiet. Alison watched through the banisters as the orchestra tuned up. Bill studied the programme notes. The choir poured themselves into tidy rows, making Alison think of school. The conductor raised his baton.

There is something so . . . *sense-stuffing* about watching music being performed, Alison thought, and she craved having her senses stuffed. Did that mean she accessed her emotions completely, or sublimated them completely? She didn't know. She'd always been a sensualist, a hedonist, an addictive personality type, according to the self-help books. Excess. You always have to go too far. She'd wanted her senses filled to the brim when she'd been nursing Beth; wanted to close her eyes and sink to the bottom of the sea, to drink herself to sleep, smoke till her lungs hurt, fuck her brains out. To turn the stereo up until she could feel the music vibrating in her solar plexus, to dance until she fell over. Anything but to feel the sadness.

She watched now, watched and listened. Filled her eyes and her ears. The synchronised movements of the choir as they silently turned the pages, a seamless white wave; the sawing motion of the cellists' elbows, and the sound that relayed a split second later, making more sense of the physics of light and sound than any teacher had been able to. She watched the conductor's back as he gesticulated in a code she found impenetrable, as his arms lifted and fell again, like bellows. She was glad she couldn't understand German: the words bypassed her intellect and went straight to her gut, leaving her free to bathe in the sound pictures. Bill followed the translation in the programme, and the flutter as he turned the page echoed as the pages of all the programmes in the hall were turned.

She lay back again, letting the music wash over her. Why did it make her so sad? Think so much of Beth? Knowing how much she'd have enjoyed this, for a start. What a kick it would have given her. That had been such a regular source of sadness over the past eighteen months. All the times she felt happy had been compounded by the knowledge that Beth couldn't share it; 'Oh, Mum would have loved this' the bitter sweet thought that accompanied any pleasure – a film, an exhibition, a good meal, a joke. And Beth had such a capacity for enjoying herself. A unique capacity. But it keyed into the grief, too, this sublime noise.

It is Good Friday. The procession leaves the church, and Alison finds herself tagging along behind. The band that came by coach from somewhere else plays sad strange music on sad strange instruments, and the statues of Mary and Jesus are carried from the church on the shoulders of men. Lumbering painted plaster, they teeter precariously.

If Beth were here they'd be respectful, but they'd probably giggle, too; find a bar for a drink after it had moved out of sight. But she's not here. She died less than a week ago, and Alison hasn't really cried yet.

She follows the crowd as they walk around the village and feels the tears pouring from her eyes. She is weeping easily, and she feels like a fraud: people will think she's weeping for Jesus, when she's weeping for her own loss.

Her mother is dead.

She feels this as if until now it hasn't been true, and she is bereft.

A woman close by, her head covered with a scarf, whispers to Alison in Spanish. She speaks calmly, coos to her, 'Whatever it is, it will pass.'

The moon is almost full. It illuminates the landscape all the way down to the sea. That's where she'll be. As soon as they can arrange it. She promised.

The music ends with the chorus singing as one complex creature, pulling together the melodies that have seeped through the hours of sound; the undulating streams and gushing rivers of emotion culminating in this ocean of pure sadness. Alison doesn't need the programme notes to tell her what has happened; the story is in her bones. It makes perfect sense. This is what therapy calls closure. What the Greeks called catharsis. Passion; the word means agony. To swim in grief and be purged by it, and by that process to be healed.

Sad ending, happy ending, never ending, the end.

10

Alarm

*The clutches of a drowning person are deadly in the extreme, and unless
the rescuer is well versed in water wrestling he will in all probability be
imperilled . . . at times pain may be the only means of obtaining release.*
Lyba and Nita Sheffield, *Swimming Simplified*

Jacques swallowed a yawn as he watched from the high chair on the
edge of the pool. Some kids were clowning around, but they weren't
a problem. He fingered the whistle that hung from his neck, alert
through habit even though he was running on a couple of hours'
sleep. He'd saved lives in here. Dragged limp bodies from the water;
thumped their chests and put his lips to their snot-covered faces.
The kiss of life: so romantic to say, so unpleasant to administer. On
days like these, it was hard to believe anything so critical happened
in here.

He watched a mother and son in the shallow end. She moved
away, arms outstretched, and he thrashed the water to reach her.
He'd get it in no time. Jo was already doing widths by his age, but
she'd started early. His first ever sight of her as the midwife eased
her from Hannah, this slippery creature that swam into the world.
Jacques couldn't understand what was so radical about water births;
to him it seemed right to travel from liquid to liquid.

He'd taught Jo to swim when they were in Spain, while Hannah
looked after her mum. His flat hand had supported her stomach as
she kicked and splashed. Her face screwed up in concentration as
she doggy-paddled towards him; unsmiling, utterly serious. When

she reached him, he caught her up in his arms and hugged his slippery mermaid, carrying her through the waves, her clinging to him like a limpet. In the shallows they practised their breathing, holding their noses and blowing bubbles into the warm sea till they got the giggles.

Jo had Hannah's laugh, and the same mixture of serious and daft he'd first fallen for. In fact, he thought with some pride, they'd passed on the best of themselves: Hannah's legs, Jacques's eyes; her skin and hair a blend of them both, her temperament a combination of Hannah's sensitivity tempered by his calm.

Jacques suppressed another yawn. Last night had been a long one. Jo had gone off without a grumble. He and Hannah had brushed their teeth standing side by side, pulling stupid faces at each other in the bathroom mirror. They'd thrown off their clothes and climbed into bed; Hannah's back fitting comfortably into his front, their fingers laced together, his face against her neck. And then the car alarm went off across the road.

It had happened before; they knew it would stop eventually. You just had to try and ignore it. But Hannah lost it; bundled on a coat, and stormed outside, kicking the wheels. It was Hannah not the car alarm that had woken Jo. She'd climbed into bed with them. Jacques had given up and slept on the couch.

He knew what it was. If Hannah could do something to make a difference, she could cope. Just.

11

Eau de Nil

This is much nicer than the Brixton Rec, Alison thought as she floated, letting the water support her in the blood-warm pool at Clapham Manor. The mood was less frantic. There were no people on treadmills; there was no working out, just a couple sitting in the gallery. The sun leaked in through skylights in the barrel-shaped roof. A frieze of elaborate white plasterwork, a relief pattern of oak leaves ran round the top of the walls, not in the least sporty; languorous. She thought of the old adverts for Imperial Leather, the whole family in luxurious tubs, soaping themselves into a rich lather before the days of home Jacuzzis. She let the water fill her ears so all she could hear was her own heartbeat and the distant muffled clanging of motion.

Sometimes she felt overwhelmed by the memory of Beth. It didn't always make her sad, but it still preoccupied her. She couldn't believe there would ever come a time when she'd be able to go about her day and not be reminded of her. Or maybe she was terrified of that time. Her main concern used to be that her memory of Beth would be permanently stuck with the haunting last few weeks and days; that she'd never get back to remembering her healthy and happy. Thank God that had passed. Beth still filled her head through associations with practically everything, only now she could remember sweet things, too. And the sweeter they were, the more sorely she missed her.

Foolish things.

The smell of sweet peas, old Scrabble scorecards, nail files, lemon curd, strawberries, Lancashire accents, Lancashire cheese.

The water splashed against the chunky white tiles and into a gully. The water depth was marked on special tiles in a deep cobalt glaze. Alison ran her finger inside the '8ft'. The recess just fitted her finger, and she traced the loops up and down, the symbol of infinity turned on its side.

The showers were nicer, too. They stayed on until you turned them off, probably very wasteful but so much more enjoyable. It was that magical time of day when schools had already left, working people still worked, and she had the whole communal shower to herself. She peeled off her costume and switched on all four showers, full pelt.

Rita Hayworth is in her eau-de-nil boudoir. Like a nineteen-fifties American *Vogue*, it is understatedly stylish and sumptuously feminine with jade velvet upholstery, wispy turquoise chiffon and subtly opulent gilt detailing. She strips behind a decorated screen and, without revealing more than a tantalising glimpse of her body, enters the circular shower. The camera zooms in and we see Rita from her beautifully defined collarbone upwards. The water splashes in a hundred rivulets, enveloping her in a fountain which falls on her skin like kisses. She strokes herself with soap, her eyes filled with lust.

'Oh we thought this was the most elegant thing ever when we saw it at the pictures,' Beth says. 'A circular shower! So decadent. She was older than Sinatra, of course, but such a sexy woman. She married the Aga Khan, you know. They had a house in Mombasa.'

A certain day came and went when, without even knowing it, Beth immersed herself in water, and it was for the last time. She didn't mark the day because it was only with hindsight that it became *the* day. When had it been? As she soaked in a deep bath until her skin got pruny? Or swimming in a pool one sweltering day to refresh herself; lengths of her inimitable breaststroke, smiling, her head remaining above the water, turning from side to side, her hair staying dry. Maybe it was in the sea, after lying in the sun, edging in slowly, feeling the delicious cold taking the sting out of the day's heat, then plunging herself into clear water. They hadn't been red-letter, last-time occasions. They had been an insidious series of penultimates and ultimates which one day were taken for granted, and the next, not.

From being a complete body with an entire wrapping of skin, Beth had been medicalised into parts which were OK, parts which were not so OK. Parts which had to be kept dry. And if she had known, if she had been given the foresight to realise 'This is the last time that I shall experience x, y and z', how differently those experiences would have been coloured, how heartbreakingly infused with resonance. Live each day as if it were your last. Who really could?

12

Jerusalem Rose

Sam and Alison met for an early lunch at Eco's in Brixton Market. It was still only twelve thirty, so they easily found a table. They sat outside in the covered arcade, Alison with her back to the window, watching Brixton shop. People mooched past with trolleys and children, bags and dogs. Fairy lights hung from the glass roof; red, blue and yellow. Opposite, a stall spilled cosmetics and hair accessories. Next door was a nail bar, where people in surgical masks extended women's fingernails to improbable lengths. Alison wondered how it must feel deliberately to disable yourself from wiping your arse, typing, masturbating. The waitress placed two cups of coffee in front of them. Alison wrapped her hands with their stubby nails round her latte, and turned her attention to Sam.

'Fucking hell, Sam. Nice hickey.'

'Is it that bad?'

'Er, well, compared to what? It's the kind of bad that would have got me a clout twenty years ago. Come to think of it, that's about the last time I had one.'

Sam felt her neck, touching the spot. A mouth-sized bruise nestled between her ear and the neckline of her skinny-rib jumper. She looked around briefly and smirked at Alison before pulling her jumper down and flashing a glimpse of the skin beneath. A diminishing series of love-bites formed a sequence of stepping-stones which led to and disappeared under her bra.

'Bloody hell,' said Alison.

'Quite.'

Sam poured sugar into the teaspoon she held over her cup. It spilled over the edges of the spoon and sank, and she absently stirred it into her cappuccino. The brown chocolate powder swirled into the milk foam.

'So? Come on – who, when, where?'

Sam lifted the cup to her lips. 'You know I was doing the sleepover thing at the British Museum?'

Alison nodded, waiting. Sam grinned at her, a faint chocolate moustache on her top lip.

'You didn't!' Alison sipped as she stared at Sam, incredulous.

'Under the Elgin Marbles,' Sam said.

Alison spat latte across the table. 'Jesus!'

'I know.'

'And there was me thinking, how nice of Sam, what a dull way to spend the weekend, with a load of geeky kids.' Alison wiped the table with a handful of serviettes. 'Christ, Sam, it wasn't some geeky kid was it?'

'No, course it wasn't. I do have my limits. No, it was their teacher's assistant. The guy I told you about – Jonathon – the one who roped me into going.'

'You bitch. So what was he like?'

'Not bad,' said Sam. 'Not bad at all.'

Alison sat back and surveyed her best friend, full of admiration. Sam had turned casual sex into art.

After lunch, Sam and Alison wandered through the arcade. A couple of doors down from Eco's there was a Mexican shop selling candles and love potions. They stood outside looking at the window display.

'Brixton needs another candle shop like it needs a few more nutters outside the tube,' said Alison.

A bottle labelled 'Evil Go Away' was displayed alongside 'Money Come to Me'. Next to that, a candle for 'Legal Troubles'.

'Wouldn't it be nice if life was that simple?' said Sam, 'Come on, let's take a look. Maybe there's one called "Get Over It"; I could buy some for Bill.'

The woman behind the counter was chatting on the phone when they entered, and continued her conversation as if she were in her own front room. Aretha sang something gospelly on the tape deck; the kind of singing that makes you wish you had faith, Alison thought. The shelves were crammed with tiny paper packets printed with flowers and hearts. 'Amor, Ven a Mí'. Alison translated as she read: 'Love, Come to Me'. There were bags of herbs, packets of joss sticks, incense, and bottles of something that could be used either for spiritual bathing or as a cleansing floor-wash. In a basket by the till were some dry balls of fern. The basket was labelled with a piece of white card, handwritten in black marker pen: 'Roses of Jerusalem'.

'I haven't seen these since I was a kid,' she said.

Sam came over and picked one up. She examined the fist of dead-looking fern, some old roots at the base holding the thing together.

'What are they?'

'I don't think I ever knew what they were called before, but I remember Hannah and I were given one each when I was about six. Can't remember who gave us them. We had to put them in a saucer of water.'

'What for?'

'They come back to life. The roots take up the water, and all this stuff fans out. Some kind of desert survival mechanism, I guess. But I remember it feeling like magic.'

13

Egg

As the water started to bubble around the egg, Bill looked out of his kitchen window to note the position of the pod nearest the local library's roof. It was just beginning to ascend. He pressed the bread into the toaster and counted pods. As the fourth pod lifted away from the roof, allowing the grey sky to show through, Bill scooped the egg out of the pan, buttered his toast and sat down at the counter. The egg was perfect: firm white and still-soft yolk.

The London Eye had given Londoners a beautiful egg timer that you could ride in. In fact, he pondered as he dipped his toast into the runny yellow, it had redefined London. For one thing, there was the South–North divide; the way it went clockwise or anti-clockwise, depending on your perspective. Bill was without doubt a clockwise, South London boy. He loved the Eye. He'd loved watching its progress as it gradually took shape on the South Bank.

The day it had been hoisted into vertical, he and Sam had snuck into the Marriott Hotel, the old County Hall. The lifts were operated by hotel-issue credit cards, so Bill and Sam had hung around by the gift shop and casually followed a couple of Japanese guests in as the lift doors parted. When the others got out on the third floor, Bill and Sam continued up to the sixth. The corridor was decorated with innocuous prints of Old London, and the carpets were thick and fawn. The windows were so close to the wheel you could practically lean out and touch it. They watched as it was slowly levered upwards, towards them.

They'd been disturbed by the ping of the service lift, and had seen a girl in hotel uniform emerge from the opening doors pushing a trolley load of towels and soap. She returned the trolley to a supplies cupboard and took the lift back down. Sam grabbed Bill's arm and led him along the beige corridor into the walk-in cupboard that the girl had just left. They fucked standing up between the shelves of fluffy white towels. Sam filled her pockets with souvenir soaps and individual sachets of Nescafé. She could never resist a freebie.

Bill inverted the shell in the eggcup, an April Fool's egg.

'April Fools!' he said aloud, as he raised his teaspoon and smashed the empty shell.

14

Benches

Alison and Sam had entered Brockwell Park from the main gates at Herne Hill; passing the group that Bill had christened 'The Late Show'. He had joked with Alison that they could replace Paulin, Parsons, Greer and Lawson as guardians of the arts. Transmitted live on BBC2 as they sipped from their cans and ponced roll-ups off the runners, they would be watched by the nation: eulogising on the current state of the novel, and the implicit poetry of the latest soap opera. Alison had laughed, saying that it was almost certainly already being pitched to some media executives, and the name had stuck. She told Sam this as they made their way up the path.

'He's such a cynical git,' said Sam.

'When are you going to give him a break?' asked Alison.

They had been like this for the past few months, and it was hard work. A woman walking an Alsatian passed them. On her sweatshirt was a printed photo of the dog.

'Did you see the top?' asked Sam.

'Don't change the subject.'

'Oh, I don't know. When he grows up.'

Sam had dumped Bill. On April 1st. That hadn't helped, because he had thought she was being April foolish, when in fact she hadn't even been aware of it being April Fools' Day, just the day when she'd taken a deep breath and told him that she was so, so sorry but she'd made a big mistake, and that one day he'd thank her for it.

*   *   *

The café was steamy hot after the cold of outside, and noisy. Sam and Alison had to negotiate their way through the barrage of children and buggies and parents to join the queue for drinks. This place was the best antidote Alison knew to feelings of broodiness. The noise of it all, and the endlessness of needs exhausted her. She felt all cared out.

'This is a bit of a busman's holiday; it's a right mother's meeting,' Sam said. She had a business called Bloomers, photographing pregnant women. "I did another Cleopatra last week. Hey, I haven't told you, have I? I've been to see a studio.'

'Great. Where is it?'

'West Norwood, ten minutes tops by car. You must come and see it. You'll love it; it's right next to the cemetery.'

'Sounds right up my street.'

'Oh, sorry, Al, I didn't mean it like that. I just meant . . . Oh, never mind. Me and my mouth.'

Two dogs were chasing each other on the stretch of lawn below the café. They wagged their tails, sniffed each other's arses and ran off.

'Why can't we be more like dogs?' said Alison.

The flower garden was in a state of flux. Chinese lanterns hung tissue-paper orange over the rotting remains of summer, and final white roses bloomed on leggy stems. They walked in the space between two newly flat-topped box hedges, shoots of lime green growth poking out from the deep Harrods green. Ahead of them, a woman about Alison's age appeared from the tunnel cut out of an arched hedge. She was walking arm in arm with a woman the age Beth would have been. Alison felt a surge of sadness – a physical pain in her chest. She and Beth had ambled arm in arm around these gardens when she'd been to stay, and now she felt panicky that she couldn't remember what they would have been talking about, what they would have been wearing. Certainly, Beth would have casually nipped the dry seed-heads from the flowers they passed, and later she would have put the seeds into Basildon Bond envelopes, but failed to label them. Alison still had the evidence. She felt a burning jealousy of the mother and daughter. She breathed hard, filling her lungs with the damp autumn air until her eyes watered.

They headed towards the centre of the walled garden, past flowerless primulas planted with allotment precision. Some bedding segments had been cleared and the earth freshly turned, leaving the lumpy soil framed with an edging of terracotta twisted brick that looked like a long loaf of glazed bread. They walked round the lily pond, reading aloud the inscriptions on the benches. The last ones had been torched so that only the cast-iron stumps remained, cemented into the paving. On one of the replacements were two men's names, their dates of birth and death.

'Ah, look,' said Sam. 'They were only in their thirties.' They sat down on it. 'I expect,' she said, 'that we'll still be doing this when we're in our nineties.'

'Yeah,' said Alison. 'When all our friends are benches.'

15

Maybe

*I have had good aluminium pans for about fifteen years and I only wish
I had a daughter to inherit them.*

The Constance Spry Cookery Book

The bargain hunters had queued outside Patcham village hall in the
drizzle. They paid twenty pence each on the door, took in the room's
layout, and charged towards the tables, not quite running. Their
footsteps rumbled and clattered over the old wooden floorboards, and
the damp seeped from them and into the fusty mounds of clothes.

Hannah picked over the greyish-brown mass of material. It all
looked pretty grim, but then she spotted a cardigan and pulled it
from the pile, holding it at arm's length. It was good cashmere, a
brown paisley design on a cream background. Her stomach fluttered, but on closer inspection she saw the wool was bobbled and
the neckline grubby, so she tossed it back. She hadn't the heart for
this today. She felt irritated by the pushing and shoving.

The woman opposite was wearing white cotton gloves. They
looked incongruous with her jeans and jumper, but Hannah
supposed it was sensible, all those minuscule particles of so many
people. Detritus. The word made her itch. The woman bent down
to pick up the clothes that spilled over her side of the table, and
returned them to the top of the pile. Hannah thought of the seaside
arcades, the glass cabinets with sliding shelves of fat brown two-
pence pieces that ebbed and flowed. If you dropped a coin in at the
right moment, a few slipped over the edge.

There were three in the bed
And the little one said,
'Roll over! Roll over!'
So they all rolled over and one fell out.
There were two in the bed . . .

She pushed her way from the table and looked for Jo, spotting her on
the floor between the raffle and refreshments, rummaging through a
box of toys. Hannah had given her fifty pence to spend, and it looked
like she was spoiled for choice. There were plenty of orphans for her
to rescue here. Her bedroom was getting to look more like a refugee
camp each day, with one-eyed teddies and ugly, awkward-limbed
dolls. She had a knack of finding them, the really tragic-looking ones.
It was really for Jo that she'd come; she wouldn't have chosen to
spend her Saturday morning trawling through other people's cast-
offs. There was a time when she'd loved going to a good jumble sale.
She, Beth and Alison would all go together when Beth was over,
sometimes to two or three in a day. They'd get the local paper and
work out their itinerary. The best one had been an annual Scouts'
jumble sale one sunny August Saturday when they'd left with a Susie
Cooper tea service, some Sarah Vaughan and Nat King Cole LPs in
mint condition, and an armful of designer dresses. Beth had found a
classic Homeware teapot, complete with its original silver cladding.
When she'd returned to Spain that time, she left it as a surprise for
Hannah, all polished up, the tea stains inside bleached away.

But people's crap had become crappier. It was partly the fault of
the *Antiques Roadshow*, and partly down to car-boot sales. Nowadays
people kept their junk to sell for themselves. And the few jumbles
that remained had lost their innocence. There were the profes-
sionals; she'd spotted them this morning, the ones there to supply
their trendy second-hand shops in the Lanes, turning Patcham
jumble into 'vintage clothing'. Just like that.

The man in charge of bric-a-brac was trying to drum up trade, pointing out the items behind him – an old television set, a vacuum cleaner, a darts board and a couple of suitcases. Nobody paid any attention to him. Men were always put on bric-a-brac, as if it were the only place where they could be trusted not to fuck up. Maybe it was because they were unrealistic about what to charge, or was it that used clothing was too intimate? She scanned the items on the table – prescription spectacles, heated rollers and a sandwich toaster – picked up a mug printed with a portrait of Prince Andrew and Sarah Ferguson, put it down next to a stack of *Reader's Digests*. A man in an anorak was leafing through a pile of records. Hannah could tell, if there were any good ones he'd find them, so knelt down and poked about in a box full of shoes, belts and handbags. Right at the bottom she spotted a tin. It was an old rectangular biscuit tin, salmon pink with a photograph of a woman's face on the lid. Hannah studied the face. She looked a little like her aunt, Beth's sister Margaret, and also a little like Alison. Maybe the eyes. She was a classic English beauty in the nineteen-fifties style. Peaches-and-cream complexion, fluffy peroxided hair crimped into waves, brown eyebrows pencilled in over grey-blue eyes, and coral lipstick on slightly parted lips. The kind of girl who might have won Miss Butlins, or made it into Rank Charm School. Her lacy white collar disappeared into a confection of flowers. Pink and yellow, purple and white, they were old-fashioned flowers, the sort that would have been tortured into complicated table arrangements.

The tin was surprisingly heavy, and the contents rattled as Hannah lifted it onto her lap and prised the lid open. She read the paper labels on the wooden reels of cotton. Dewhurst's Sylko 100 yards. Violet, Biscuit, Apricot, Irish Turf, Hunters Green.

She pushed the reels aside. Underneath was a half-used sheet of hooks and eyes. Further down were sturdy black pinking shears, navy bias binding wrapped on a card, and a plastic bag of buttons.

There were dozens of them: shirt buttons with their square of neat holes, toffee-like leather knots, delicate silver and pearl sweets. Hannah imagined the clothes they'd once been attached to; the people who'd worn the clothes. People didn't do this any more, she thought. They didn't make do and mend; they bought new. She rummaged deeper, finding skeins of embroidery thread in colours that washed over her with memories – the deep green, the fleshy peach, coffee brown – each secured with the familiar paper Anchor seal.

Beth had been a pretty erratic seamstress, but she'd always made the effort. She'd sewn sequins onto leotards for Alison's dance classes, and she'd made them costumes for their local carnival each year, only rarely resorting to glue and staples. They had been pirates with metal curtain-ring earrings and gypsies with wooden curtain-ring earrings. She had a photograph of herself as 'Miss Hit' in a costume Beth based on *Juke Box Jury*. In the photograph she's grinning, squinting into the sun. She's dressed in a black and white tunic and holding a sign like a lollipop lady's which, she remembered, said 'Hit' on one side and 'Miss' on the other. Thinking about it now, Hannah wondered if the costume had been made in black and white because they had black-and-white television. It had never occurred to her before. Anyway, it had won her first prize.

But hit and miss was about right. She remembered clothes of hers that had the scars of Beth's running repairs. The lanky tacking stitches she never got round to doing properly, the angry reversing of machine stitch where the material didn't behave. And she'd always made little improvisations from the Buttericks pattern – a strip of Velcro instead of a zip, a panel of contrasting material where she ran out. Hannah had inherited that slapdash approach to both sewing and cooking. She tried, but she hadn't a great deal of patience. Every Christmas she set out to create the cake that appeared in her imagination, with its smooth top and tidy piping. But they always ended up with snow. She used the snowmaking technique she'd learned as a child, watching Beth bounce the flat edge of a palette knife over the surface, and adding a handful of plastic snowmen and trees for good measure.

Hannah still used the same needles to sew Cash's name tapes onto Jo's uniform that Beth had used for hers; sewed with the same thread that had embroidered Hannah's name in pink chain stitch on her pump bag. These were things she would no more throw away than Beth's recipe books with their sticky pages denoting favourite cakes, and their idiosyncratic floury notes: 'Could add cocoa here', or 'Save the juice of the lemon!'

And yet this tin was the intimate story of someone else's mum, someone else's daughter. So how had it come to be here? Why had it not been cherished? She raked through the rest of the contents. The Quickunpic, the squares of felt, the blue flint of tailor's chalk, the stainless-steel thimble, and a card printed with a picture of flowers in a basket. Hannah knew without opening the card that she'd find inside it a selection of needles attached to the shiny red and green foil. The thick, curved upholsterer's one that never got used, the ingenious loop of fine wire on a circle of tin for threading needles, these were so familiar. How could someone do that? And then she thought of the things she and Alison had thrown away in the days following Beth's death. When they hadn't been thinking straight, but had tried to be practical. God knows what they had chucked, the state they were in. Maybe someone was finding things of Beth's in some charity shop in Spain. Or maybe, she thought, as she secured a loose thread into the diagonal slit of the wooden reel, maybe this woman had no children. Maybe she'd died alone and had only been discovered days later, when a neighbour noticed that the milk hadn't been collected. Maybe a professional house-clearance company had thrown her belongings away.

Jacques despaired of Hannah when she did this – invented

scenarios which she then embellished with more and more con-
vincing details until they reached a terrible crescendo. And Hannah
knew what Jacques's version of this would be. He'd say that a very
happy old lady was probably enjoying a ripe old age and had just
decided to have a clear-out. It wasn't even a case of Jacques seeing
the glass half full – she saw it spilled all over a beautiful damask
tablecloth, ruining it. Or poisoned, or something. But she couldn't
stop herself; couldn't allow herself nice stories with happy endings.

She organised the contents of the box so that the lid would shut,
and paid the man the one pound he asked. Had he any idea how
much a reel of thread cost? Probably not, she thought, looking for
Jo.

'I can't decide.' Jo sat on the floor cross-legged, her brow knotted
in concentration. 'This one seems really sad.' She held up a naked
brown doll, its hair brutally chopped, felt-tip scribble on its arms.
'She'll be so cold without any clothes on. But if I buy her, her friends
will be lonely.'

Hannah looked at the line-up of three more manky dolls and a
balding teddy. They seemed to be waiting for her decision.

They left the hall with the five new orphans stuffed into an old
carrier bag. Tonight, they agreed, they would make them all new
clothes with the threads and felt that Hannah carried under her arm
in the salmon-pink tin.

16

Monkey Puzzle

'What do you think?' Sam asked.

Alison took in the enormous white room. 'It's fantastic; all this space. I'm jealous.'

'Isn't it great? It'll probably be freezing in winter; I guess these are a clue.' She kicked one of the pair of Calor Gas heaters that sat in the corner, already looking hopelessly inadequate, 'And boiling in the summer. Well, it's hot enough today. But the light is so . . . light!' She hugged herself as she looked up at the sky through the glass panels in the roof, 'Oh, it'll be so nice not having to kneel under beds searching for a spare socket. Knowing where my light source is in advance, imagine! And best of all, no more dragging my gear across London every shoot.'

'Are you going to do all your Bloomers work here?'

'I've still got some commissions I've agreed to do on location, but that's the idea. I want to try shifting all future clients here.'

'They'll probably like that, too. I mean, it'll be easier for them to let rip if it's away from their homes.'

'Do you think? That's the one bit I'm not sure about. I think maybe they feel safer in their own space; more in control. We'll have to see.' She looked around the room. 'I'll have to make it more comfortable, get a decent fan and better heating, and I'll need a screen, and a sofa.'

'Will you do my portrait sometime, Sam?' Alison hadn't been planning to ask her, but the thought popped out.

Sam was still mentally sizing up the space for furniture, but she spun round and faced her. 'Oh, my God, are you trying to tell me something?'

Alison frowned at her, then laughed. 'No, I'm not pregnant, you fool. Not likely to be, either. You need to have sex for that, apparently. Bit of a drought there. Why, are you strictly limited to pregnant subjects?'

'No, not at all. Of course I will; it'd make a welcome change, seeing a flat belly for once. I'd like to.' She thought for a minute. 'It'd have to be collaboration, though; I'm not just going to tell you what to do.'

'OK, it's a deal. Although I wouldn't go overboard on the flat-belly bit. I mean, I may not be pregnant, but we can't all be skinny like you.'

'Leave it out, will you? You've got a great figure; you're tall enough to take a bit of weight.'

'Ah, that's just what Mum used to say. I guess I've lost my confidence.'

'You know what you need? Some good old-fashioned shagging.'

'Mmm,' Alison said. 'I might, but not all the stuff that goes with it.'

'What stuff?'

'You know.' Alison picked up a contact sheet and glanced at the sequence. 'It's too intimate,' she mumbled.

'Doesn't have to be.'

'I know. Well, I knew. I just don't seem to be able to . . . I dunno . . . let go. My head won't let me.'

'Why not?'

'I can't explain. Maybe I'm like your clients, maybe it's about control.'

'I love losing control.'

'I know. That's why I envy you.'

'Me?'

'Yes. You're so good at being . . . I don't know . . . spontaneous. You take risks.'

'Maybe I'm just a bit stupid.'

'I don't think so; I think it takes courage. I wish I could be more like that.'

'Maybe you think too far ahead.'

'I don't know.'

Alison left Sam measuring up the space and making calls to suppliers. On her way to the bus stop she saw the open gates of the cemetery. It was one of the more famous Victorian ones. The stone angels perched on the rooftops of the mausoleums seemed almost to be waving to her. She crossed the road, deciding to take a look. She walked through an ornamental garden, past an electric buggy parked by the gatekeeper's house, and went over to the notice board. Next to a map of the grounds there was a letter apologising for the unkempt look of the place, explaining that it was due to the weather, and that they were doing their level best to get things back under control. How British, Alison thought, walking past some straggly rosebushes; everything is always because of the weather. Everything is always supposed to be under control. Alison considered what Sam had said about losing control and about her thinking too far ahead. She'd always imagined it was more a case of being too wrapped up in the past, but maybe it was about the future. There's a real art to living in the moment, she realised, as she walked along the pathways between the hundreds of dead in the bright sunshine.

It had been such a strange summer; rainy through July and August and now, suddenly, this tremendous heat. Everything was wonderfully lush. The tombstones were almost hidden in the tall cow parsley, and bees buzzed round a bush of lavender that grew in front of a heart-shaped stone. She read the inscription. The deceased had been only a baby. Which was sadder, she wondered; losing someone you'd grown to love and need, or losing someone you'd never had the chance to know? Both were sad in their different ways, she guessed. It wasn't a competition.

Alison was amazed Sam had asked if she was pregnant; she couldn't even imagine it. A thought came to her, and not for the first time: what would be the point in her having a baby now, with no Beth as grandmother? She knew how melodramatic that sounded; it was probably the effect of the graveyard. Just as well she had Sam there on maudlin alert. And anyway, it wasn't even true. She didn't want a baby. She wanted her own life back. She wanted to get Spain over with, and to feel something other than this, this not-feeling.

She settled in the deep blot of shade under a lolloping monkey-puzzle tree, and remembered the one they used to pass when she was a kid. Where was that? It was on the way to somewhere or other, in a front garden. They used it as a sign that they were nearly there. But she couldn't remember where.

17

Rink

Amelia mixed the mustard,
She mixed it good and thick;
She put it in the custard
And made her mother sick.'
                    A. E. Housman

Alison threaded the laces through the eyelets on the hired white skates, pulling them tight and wrapping the excess cord round the top of the boot. She lifted one booted foot, twisting her ankle so that the blade caught the light. She turned to Sam, who was having difficulty getting her boots on.

'Sam, why don't you take your gloves off?'

"Cos I know I'm going to fall flat on my face.' She tied her laces in double bows, and they hobbled over the wet lino to the edge of the rink.

The advanced couples were finishing their session, older pairs who knew and anticipated each other's moves instinctively. The men expertly twizzled their partners away from them, the women spun out, performed little kicks, returning to find the men's hands ready to take, and resumed their matching footwork.

'I'm going to hate this,' Sam said.

'I can't believe you've never been skating. Didn't you ever go when you were little?'

'Nope.'

'Mum used to take us on Saturday mornings.'

'I can't imagine my mum doing anything like that with me.'

Sometimes, Alison wondered if she attracted motherless people into her life. Not literally motherless, but without any bond. It made her uncomfortable. She had to stifle her frustration at the unfairness of it; that Sam's rubbish mum was alive and kicking, and Sam didn't particularly care. She wanted to bang their heads together.

'We were really crap, all three of us.' Alison almost apologised for the memory. 'We never seemed to improve.'

'So you finally decided to get some lessons?'

'Yeah. Mum and I got really hooked during the winter Olympics, although neither of us had a clue what a triple salcho or a lutz was – I still haven't. We just enjoyed the kitsch costumes – those men in fitted nylon trousers that cover the skates so they look like they've got hooves, and the women in American Tan tights.'

'Oh, American Tan. I can see you in those.'

'I wouldn't hold your breath – I don't imagine I'll ever be any good, but it's a laugh. I enjoy it, all of it – the bad acoustics and the cheesy music, like this.'

They listened as 'Yellow Bird' wheezed from the speakers, a relentlessly jolly cha-cha-cha; a nostalgic, gone-to-seed organ sound that fitted perfectly with the down-at-heel surroundings of Streatham ice rink.

Alison continued, 'That and synchronised swimming were the only sports we watched.'

'Yellow Bird' ended with a final cha-cha-cha, and the couples coasted to the exits and cleared the ice, leaving it scored with their tracks; circles looping inside wheels, arcs sweeping the circumference of the rink.

'Did you used to have Spirograph?' Sam asked.

'Oh yes. I'd forgotten. With a green Biro.'

'I nagged my mum and dad till they got me it for Christmas, but the pictures never came out like they were supposed to. They were never perfect.'

They watched the skaters hobbling on the lino, suddenly no longer graceful but old and normal. The music changed, and Barry White's deep groan rumbled from the sound system. Immediately, a flurry of skaters appeared on the ice.

'This is it,' Alison said. 'Ready?'

'Ready as I'll ever be.'

Alison held Sam's elbow as they left the mat and stepped gingerly onto the grey ice, which smelled like the inside of a freezer. Sam immediately tugged Alison down; Alison yanked her up again, keeping her balance.

'Steady.'

'I'm OK,' Sam said, lunging towards the railing. 'Go ahead, impress me.'

'Sure?'

'Yes.'

Alison tipped her weight from side to side, moving from the hips as she'd been taught. In her very first class they had concentrated on learning how to fall safely. Once you knew that, you could take risks. It was 'Feel the Fear and Do It Anyway' On Ice. She loved the fact that no matter how bad you were there was always someone worse, and however much you improved there was always someone better, something to aspire to. Skating between the precocious kids – who didn't yet understand pain and had the sublime confidence of ignorance – and the tentative late starters, arms flapping like penguins, Alison felt as if she was part of a diagram of the evolution of species.

After serious consideration Beth decides not to have chemotherapy. It's scary rejecting conventional wisdom, but she's done her research. She reads that the treatment originated from mustard gas trials in the First World War, and she concludes that it's no more accurate now: shoot everything, ask questions later; some of the bad guys will get hit. It's like finding a needle in a haystack. No. She'll follow her instincts and work with her body. Change her diet, cut out toxins and stress, take juices and herbs and minerals and vitamins. Be kind to herself. The doctors are appalled – a woman – a middle-aged woman – who can't even speak their language fluently, refusing their advice, and they tacitly wash their hands of her. The feeling is mutual.

A friend suggests visualisation.

'The bad cells are red, the good cells are white,' she says encouragingly. 'They are soldiers in battle. Imagine the white cells at war with the red. The white cells shall be victorious.'

Beth tries, but can't get into it.

'It's just so . . . aggressive,' she says to Alison.

They work to find a middle ground. A visualisation that takes on board the fighting, only some other way.

'I've thought of one,' Beth announces. 'Ice skaters.'

The white cells are skaters. They're dressed in beautiful white chiffon costumes, and they skate in formation. They use their sharp blades to slice into the bad cells. They kick as they spin. Their costumes swirl as they lean back in perfect spirals. The bad cells haven't a chance.

The skaters disappear behind the lace curtain that is the stomach lining. Beth has seen it in her X-ray. They change behind the curtain, reappearing as swimmers in white swimsuits and sleek white swimming caps. Beth's body is a pool, and they swim through her in pairs, perfectly synchronised. They carry a long net between them, and as they move along, they gather up the destroyed bad cells, placing them in the net, moving along the stomach, bright smiles, clear eyes, hands dipping, toes pointing, flushing away all the debris.

'My feet feel like lead,' Alison said as they walked out of the building.

'I'm just glad to be back on the ground,' Sam said. 'Streatham High Street never felt so good.'

'You weren't as bad as all that once you got going. You'd pick it up in no time if you stuck at it.'

'You know me and sticking at things.'

'Don't be so hard on yourself,' Alison said, touching her arm. 'Look, someone's left their light on.' She walked over to a bicycle chained to the railing. The orange backlight flashed on and off. 'I can't find anywhere to switch it off.'

Sam joined her. 'I bet you were in the Guides.'

'Brownies. A good deed every day. "To serve the Queen and help other people,"' Alison said, fiddling with the light.

They traced the wiring from the light along the frame of the bike.

'It must be a dynamo. It's still charged from the cycling. It'll be fine,' Sam said.

They walked away from the bike, its orange light still blinking.

18

Pepe's

The brown gloss paint on the window frame at Pepe's café was so thick that it looked as if the woodwork was melting. Geraniums in yoghurt pots lined the ledge, spilling flowers of tangerine and cerise. Alison sipped her tea, waiting for her beans on toast. She was surprised Sam hadn't been at her studio; she was sure she was meant to be doing a shoot today, but it didn't matter. Recently, she'd been using the excuse of meeting Sam for lunch as a reason for spending time walking around the cemetery. Even after a dozen visits, it threw up new surprises.

At first, without any particular grave to visit, she'd felt like an impostor. But after a while she'd started to recognise the people sitting on the memorial benches, eating their packed lunches. And people had started to recognise her. The man who drove the electric buggy that took mourners from the entrance gates to the chapel nodded when he passed, and the three men employed to cut back the undergrowth were on first-name terms with her. Not that they were making much of an impact on the place; in some parts it was still wild enough to get completely lost. The trees and shrubs were rampant. The place felt quite joyous, it was so teeming with life.

She'd started to check the floral tributes that were left each day on the clipped grass lawn by the chapel, the markers naming the deceased like those at buffets saying what fillings are in the sandwiches. Flower heads were used to create pictures, like the shark she'd seen last week, the attached card from friends at the dead man's angling club. Today there had been a pint glass in rust-coloured chrysanthemums topped with a row of white. Alison guessed it must have been his service that she'd seen the mourners leaving; a tape of 'My Way' playing him out.

Say it with flowers. Alison remembered Beth describing a man she'd overheard in the florist's. Asked what message he wanted to enclose, he'd thought a while, and then decided: 'Yeah, put "You're the business."' Alison smiled. Beth would have enjoyed walking here in the late-summer sunshine. But she'd have been disappointed by Mrs Beeton's memorial. Alison imagined a large marble rolling pin, or a granite pie with 'First catch your hare' in gothic script round its circumference. Hidden in weeds, she had been a mere footnote on her husband's headstone: 'Also his wife, who contributed to some of his projects'. Bloody typical, Alison could almost hear Beth saying.

During her walks, Alison had known she was searching for something. Eventually, she'd found three graves; one with Beth as the name of the deceased, one with Beth's date of birth, and another with her date of death, only a century earlier. Having found them, she'd felt depressed. Not one could she adopt as Beth's. All three had left her cold: they were just other people's dead. She'd tried again, this time looking for a stone so weathered that she could fill it with the idea of Beth. But she hadn't found it. Until now.

Her beans on toast arrived and Alison tucked in, reading the handwritten list of fried breakfasts. This morning, it had felt as if she'd cracked a code.

Reading the inscriptions she'd tried to imagine who these people had been. Some had details of their career, or how they'd met their death; a few had clues through the choice of headstone – a ship for a mariner – or by the floral tributes – maybe their team's football colours, but these were the minority. For the most part there was nothing that could be deduced about who *they'd* been, other than in relation to those who had survived them. They were someone's father or son or sister or grandparent, and Alison had understood something obvious: the graves weren't for the dead; the dead existed as losses to those who survived them, and that was who the graves were really for. And she knew with absolute clarity why Beth had wished them to scatter her ashes.

Almost as soon as she'd realised that, she found The Place. It was hidden away in a part she'd only discovered today; a Greek chapel and grounds within the main cemetery. There, reaching out from the chaos of undergrowth was the statue. The young woman was sitting legs akimbo, and her daughter leaned back against her. The girl, five or six years old, was naked; her young mother draped in folds of cloth that touched the ground. In her left hand the mother trailed a stem of ivy, as if she'd just picked it and had forgotten she was holding it. Her right hand held her daughter's, their fingers interwoven, their touch light but assured. The mother leaned forward slightly, so her breasts just touched her daughter's back. They both looked out to something on the horizon. Alison had tried to follow their gaze, but couldn't see what it was that absorbed them so.

Alison pronged the last of the beans with her fork, satisfied. The statue was so beautiful, so quiet; the relationship between mother and daughter so evident yet private. Alison knew; this would be where she could visit, where she could best feel close to Beth. Best, at least, until her ashes were in the sea.

19

Diddly Dee

'Good morning, London. My name's Robert Elms.'

He always said that, as if London were a person, or as if every listener was generically London. The taxi drivers, the parents dropping kids off at school, people prepping vegetables in restaurant kitchens, or hanging out washing, or shaving; everyone. For the first time since *Junior Choice* Alison felt included in the demographic. That was his real knack.

Robert Elms's listeners shared his enthusiasm for London. Each day they phoned in with their notes and queries – anything from pyramid-shaped milk cartons to smells from factories on certain roads; odd buildings, extraordinary people, obscure parks, apocryphal events and once-seen sights.

Alison put the kettle on, humming along to 'Come Fly with Me'. As the song ended, she heard the voice of an elderly man.

'Hello, Robert. First of all, I'd like to say what a treat it was yesterday, hearing that Duke Ellington tune. Splendid.'

'Thank you. Anyone who wasn't listening yesterday, we dedicated the last half-hour of the show to train music, and I played Ellington's sublime "A Train". But I believe you have a question for us, Derek; the first of today's London Queries?'

'Yes, I do. When I was young, my parents had a wonderful collection of 78s, which they misguidedly got rid of in the sixties.'

'Big mistake. Hang on to your vinyl – and your shellac.'

'Well, among them was a spoken-word piece, which I have no

information about, except that it included the line, "Diddly dee, diddly dum."'

Robert Elms laughed indulgently. ' "Diddly dee, diddly dum"?'

'Yes. I was reminded of it by your feature on trains.'

'So "Diddly dee, diddly dum" was the sound of a train?'

'Yes. It was a piece for children about a train journey, and I'd dearly love to find out if any of your listeners can remember it, and if I can still get hold of it.'

'Well, sir, you've come to the right place. If anyone can track that down, no pun intended, it's our listeners.'

'Thank you. Unfortunately my parents are no longer with us, so I can't ask them.'

'So, if you think you can help identify "Diddly dee, diddly dum", give us a call on . . .'

Alison poured milk into her coffee. No doubt someone would be able to help. That was why it was such a successful format: people were given the chance to shine for knowing off-the-wall facts which normally only got aired down the pub among a table of mates. The listeners were all at the same metaphysical boozer, sat round one enormous table, arguing the toss.

But that wasn't what had brought a lump to her throat; it was what the man had said about not being able to ask his parents. She knew that feeling so well. All the things she hadn't asked Beth. Things it hadn't occurred to her that she would want to know – or that she'd forgotten, always assuming there would be another time. There was so much she wished she'd asked. Like, did Beth always know she wanted to have children, or would she do things differently, given her time again? What had it felt like, being a single parent in the sixties? How had she made that courgette and tomato bake? When had she noticed her first white hair? And there was all the stuff she didn't know about her own childhood. How long had she been breastfed? Had she been fed on demand?

Who could provide her with answers to questions like that? Not even Robert Elms's listeners could help her there.

She turned the radio off. The printer had finished chugging out the half-dozen pages she'd been working on. She picked them up and sat down with her coffee, reading through.

The sleeping bags are nylon, slippy, slightly musty-smelling. The chunky zip has etched into my skin. We whisper to each other in the dim light of the gallery, a pair of caterpillars. I take your hand, pulling it down into the nylon warmth . . .

. . . I crawl over your body, an inch from your skin, trembling with the effort of sustaining the perfect distance. I photograph your big blue eye, your baby-fat lips, and your fleshy pink nipple. Each image fills my viewfinder; spills over it. I lean over your generous belly button.

I take the jigsaw pieces of your flesh. I want to superimpose you on me.

In the photo booth, I adjust the seat, select the background, and feed my coins into the slot.

Flash! Flash! Flash! Flash!

I study the four pictures still acrid with chemicals. First, my face – our face – identikit eyes, one of mine, one of yours. Look! A bastard child collaged out of us. Then my mouth, lost under you, kissed with the paper of your lips. You delete me. Next, top lifted, flashing for the camera's flash, your nipple grafted over mine. Finally, across the skin of my stomach, hiding the knot of scar tissue where I was once-upon-a-time connected, is this new, strange, transient union . . .

. . . It is called a Death Spiral. It looks beautiful, impossible. I think the ice burns my skin, but can't say for sure. Can't

59

distinguish between hot and cold; can't say with any authority whether I'm feeling pleasure or pain.

And if I say it is one, how can I tell whether it will remain that constantly? Not metamorphose into its opposite number? What's the difference?

I let you spin me until I'm dizzy as washing. My hair touches the ice, becomes wet with it. My back is arched like a cat's. I feel the cold air rising; hear the rush of it. I know that if you were to see me from above, I would not register as me. I would be an undulating blur, like a plate on a potter's wheel.

I want to press the blade of my boot hard against your skin.

To see if it hurts.

I want cause and effect.

When the phone rang, Alison took a moment to register. She put down the pages and picked up the receiver, still half in the world of her words.

'Alison?'

'Yeah. Hi, Hannah. How are you?' There was a silence. Alison waited. 'What is it?'

'I've been thinking. It's about coming to Spain.'

20

Easter Island

As Bill left the Tate he rewound his Dictaphone and listened again to the curator's talk he'd just left.

'He came to attention with the extraordinary photographs of his family. His alcoholic father and his, um, overweight mother, in a tower block – or "high rise".'

Bill fast-forwarded. 'There's a kind of new aesthetic quality to it . . . um, wonderful colours, the colours of the wallpaper and the bedspread that the artist has particularly, um, kind of used, I think.'

'Christ,' Bill said to the black box.

He realised that he enjoyed walking through London streets more than any exhibition. In a gap between the uniform Georgian houses built in the square facing the immaculate cricket pitch was a single modern house. It stood out like a gold tooth. Someone walked past, and Bill instinctively said, 'Yep,' pretending the Dictaphone was a mobile. He'd heard a Radio 4 programme about people who hear voices. There was a help-line they could phone, and he'd wondered how the fuck that would work. The expert had said, if you felt compelled to answer the voices back, it needn't be embarrassing; you should just carry a mobile and pretend you're having a conversation. The curator on Bill's imaginary mobile droned on.

'Also, you'll notice that he veers between extreme close focus on his father's skin and face, which produces the most extraordinary effect – I mean, at one point he looks like a kind of Easter Island statue lying on his back, you know with pitted, um, skin – and passages where the whole thing is blurred, almost abstract.'

Bill thought of his own dad. He hadn't looked like an Easter Island statue the last time he'd seen him, he'd looked like a man who'd fucked his liver to fuck. The colours hadn't looked wonderful in his private hospital room. They'd not inspired him. He snapped the tape off, and pulled open the door of the old-fashioned red phone booth. He was just about to leave a message when Alison picked up.

'Hi. I'm here, I'm just screening.'

'I'm honoured, then,' Bill said.

'I've just hung up on Hannah; I thought you might be her.'

'You OK?'

'Not really. She's not going to come with me to do the ashes. I've waited more than a year. I've waited – Mum's waited! And now she says I should do it without her.'

'Shall I come round?' Bill asked.

'Can you? That'd be great.'

The top deck of the bus was practically empty, which meant Bill was able to sit at the front and get the full value of the view as they crossed the river. He always felt cheated if he was so caught up in a book or paper or just daydreaming that he missed it. Today the river was dark and glossy. The tide was high and a police boat sped east, churning up a thick foaming V in its wake. Above it, the London Eye was an O written with a thick, calligrapher's nib, pivoting as they moved farther south. The bus went through Vauxhall and Stockwell, past the Portuguese cafés and Irish pubs. As it pulled up at a stop, Bill saw tangled ribbons of cassette tape fluttering from the branches of a tree. He imagined someone collecting the stray tape from all London's trees, and splicing it into a monumental sound installation. He still had some old answerphone tapes with Sam's messages on. Her disembodied voice saying silly, inconsequential things; private jokes. He could contribute those to it. It could become an endless soundtrack of messages heard too late, or saying the wrong thing, or the right thing at the wrong time or by the wrong people.

The bus hit traffic when it reached Brixton. As it crawled along past the Ritzy cinema, Bill couldn't stop himself checking for Sam's car on Rushcroft Road. He didn't think he was half as bad as he had been, and he reasoned it was a natural enough thing to do, but he had a sudden flash of himself as a young boy sitting in the passenger seat next to his father, watching as he – oh so casually – checked as they drove past a certain house. It wasn't anything obvious, but something in Bill's own gesture had brought the association to mind. He shuddered. As it happened Sam's car wasn't there, and Bill in spite of himself began to concoct the various places she might be, the things she might be doing.

Alison answered the entryphone and buzzed Bill in. She was wearing faded navy pyjamas with a jumper over them, and she looked as if she'd been crying. Bill offered her a carrier bag.

'What's this?'

'Research. And supplies.'

She removed the two bottles of wine and tipped rest of the contents onto the settee. She picked up the videos: *Snow White*, *Dumbo*, *The Lion King*, *Bambi*, *The Little Mermaid* and *Fantasia*.

'OK, I'm guessing regression therapy?'

'What the fuck is this?' Bill asked, poking at a fern. The outer fronds spread over the edges of a saucer that it soaked in, and the centre opened out like a prehistoric flower, its petals like hunks of seaweed.

'It's called a Jerusalem Rose. Hannah and I had them when we were kids. I hadn't seen them since.'

'I'm not surprised.' Bill touched it cautiously at the edges. The paler sand-brown tips were still dry and folded in like curled fingers. 'It's scary.'

'So, what's with the Disney?'

63

'Oh, it's this article they've asked me to think about for Disney's centenary. They want a fresh angle – "something cynical and controversial" is how they put it. So which one shall we watch first?'

Films had featured almost from the very beginning between Alison and Bill. They'd first met when they were both still students. Alison had been rooting around in a junkshop on Coldharbour Lane. She was leafing through a book when she heard someone ask if anyone knew of a doctor nearby. Alison did, and said so. The person who'd asked was Bill. He'd been stung, he wasn't sure by what, but he believed he was allergic to wasp stings. He swelled up, he told Alison as she led him to the A and E department of King's College Hospital. She ended up waiting with him, unsure if it was safe to leave him. After a good few hours, he was given a shot of antihistamine and discharged. Bill thanked Alison and took her phone number. A week later he phoned, inviting her to see a Tarkovsky film in a cinema on Oxford Street. She hadn't been sure if it was a date, or if she wanted it to be, but she agreed to go out of curiosity. They sat through an hour of the film. All Alison could remember of it later was how cold and miserable everyone in the film had been, and that the usherette had been perched on a stool, knitting a long orange and green striped scarf. Just as Alison was twitching for it to end, Bill had leaned over and whispered, 'It's in the wrong order.'

The projectionist had got the reels in a muddle, and Bill had been the only one to notice. Alison could have hugged him. She still had no idea how it ended (or was it started?), nor did she care. Alison and Bill had walked to the Blue Posts on Rupert Street and spent a much more pleasurable afternoon getting very slowly drunk. And that had been the general pattern of their friendship ever since.

'Al, come and watch this. It's great.'

Bill was sprawled on the settee, holding the remote. He rewound and watched as the mermaids sped through their routine in reverse.

Alison came back from the kitchen with a bowl of hot, salted popcorn, which she placed between them, slumping down next to him. Bill pressed Play and the action resumed.

'Under the sea,' they sang.

'I used to wish I was a mermaid,' Alison said, dropping popcorn into her mouth. 'I loved the whole long-hair thing – that and the swimming. Then I thought about how they had no genitals. It's like a metaphor for Chinese foot binding. Or female circumcision. The little mermaid has to give up her voice in order to have legs.'

'So she can't have any screaming orgasms.'

'Exactly. Or tell them what she really thinks. When I read it to Jo it was so disturbing I had to ad lib the ending. First there's her painful feet, then she can only get a soul if the prince marries her, which he doesn't as she can't talk, then she can't bring herself to kill him – even though all her sisters cut off their hair to get her a knife – so in the end she becomes foam. How crap is that? Foam!'

'Yeah. Grim.'

They ate popcorn as Ariel sang, 'What would I give to live where you are?'

'Pathetic,' Alison said, taking the remote and fast-forwarding.

'Maybe her sisters become militant feminists.'

'I hope so.'

'OK, let's try something else,' Bill said. 'You've ruined this for me now. What next?'

So far, they'd watched *The Lion King* and *Fantasia*. Alison's tiny TV hadn't done *Fantasia* justice, but it was still quite trippy, and they'd searched for the subliminal Mickey's Bill had read about on some Disney freak site. The 'Sorcerer's Apprentice' scene had set Alison's teeth on edge, when Mickey and the army of brooms flooded the workshop.

'It's like *Some Mothers Do 'Ave 'Em*. Mum used to hate that. All the waste.'

'What waste?'

'You know, everything getting broken and falling apart.'

'I never thought, What a waste. I always thought, What crap props.'

'I guess it came from rationing. She used to have to leave the room. With me it was the plate-spinning acts in those Variety Show Specials. You'd sit there, knowing the one on the end was losing momentum, and you'd want to yell, "Behind you!" Then crash! Just thinking about it now makes me feel sick.'

'That's the control freak in you.'

'Yeah, maybe.'

'You know, I can't hear this music without seeing these pictures. What year was it made? Nineteen forty something? It must have been the first ever music video. Just think, we've Disney to thank for MTV.'

'God bless him. Mojácar's most famous son.'

'What do you mean?'

'That's what they say – that Walt Disney was born in Mojácar.'

'But he was American. He was about as American as it gets, surely?'

'Well, apparently not. Don't ask me why, but that's what they say.'

'I thought it was Spaghetti Westerns southern Spain was famous for.'

'It is. But legend has it that Uncle Walt was born there, too.'

'That's incredible. Are you sure?'

'"Course I'm sure. I mean, I'm sure that's what they say. I haven't a clue whether or not it's true.'

Bill looked through the stack of videos. 'Are you up to watching the Big B?' He held out the video of *Bambi*.

'Oh God, I'm not sure. All I remember is there's a fire and Bambi's mum dies.'

'No! And I thought there was a car chase.'

'Oh, go on, then, stick it on.'

By the time the credits rolled, Bill and Alison had consumed a whole tub of Häagen-Dazs and were feeling sick as well as emotionally purged.

'Phew!' Alison said. She reached for the tissues and blew her nose noisily. 'When we saw *Bambi* as kids, Hannah took a biscuit tin with an egg in it. She'd found it in the fields across from our house – a cuckoo must have booted it out or something. She'd rescued it and was incubating it in cotton wool inside this biscuit tin. She was convinced it would hatch. Took it everywhere.'

'What happened?'

'Can't remember, but I'm sure I'd have remembered if it had hatched – that would have been a bit memorable. I guess Mum managed to prise it from her after it started to smell. Isn't that extraordinary? I couldn't remember anything about the film, but I remember that.'

'It's totally different now how kids see films,' said Bill. 'We hardly ever saw a film more than once, unless it was on telly at Christmas. Now kids watch the same film over and over. The same scene, even. They prepare themselves for the traumatic bits, knowing that if they endure it it'll all work out. It's like trauma immunisation.'

'That's true. Jo can recite most of *The Wizard of Oz* by heart. I suppose fairy tales for us were like videos are for them.' Alison looked outside. It was getting dark. 'My God, how long have we been sitting watching films?'

'Hours and hours.'

'Look at me – I'm still in my pyjamas. Well, it's not as if I was going to get much done today.'

Bill ejected the video and returned it to its case.

'So how did you leave things with Hannah?' he asked.

Alison sighed. 'Oh, it's something and nothing, really. She doesn't want to be responsible for stalling the ash scattering, but there's always been some copper-bottomed reason that's prevented her.'

'Do you reckon she's making excuses?'

'No, it's not that. That's why it's so difficult. I know she believes absolutely in the reasons she gives. But I think she's run out of reasons, and this time she's called my bluff. If I want to do it sooner rather than later, as far as she's concerned I should just go ahead and do it.'

'Without her?'

'Yep. She doesn't want to be blamed for holding me up.'

'So the ball's in your court.'

'I suppose. I just wish she'd said that a year ago.'

'But a year ago she probably didn't realise that.'

'Do you always have to play devil's advocate?'

'What do you mean?'

'I mean I know that, I just want you to be on my side, even if I'm not being reasonable.'

'OK.'

Bill watched as Alison got up and went to the kitchen. He heard her pick up the kettle and fill it with water, then click the electric ignition to light the gas. Click click click click, bouf. She walked back through to the living room.

'The thing is, I can't do it without her,' she said, pushing the empty wine glasses together and tidying around. 'I mean, for one thing I can't drive.'

'What's that got to do with it?'

'Everything. Mum wanted her ashes scattered in Manacar. That's this really remote beach. The only way you can get to it is by car. She knows that.' Alison shot a glance at Bill. 'I mean Hannah, not Mum.'

The kettle started whining like a petulant child. The whine gathered volume and turned into a shrill scream. Bill winced, itching to go through and turn off the gas. Alison seemed not to hear it. She picked up the glasses and walked back through to the kitchen. Bill let out his breath as the gas was turned off and the kettle silenced. Alison had never learned to drive, and he knew there was no point going over that again now. Bill and Sam had both tried to persuade her to take lessons – Sam had even offered to teach her – but it was a subject where rational argument was useless: it was her one phobia. It puzzled him though; she was such an in-the-driving-seat person. Alison returned, dressed in tracksuit bottoms and a sweatshirt, with a cafetière and two cups on a tray. It appeared they were officially sobering up.

'Looks to me like you've two or three options,' Bill said, clearing a space for the tray. 'Either you hold your horses and wait till Hannah's good and ready—'

'Which may never happen. Or?'

'Or you scatter the ashes somewhere else.'

'Impossible. What's left?' she asked, plunging the cafetière, forcing the coffee grounds to the bottom of the jug.

'You go with someone who can drive.'

21

Worldly Goods

Ground floor: perfumery, stationery and leather goods, wigs and haberdashery, kitchenware and food. Going up.

> David Croft, *Are You Being Served?*

'What, so Bill has actually volunteered to go with you?'

Sam had to shout over the noise of the industrial shredder that had just been activated in the disused C&A on Oxford Street. Alison mimed to Sam she'd tell her later, and they gave up trying to compete with the racket, and turned their attention to the artist in blue overalls who was in the process of destroying all his possessions.

There were thousands of things. Inventories were displayed on the walls under various headings: Clothes, Artwork, Electrical, and Furniture. Alison read the descriptions of the individual items that added up to the sum of a person. It reminded her of *Desert Island Discs*: the final question, when the interviewee is asked what luxury item they'd take. Their choices always revealed more than an entire database could. But this guy wasn't selecting anything; he was removing every trace. Nearby, an original sign left over from the shop was still fixed to the wall. It read, 'Everything Must Go'. She turned round again. Sam was looking on wistfully as a mechanic dismantled a red car, placing the components in yellow trays that moved slowly around a long, winding conveyor belt. A team of helpers removed pieces from the trays and broke them down even further. One of them peeled the plastic coating from an electrical cable, putting the bare copper wire in one tray and the insulation in another. Alison was struck by how immensely complicated throwing away the simplest thing was. It was a kind of inverted alchemy, reducing complex structures back to their base elements, and it made her dizzy.

She and Sam moved around the room with the rest of the spectators, Alison wincing as one of the helpers picked up a pile of snapshots, scribbled on them, tore them into pieces and returned them to a tray. A koala-bear slipper travelled the length of the belt; a slow ten minutes away from being deconstructed and granulated. It was like *The Generation Game* in reverse, she thought, only it was deadly serious. This was so calculated, so scrupulous. Who would you be if you had nothing? Alison watched as Sam took photos. At least she could salvage something; they would still exist for her, at least.

'I can't bear this, Sam,' Alison said when the shredder was switched off and they could hear themselves. 'Can we go, please?'
'Sure.'

They headed through the crowds and towards the doors. David Bowie was singing from the soon-to-be-destroyed ghetto blaster as they found their way onto the street. The doors swung to behind them and Sam turned to Alison. A fine sweat covered her face.

'Hey, Al, are you feeling OK?'

'Not really.' Her voice was teary and she took a gulp of air, trying to collect herself. 'That was so upsetting. How can he bear to do it?'

'I don't know; maybe the fact that it's his choice.'

'God, I can't even clear out clothes,' she wailed, 'and that's when I have a chuck-out for charity, so at least then I can feel it's useful. This was so . . . so wilful.'

'I know. I kept wanting to rescue things. Well, to steal things, if I'm honest. Did you see those kids nicking stuff?'

'No, but I don't blame them.'

Shoppers bustled by as they walked towards Tottenham Court

Road. Alison looked at all their carrier bags full of stuff; stuff they needed to sustain being who they believed themselves to be.

'Where to now?' Sam asked as Centrepoint loomed into view. Alison didn't answer, just walked on in a daze. Sam took her arm. 'You look like you could do with a drink,' she said, steering her down a side street. 'Come on.'

In the lounge at Bradley's, Sam pressed the numbers on the old juke box, and 'White Horses' started to play. She sat down opposite Alison at a cramped corner table, picked up her vodka and orange and sighed. 'Ah, that's better.'

Alison smiled weakly. 'I love this song. It's like cocoa; it makes you feel all safe and secure.'

They listened, letting the words wrap round them like a big, soft blanket.

> On white horses,
> Snowy white horses,
> Let me ride away.

Alison glazed over, transported back to a vague memory of Eastern European children's programmes. When the tune faded out and the horses cantered off into the distance, it all came back to her, and she felt her stomach clench. The artist had really got to her; she felt he was criticising and ridiculing her personally.

'Oh, there were so many nice things,' she said. 'I'm such a hoarder. I mean, I can't even get my hair cut. It's like I don't ever want to narrow down my options by deciding what to part with.'

'Yeah, but then that becomes a choice: you're choosing not to choose.'

'That's a bit philosophical, Sam!' Alison looked up at her, but Sam just shrugged and pulled a packet of Golden Virginia from her bag. 'I don't know,' Alison went on, 'maybe that's true. But everything! Even his dad's sheepskin jacket – how could he bear to do that?'

'I know. The Saab.'

'The paintings.'

'The Saab.'

'Yeah, well. That wouldn't be much use to me.'

'No, I guess not. Al, why won't you learn to drive?'

Alison lifted the Guinness to her lips, took a mouthful and deliberately set the glass back on the beer mat. She directed her reply to the glass.

'Living in London I never felt the need.' Sam waited. 'I didn't exactly have a lot of warning I'd be in Spain for two years. That was tough. Mum always used to drive when I visited, or Hannah when she was over. It just hadn't been a problem till then.'

'So couldn't you have learned then?'

Alison looked up at her. 'Sam, I hardly had time to think. Anyway, you need to be a resident to take your test.'

'I'm sorry; I didn't mean to be insensitive. But you could learn now. You know I'll teach you.'

Alison studied her glass, poking her finger in the froth on her Guinness. 'It's not that simple.'

'But if you passed your test you wouldn't need anyone to go with you to sort out your mum's ashes.'

'I know.' She looked at Sam again, willing her to drop the subject. If she started to untangle the logical from the illogical, it would all fall around her ears. Now wasn't the time. Later, after the ashes, after Spain, would be soon enough. 'I can't explain it,' she said. 'As soon as I even sit in the driving seat . . .'

Sam rolled the tobacco between her fingers, waiting for Alison to continue. 'Were you ever in an accident?' she asked eventually.

'No. It's not anything logical. I just can't.'

'So what's that all about then?' Sam asked, licking along the edge of the paper.

Alison blew air from her lips, sick of answering the same question, but knowing she'd never found a good enough answer. She didn't want to think about it that hard. Not now, not yet.

'Mum used to try and tell me that nobody else wants an accident, but I guess I don't believe it. No matter how carefully *I* drive, I can't do anything about the other people on the road. That feels like a big risk to take.'

Sam lit her roll-up and inhaled. 'Well, I'm with your mum on this one. You just have to have faith.'

'Yeah, well, that isn't something you can just get. If you don't have it, you don't have it.'

'Which is why you need a driver to come to Spain with you.'

'Yep.'

Put like that, Alison felt foolish. It was like telling herself as a child, *If I get all the way home without walking on the cracks in the pavement, nothing bad will happen.* Recognising this didn't make it any less real, though; she still wanted to avoid the cracks and get safely home.

'Al, you know I would if I could. If you could wait a month I could free up the time, but these damn babies will keep being born to a nine-month schedule.'

Babies. Babies were such an intractable reason, Alison thought. Who could argue with an excuse like babies? They were the royal flush of reasonable reasons.

'I know. It's OK, and thanks anyway.'

'In the next three weeks I've got five shoots, all in their eighth month. They always like to leave it till they're practically about to pop. One of these days I'm going to end up at a birth, I just know it.'

'Well, like I said, Bill wants to come. He's following up this Disney thing. I don't know if he's serious about needing to research it, or just saying that to make me feel better.'

'You never can tell with Bill. Either way, it's good of him.'

'Yeah, it is.' Alison looked at her and laughed. 'That's about the nicest thing you've said about Bill since you split up.'

'I know. He's a lovely man, I realise that. Maybe he was just too lovely.'

'Not enough of a bastard?'

'Well, I don't think I go for bastards, exactly.'

'What, then?'

'I don't know. He faffed about with things. If he was heating up a pizza, he always had to fiddle with it, put some more olives on or grate a bit more cheese on top.'

'OK, that makes sense. How could you ever consider getting serious about a man who embellishes pizza? God, Sam.'

'I know. Pathetic. I couldn't suss out his sell-by date. There wasn't any good reason for us ever to split up. To begin with, that felt nice, but then it scared me. It felt too . . . permanent, like "Is That All There Is?"'

'But you can never guarantee anything. You never know what's round the corner.'

'No, but it felt like I could, which felt, oh, I don't know, claustrophobic. I suppose it's easier to dump than be dumped. To chuck it all into a big industrial shredder before it gets spoiled.'

'Well, that's logical.'

'It's as logical as your reason for not wanting to drive.'

'It's the opposite of my reason: you believe you can guarantee the future; I believe you can't.'

'Well, it amounts to the same thing.'

22

Baby Moon

Though worlds of wanwood leafmeal lie;
And yet you will weep and know why.
Gerard Manley Hopkins

'OK,' said Carla after a few moments' consideration. 'Now, I think the best oils for you today, bella, are Roman camomile to calm and help with your feelings of frustration and anxiety; coriander for fear of failure and to help balance you; cedarwood for the sense that I feel in you of general worry and mental strain, and rose to help you feel the mother love that I can tell you're missing so terribly. How do you feel about that?'

Hannah felt on cue: frustrated, anxious, unbalanced, worried, strained. A motherless child. Only, now, she also felt she couldn't breathe. She nodded feebly. Carla leaned across and touched her arm, and Hannah felt as if she'd been given an electric shock. She was tense, all right.

Jacques had given her this aromatherapy massage as an anniversary gift, and she'd put it off and put it off. But here she finally was, in this calm room with drawn curtains and subdued lighting, a massage table at its centre, and a little arrangement of fresh flowers on the writing desk near where Carla sat opposite her. Carla had a wonderful, soothing accent. She was from Italy, and she unconsciously peppered her sentences with 'Eco' and 'Va bene'. Hannah had found it easier than she'd expected to give Carla her case history, as if they were not facts about her but a story she was telling about someone else. From time to time, Carla had prompted her with questions, and taken notes.

'Va bene. Now I shall leave you to undress. I think the room should be nice and warm, but please don't hesitate to say if you feel cold or at all uncomfortable, OK?' She looked at Hannah and gave her arm a little squeeze. This time Hannah didn't flinch. 'As soon as you're ready, hop onto the table. We'll start face down. If you can put your head through the hole here' – she pointed to a head-sized hole in the top end of the table – 'that way, you don't have to twist your neck. And there are some warm towels on the side there for you to cover yourself with when you're ready.'

Carla left the room and Hannah remained seated for a moment before getting up and doing as Carla had instructed. After removing her clothes and folding them into a neat pile, tucking her knickers and bra into the pockets of her tracksuit bottoms, she clambered onto the table and covered herself with a thick towel. She lay down on her stomach, wriggled her face into the hole and looked down. On the pale-blue carpet directly below her were some semi-precious stones arranged into a spiral. She didn't know the names of all of them, but recognised the amethyst and remembered a chunk of it that she'd had since her childhood, a souvenir from the Lake District. She wondered abstractedly what Jo was doing at school, and could see her in her mind's eye, sitting at a table with a group of children, some books in front of her.

Carla returned and quietly closed the door behind her. 'Comfortable?'

Hannah said, 'Yes,' but her mouth was on one side of the table through the hole, while her ears were on the other, making her voice seem very far away. She heard Carla speaking to her.

'So, bella, we have a whole hour now, and please, anything you feel, any noises you make, don't try to stop them. And if you want to cry, please do. Tears are my friends.'

This phrase clung to Hannah. Tears are my friends. Tears are my friends. It danced around her ears and crept inside her head.

Carla rang a little bell three times. It had a high, pure sound which resonated for a long time. Tears are my friends. Then Hannah felt the hands begin to work on her back. Soothing, assured. She tried to see herself from above; to map out exactly what Carla was doing, where she was touching, but she couldn't. The hands were firm on her, but elusive, too. At no time was connection between Carla's hands and Hannah's flesh lost. Carla seemed to be magnetically fixed to her, so that even when Carla moved from one side of the table to the other, Hannah was unable to work out how. After a while she stopped trying to work it out. She stared at the spiral of stones below. Turquoise was there, and rose quartz and malachite. She closed her eyes.

Beth's top drawer
When I looked in Beth's top drawer, I found
A pair of lacy knickers
When I looked in Beth's top drawer, I found
A pair of lacy knickers and a toy gun
When I looked in Beth's top drawer, I found
A pair of lacy knickers, a toy gun and a brown comb with a strand of her hair
When I looked in Beth's top drawer, I found
A pair of lacy knickers, a toy gun, a brown comb with a strand of her hair and a recipe for lemon curd
When I looked in Beth's top drawer, I found
A pair of lacy knickers, a toy gun, a brown comb with a strand of her hair, a recipe for lemon curd and a sewing kit
When I looked in Beth's top drawer, I found
A pair of lacy knickers, a toy gun, a brown comb with a strand of her hair, a recipe for lemon curd, a sewing kit and some airmail letters

When I looked in Beth's top drawer, I found
A pair of lacy knickers, a toy gun, a brown comb with a strand of her
hair, a recipe for lemon curd, a sewing kit, some airmail letters and a
pot of Age Defying All Day Lifting Foundation
When I looked in Beth's top drawer, I found
A pair of lacy knickers, a toy gun, a brown comb with a strand of her
hair, a recipe for lemon curd, a sewing kit, some airmail letters, a pot
of Age Defying All Day Lifting Foundation and a malachite egg
When I looked in Beth's top drawer, I found
A pair of lacy knickers, a toy gun, a brown comb with a strand of her
hair, a recipe for lemon curd, a sewing kit, some airmail letters, a pot
of Age Defying All Day Lifting Foundation, a malachite egg and a
torn piece of paper with the words 'Baby Moon' written in her hand.

Carla kneaded and unlocked and stroked. Secrets that she had
stored in her ribs; residual sadness in her armpits. Things lost in the
small of her back. Pulling, coaxing.

Hannah did not feel the tears as they fell from her and ploshed
down, wetting the semi-precious stones, making them shine.

23

Air Con

Manuel Martínez sat at his desk in his small office in Garrucha. It was ten o'clock and the post had just arrived. He'd seen the postman through the window, a young man he didn't recognise, and had waited till he was sure the risk of conversation had passed before opening his door and unlocking the box attached to the wall outside. Retrieving the half-dozen letters, locking the box and returning to his desk, he held the wad of envelopes with a familiarity he guessed he'd never lose; expertly sorting them into a natural order of precedence. He put the one that was handwritten at the bottom of the pile.

It was still something of a novelty having post delivered and not collecting it from the post office. He felt guilty that someone was burdened with the whole town's letters to deliver, including his own, when he was perfectly capable of popping out to collect them himself. It was like having breakfast in bed if you weren't sick – it was an indulgence.

'Life moves on,' he heard his mother say. She'd had no qualms about taking her breakfast in bed. She'd been all for change – which she'd regarded wholesale as progress. He pondered how this had happened. Right up to her death, she'd happily embraced the new. It was her who'd pestered him to get satellite TV; even brought a tray of refreshments up for the men who'd come to install the white dish high on their pretty roof terrace. Cans of Coca-Cola and a plate of madalenas.

Her philosophy had been 'Off with the old and on with the new.' Why not take advantage of the things that made life easier? She'd say, why bother with the little vegetable shops for a couple of onions, and the bread shop for a loaf, when you could get everything in one simple trip to Komo Komo?

Why, for example, did Manuel insist on keeping his father's old Seat, when he could perfectly well afford a nice new car, one with air con? He was such a stick-in-the-mud. She thought his trips to José for wet shaves were, frankly, ridiculous. And she hadn't understood why he'd made such a song and dance about the changes at work, letting this new man, Ramón, get up his nose, as she put it.

'Get over it, Manuel. What's so wrong with him making sure you're at your desk by eight, if that's the time you're paid to be there?'

'It's the principle of the thing. Before Ramón came along, we got the same amount done – more, probably – but we'd have a chat over a coffee first. We knew what was going on in each other's lives, and we cared.'

'Looks to me like your Ramón cares, too; about getting a full day's work out of you lot. I don't see why you have such a problem with that.'

Manuel knew he'd never make her see, but he couldn't stop himself trying. Couldn't save his breath, as she'd have said. She had a knack of making his words as insubstantial as the bubbles that José smothered onto his chin before smartly slicing through. But he'd persevered. It was in the fabric of their relationship that he persevered.

'We got to know the people who came in,' he said weakly, 'so when we saw them outside work, we'd say hello. Ramón hasn't time for that: It's not "cost-effective"; it doesn't "add value".' Adding melodramatically, 'He's sucked the joy out of the day.'

'Pah!' she said over the sound of the television. 'Pah! If you were more like Ramón, you'd get yourself an electric razor.'

Even thinking about this now, five years on, Manuel felt the acid sensation in his gut. He fished around in the desk tray for his Zantac, found the packet under a brochure for a new printing company in Vera, and took two tablets with the cold remains of his cup of camomile tea. The infusion never failed to transport him to fields of freshly mown hay. His doctor had advised him to give up coffee and to minimise stress, around the time his mother had passed away. He'd gone for a check-up, both as a reflex response to her death and because he was so accustomed to the doctor's presence at his mother's behest that he'd got to enjoy his company. The doctor had been more concerned than Manuel was used to.

'It's just an ulcer now, but it's there for a reason,' he'd announced ominously. 'Listen to your ulcer, see what it's trying to tell you. Make the changes while you still have the choice.'

Manuel had been astounded by this use of language. It seemed as if the whole town had been watching the same daytime television as his mother. Changes, changes, changes. But he'd thought about it. He'd hardly felt it decent to confess that the major stress in his life had just gone to a better place, but, as he took a walk that lunchtime, he meditated on the theme.

His method of meditation was to sit on a bench overlooking the harbour and to watch the sea. Listening to the tinkle of the boat masts, breathing in the smells of salt and fish on drying nets, feeling the warmth of sun on his skin, thinking of nothing. When he returned from this state, the answers usually suggested themselves as if they had been patiently waiting for his attention. The answers that were waiting after this particular sojourn meant that he had gone straight home and dismantled the satellite dish. The following morning, he handed in his resignation at the post office.

After thirty years, his colleagues couldn't understand it – less still when they heard what he planned to do next.

'A funeral director? Why the hell would you want to be a funeral director?'

It was a question he still found hard to answer in a way that would make sense to anyone else. So he'd once again be able to do what he'd most loved about his old job: be courteous and kind to people; make a difference. It sounded ludicrously Quixotic, even to his own ears: to be gentle and gallant. To do something that would have made his mother go 'Pah!'

As suspected, the first five letters were run-of-the-mill, but the final one was much more promising. The stamp was English, and the words 'Air Mail' had been written in the top left-hand corner in sepia ink. The postmark was the 22nd. Manuel checked the calendar on the wall behind him. Over a week. He tutted quietly and ran the sharp blade of his letter-opener along the top.

> My dear Señor Martínez
> It's been a while. I send you greetings and hope this letter finds you in good health.
> Now (eventually!) it has arrived the time that I am able to collect the final remains of my mother from your safekeeping.
> I shall be visiting you on the 31st October 2001 and hope that this will be convenient. I shall hope to be arriving between 10 and 12 in the morning.
> Until then,
>
> > Alison Vine
> > (Daughter of Beth Vine)

Manuel held the letter for a long time. He read and reread the lines. She wrote as she spoke; in chatty, not quite accurate Spanish, so that he could hear the young woman, and picture her as clearly as if she were there in his office.

It had been spring of the previous year when she'd knocked on the door and asked if she could talk to him.

'Please, come in. Take a seat. How can I help?'

A tall woman of about thirty, she was dressed in old corduroy trousers and a patterned shirt. She had carrier bags of shopping with her, which she balanced around her feet before searching in her large

shoulder bag for a note-pad. An orange rolled out from one of the
bags, but she didn't notice. She wore chunky white sandals and her
toenails were painted turquoise. Manuel had been fascinated by
them, and had found himself staring at them when she spoke. She
was in something of a hurry, she explained, full of questions,
determined to be businesslike. She wiped the sweat from her face
and looked directly into his eyes.

'I have come to discover information to allow for my mother to
make arrangements for her funeral.'

'Of course,' he'd said. 'What do you need to know?'

She needed to know everything. What was and was not
permitted, what exactly would happen – the time scale, the paperwork, the costs – everything. As Manuel answered her questions,
she occasionally repeated his words, or asked him to explain again,
to make sure she'd understood. And she took notes; ticking her own
questions when they'd been answered to her satisfaction.

Although not the first English woman he'd provided a funeral for,
she was the first to question him in such detail. Could the deceased stay
at the house prior to a funeral, or did the law require their removal?
What did a funeral parlour look like? Was it absolutely necessary for
there to be a church service? What would the coffin be like? Manuel
had found her approach refreshing. Her strange grasp of the language
no doubt contributed to the uninhibited nature of her questions, which
in turn had a curious effect on him. He felt liberated and spontaneous.
But what he'd said next surprised even his own ears.

'Perhaps it would help if I showed you.'

She looked confused.

'Please,' he continued, 'leave your things here; they'll be perfectly
safe.'

He reached for his keys and went to the door that led out onto
the street. Bright sunlight bleached the pavement outside. He
waited for the woman to follow.

24

Seat

Alison checked her reflection in the passenger mirror, flipped up the visor and replaced her tortoiseshell Ray-Bans. The sunglasses had been Beth's and were slightly loose on her. She'd not got round to having them adjusted, although she kept meaning to.

'I've arranged to visit the funeral director before lunch,' she told Bill, 'Señor Martínez – he's been looking after the ashes since the cremation. Such a lovely man. I went to see him about a week before Mum died. He was brilliant. He took me to this lock-up where he kept his coffins stacked on Dexion. There was this little pea-green Seat parked in the middle of everything, same colour as his eyes. Must have been forty years old, but in immaculate condition.'

'For a non-driver you seem to know a lot about cars.'

'Only old cute ones. I haven't a clue what this one is.'

Bill was driving the hired car that had been waiting for them at Almería airport. It was a newish Peugeot, and they were in the central lane of a new motorway flanked by dusty bushes of oleander. He overtook a three-wheeled white truck that ambled along to their right with two old men in the front and a goat in the back. Lorries hurtled past on the left, and Bill instinctively reached down with his left hand for a gear stick that wasn't there.

On either side of the road were polythene-covered structures the size of warehouses. The air, all of a sudden acrid, caught in his throat.

Alison coughed. 'Quick, close the windows.'

Bill fumbled for the switch, keeping his eyes on the road. He pressed the electric control in the central panel and both windows hummed shut. He turned on the air-conditioning.

'What is it?' he asked.

'Tomatoes. See? They're drip-fed chemical shit, sprayed with pesticides, and delivered to Tesco's in charming rustic boxes. Remember what you saw from the plane?'

Bill had pointed out the squares of shimmering light in the patchwork of red earth. He'd asked Alison if they were swimming pools.

'This is your Bel Air, honey,' Alison said, in an attempt at an American accent.

This mood she was in unnerved Bill. Since their flight, she'd turned into some kind of weird tour operator. He kept quiet, letting her continue her monologue. She pulled her hands through her hair, scraping it back and securing it with an elastic band. Her sunglasses slipped down the bridge of her nose, and she pushed them back up.

'Want to know the best bit? Guess what this place is called? Campo Hermosa, which means "beautiful land". It makes you want to weep.'

They continued in silence, Bill concentrating on driving on the 'wrong' side of the unfamiliar road.

They left the motorway and ascended a mountain road, eye-stretching light appearing and disappearing as the sea came in and out of view. The grey steel of the crash barrier that wound like ribbon alongside them puckered intermittently into buckled lengths. Old cars rested among the aloe and prickly pear below. Up ahead, a man in blue overalls stood in the road holding a Stop sign. Bill slowed to a halt in front of a red and white barricade, and pulled on the hand brake. A caterpillar digger balanced on a shelf of land above them scooped away from the overhanging mountain. Red earth cascaded into the road and tumbled further down the mountain, towards the sea. The man with the Stop sign scratched himself, absently twirling the sign.

'He told me that he used to work in a post office.'

'Who?'

'Señor Martínez.'

'So how come he ended up as an undertaker?'

'Got pissed off with the bureaucracy.'

'So he decided to work at the celestial sorting office instead?'

Alison smiled. 'I guess so. He did the strangest thing when he came to collect Mum on the day she died. He asked me if he could have a cutting of donkey's tail.'

25

Dymo

Kim twisted the dial on the Dymo and squeezed the gun. She turned the dial and squeezed again. A narrow tongue of plastic started to feed out of the slit. She found a rhythm twisting and pressing, made a final punch and tore it free. Easing the plastic coating from the back, she pressed the tape to the window. It read, 'GOOD MORNING', the white capitals reversed out of the black, bruised into life. She loved this clunky word-making machine; she'd found it in a drawer in the apartment and considered it her inheritance from the previous tenants. She squinted so that her eyes focused on the view outside, then moved to the words on the smeared surface of the glass, her collection of shells that dangled on lengths of string from the curtain rail, then back to the view.

It was a good morning; the sea was sparkly, the sun just up. Mickey was still sleeping. He lay sprawled across her bed, his hair over his face. She pulled on her jeans and a tracksuit top, and pushed her feet into her old trainers, grabbing Mickey's leather jacket on her way out: it was sunny, but not hot. She shrugged it on; it felt nicely heavy and smelled of Mickey. Checking in her jeans for keys, she quietly closed the door behind her.

It was bliss being on the beach this early, the smell of morning. And she loved going out with the knowledge that there was a warm body in her bed. Reaching the water's edge, she dipped her fingers in the sea and splashed her face awake.

Kim still couldn't believe her luck that she was on a beach and not in some shit job in London. She'd only come out for a fortnight, and that was about five months ago. It had been a last-minute bargain, a package holiday with her friend Abi. Unfortunately, Abi's idea of a good time had turned out to be eating at the hotel where they were staying, nursing a courtesy liqueur which tasted of shampoo, and waiting for the phones to get cheap after ten so she could call Nathan, her boyfriend.

Everything that Kim loved had been a battle for Abi. They had even tanned differently, Kim's skin becoming easily golden while Abi's burned spectacularly. Kim remembered her angry red torso, naked but for the white ghost bikini reversed out of her like the letters in the Dymo. And whereas Kim had happily fallen into the rhythm of the days, Abi had fought it; siestas frustrating her mission to buy stuff to take home. Stuff that was difficult to pack. Stuff like earthenware casserole dishes and Lladró pottery. There was something on the menu at the hotel which had been graphically translated as 'milk-fed veal'. That image had haunted Kim; it was what Abi's Lladró reminded her of. Drippy people in long dresses the colour of mucus.

They quickly discovered that without the London routines they had nothing in common. They turned out to be a great disappointment to each other. And so, when the two weeks had ended and Kim met some guy who'd told her about a job in a local restaurant and an apartment she could just about afford to rent, she honestly hadn't been able to think of a reason not to stay on. Turned out that most of Mojácar had arrived by a similar route. Kim had nicknamed it 'the Village of No Regrets'.

Abi had swaddled her casserole dishes in tablecloths and her Lladro people in undies; and returned home to Nathan. Kim hadn't heard from her since. She'd spent the summer simply moving from one day to the next. It came easily to her – more easily than she'd have imagined, thinking of her London self – but there were no yardsticks to measure herself against here; no expectations to meet or not meet, and she discovered she liked that. She even liked the isolation of not understanding the language unless she consciously tuned in, although she was quickly picking it up without actually trying to, the way children do when they're open to new things. The more relaxed she was, the easier the words came. Strange, she'd never been any good at languages at school, but then there had never been anyone in Acton whom she wanted to speak to in French or German.

Mickey had come into her life a month or so back. She'd first seen him late one night at a concert out in the mountains. It was authentic flamenco, not for tourists; no swirling frilly dresses. The singing was like great sobs of pain, *cante jondo* – deep song – she discovered later. The words, though impenetrable, moved her immensely, and she had an overwhelming sensation of somehow having arrived. She'd got a lift there with a couple of local guys whose names she didn't know. The London Kim wouldn't have dreamed of hitching out into the unknown; bumping along in the back of a dusty car, not sure where she was heading. But she had, and it turned out she'd been right to, because there was her prize, Mickey. He bought her a drink, and they listened to the music in a horny trance. She'd returned to her flat on the back of his bike, and he'd just stayed. It was the nearest she'd allowed herself get to being in a relationship, and so far she had no complaints. He made her laugh, was a great fuck, had a sexy bike, and that, for the time being, was enough. More than enough. Her cup overflowed. Overflew.

She looked into a rock pool, fished out a bead of green glass and held it up to the light. It was perfect. Slipping it into her pocket, she breathed deeply. She must have only had a couple of hours sleep, and by rights she ought to have a hangover, but she felt fantastic. Maybe last night's tequila was still making her buzz.

An old man with white hair walked along the beach, bending down and collecting shells that he dropped into a carrier bag. Kim said good morning to him as he walked by, and watched him as he continued. It was easy to see him as a six-year-old boy doing just what he was doing now. She pictured him, not in the casual trousers and trainers he was wearing, but in a pair of red swimming trunks, with a blue bucket instead of a carrier bag. The two versions superimposed on each other; as if time had concertinaed fifty or sixty years.

Kim climbed onto a rock that was like a big black pudding; little meat-coloured pebbles embedded in concrete. She sat down, looking out to the horizon. A few fishing boats moved from right to left, returning to Garrucha, she guessed. Birds trailed behind them like the tails of a kite. She made a mental note of the word 'flotilla' to try out later on the window. Removed from the sea and placed on glass, it would look lost. She'd have to print multiples of it, spaced like the boats, and positioned just below the line where sea and sky met. Flotilla flotilla flotilla flotilla flotilla.

A sound broke through her thoughts, and she looked up. A plane cut across the sky, black and compact and incongruous. The noise ripped the air, out of sync with the motion of the plane. It hung like thunder long after the plane was out of sight. Kim felt dazed, and suddenly the glare of the light was painful. She felt in the inside pockets of the leather jacket for sunglasses, guessing where they'd be, and put them on, polarising the sea and sky. They were good ones, and she wondered where Mickey had got them. Curious, she started to pull out the rest of the contents of the pockets, laying them on the rock.

A wallet; not much cash, no credit cards; a driving licence; some phone numbers written on torn-off bits of Rizla packet; some condoms; and half a strip of photo-booth pictures. She studied Mickey's face in its two poses. He was pretty. It was his hair – not just the length of it, touching his shoulders, but the sun-bleached floppiness of it. There were girls who spent hours trying to achieve that tousled effect. She ought to know, the Saturdays she'd spent shampooing clients and sweeping their dead hair from the salon floor. Back in the day. She smiled now, looking at the pictures, minutely distinct from each other; thinking of her fingers in that hair as it fell across her thighs. The last thing she remembered him saying last night, before they both passed out, was that he wanted to sleep there, where her legs met. Who else had he used that line on? she wondered. Who had the other two photos, and where were they now? Maybe they were looking fondly at their little mementos at this very moment. Maybe he'd broken their hearts. Maybe he hadn't, and they'd binned the pictures the next day or week or month. Kim didn't care. She felt no jealousy, no desire to possess his past. Or his future, come to that.

Digging into the pocket on the other side, she felt a heavy, solid object; and as she pulled it out, last night came flooding back. She stared at the mobile phone, willing it not to be real, feeling dizzy as she remembered.

'At the third beep, the time sponsored by Accurist will be . . .'

What had it been? In England probably three or four, but in Hong Kong? And New York? And Melbourne? Oh, sweet baby Jesus, they must have called every speaking clock in the world. Mickey had said he wanted to hear time speaking.

Of course, it was the Es. She'd forgotten. Mickey had come into the Cantina early last night, at the beginning of her shift, slipping his closed fist over her upturned palm and dropping it in.

'What time are you through?'

'Tonight? It's quiet, shouldn't be too late. Say, midnight?'

'OK. Take this at eleven, and I'll take one then, too. Synchronise your watches.'

Then he'd fucked off on his bike. Kim had thought it was one of the most romantic gestures she'd ever known: making sure they were fuck-faced in unison.

When she'd finished for the night and Mickey had rocked up, everyone else had long gone, and she was already having difficulty with simple things, like closing up. She'd been entranced by the selection of keys, and overwhelmed by the security system. Mickey had sauntered in, got behind the bar and made margaritas for them both. She remembered now, he'd spent an age crushing ice cubes, slowly turning the handle on the machine, dropping shards into his mouth, then from his mouth into hers till they melted between their tongues. He sorted through the CDs while she stacked the chairs on the tables, and he'd DJ'd for her. He found the track 'La Flaca' – 'The Skinny One' – and sang it to her, nicknaming her La Flaca. They danced between the tables.

As Kim swept the floors, Mickey had rummaged about behind the bar. That must have been when he found the mobile. Kim hadn't realised till later on, after she finally sussed out the locks and they'd gone up to the *pueblo*; after they'd hung out at Pavana for a couple of beers and a game of pool; after they'd gone back down the mountain to Zig Zag till it closed. It was later, when they were on the beach, lying flat on their backs, that he pulled it from his pocket like a party trick. Stuffing it in the same pocket now, Kim headed back to the flat.

Mickey was lying on his front, still asleep. Kim pulled the sheet back and looked at him. His hips were so narrow. She kicked off her trainers and knelt astride him, tracing a finger down his spine. She moved further down the bed so that her knees were either side of his thighs, and cupped her hands round his arse. On the top of his right buttock he had a tattoo. It was a skull with Playboy Bunny ears. It was the most ridiculous tattoo she'd ever seen. When he had just his boxers on, the ears peeped out from the waistband. The first time she'd seen it, he told her it represented sex and death.

'That's all there is, baby,' he'd said.

She loved him calling her 'baby'. It was so corny, especially as she was older than him. He'd got other tattoos, some faded and some still fresh. They read like a diary of his recklessness scattered randomly across his skin. There were some little triangles and spirals on his shoulder, a fish on his calf, and a Celtic pattern that twisted round his left arm, but none of them was as foolhardy as the death bunny. She bent over now and licked it. He moved under her, rolled onto his side and put his hand over her ear, pressing her closer.

'You took Javier's mobile, you great clown.'

'Javier. Which Javier?'

'Javier, Javier. My boss Javier. My ex-boss Javier as soon as he realises.'

'How will he know it's you?'

'Me? Excuse me?'

'OK, how will he know it was anything to do with you?'

'Hmm, let's see. Javier leaves the Cantina. His mobile is where he always stashes it, and I'm left to lock up. Next day, he looks for his mobile. It's not there. He thinks back to when he last had it. I don't know, Sherlock, but I guess he'll kind of put two and two together. If he doesn't now, he will when he gets his statement.'

Mickey stroked Kim's thigh. 'I'm sorry, baby.'

'Yeah? How sorry?'

'Well, not abject, I guess. It was a crap job, and Javier's a git.'

'Oh, right. So that's OK, then.'

Mickey's hands worked their way into the waistband of Kim's jeans, and he began to unbutton them.

'Sorry, baby. I've been bad. You'd better punish me. Anything you want, baby. Name it.' he said, sticking his tongue in her belly button. Kim shivered. 'Tell me what you're going to do to me, Flaca,' he said, pushing his hand down inside her jeans.

'I'm going to cut off your hair,' Kim answered, lying back on the bed.

Mickey sat on a chair in the centre of the room, a towel wrapped round his waist. Kim had found some scissors in the kitchen drawer. They weren't very sharp, but they'd do.

She looked at him. 'You sure about this?'

'Of course. Like I said, anything you want.'

She moved behind him, lifted a fistful of blond locks, and hacked. It was exhilarating. When he was as hairless as a peeled lychee, as naked as a lightbulb, she ran her hands over her handiwork. Mickey bristled under her fingertips. It was his turn.

26

Geraniums

The quantity of cremated remains of an adult is comparable to the size of a 6-inch × 6-inch × 6-inch box, or a large dictionary. The appearance resembles crushed seashells.

www.cremation.com

Manuel Martínez was on his roof terrace, deadheading geraniums. Señora Vine's remains were on the table downstairs, waiting. It had been a long wait. Eighteen months.

After their first meeting, she had shaken his hand, thanked him, and taken away her notes, her bags of shopping, and a brochure showing the facilities in the funeral parlour. When he'd taken her to the workshop and shown her the coffins, she had insisted on no decoration – no crucifix. He'd shown her how the brass detailing was attached, how it could be unscrewed and removed, changed or added to, depending on the client's individual taste. In any case, he explained – more bluntly than he was used to – it would all be removed anyway, before the cremation. She had seemed to him incapable of being shocked, so that his usual euphemistic delicacy was unnecessary – inappropriate, even.

The telephone call had come a week later, and he was at the house within the hour. It was a pretty place, in a ramshackle fashion, out in the riverbed towards Turre. He had parked on the stretch of land in front of the house. It was early evening, the sun just setting behind the mountains, and the light was mellow. A skinny black bitch lay across his path, looked up at him but didn't move; Manuel stepped over her. He approached through the garden, the scent of jasmine pungent as he brushed past. The doctor was there; a woman he'd encountered in similar circumstances, and some people who he presumed were family – all women, it occurred to him later. There were no tears. Manuel knew this phase from his professional experience. It was too soon and they were too exhausted. They perched on chairs on the patio, mute.

The same daughter, Señora Alison, came to speak with him, and he discovered that he was pleased to see her. 'I lost my mother, too' was what he was going to say, but he stopped himself. Although true, it would have been somehow dishonest. He shook her hand, looked into her blue eyes, and smiled.

She spoke in her unique Spanish, and Manuel wondered again if she realised how bald some of her phrases were. On the telephone, she'd explained that they needed to get some rest.

'We're totally done in. We need your facilities,' she'd said. They had decided they all needed a breathing space before the funeral the following day.

'Bring my mother back tomorrow, please,' she said now.

He had nodded, opened his briefcase and explained that he would need to see the identifying papers.

As soon as he saw the photograph, he recognised her. And now that he realised, he couldn't believe that he hadn't seen her in the daughter. She was a carbon copy.

The funeral, it would be fair to say, had been unique. Manuel had returned the following day at the prearranged time. He'd not slept much the previous night. Instead, he'd sat for a long time watching the sea in the harbour.

It hadn't struck him at the time as the slightest bit odd to ask for a cutting of one of her plants. There'd been so little of the everyday to judge things against. But later he'd been ashamed at his loss of decorum.

His mother's ghost had hounded him. 'Well, well, a green-fingered funeral director, are we? Since when were you interested in gardening, anyway?'

'Since then,' he thought now.

The daughter hadn't blinked. She'd smiled, reaching into the planter to find a good, chunky length of it. His assistant, Carlos, hadn't commented. In fact, he had not said a word about the incident to this day.

Early the next morning, Manuel had been at José's before he'd even unlocked. He had needed the company of his old friend as much as the shave, and he lay back in the leather chair, his feet resting on the chrome footrest, and closed his eyes.

As José worked the soap into his face, Manuel said, 'There must be some customers you'd really miss if they never came back.'

José didn't answer for a while.

'Don't tell me you're thinking of growing a beard,' he said eventually.

Manuel smiled and gave himself up to the sensations. He knew better than to try and speak while José was at work. The smell of soap and hair and skin, the texture of the rough towel tucked into his collar, the tinny sound of the radio chattering away to itself.

He remembered sitting behind the counter at work, looking up and feeling happy. The woman on the other side of the glass, who always had the time to exchange a few words, her carefully wrapped little packages destined for England, her thanking him for his trouble. She spoke carefully in polite, faltering Castillano. Her bright blue eyes. He'd seen her once at the local fiesta, and had been delighted that she recognised him away from his desk. She'd beckoned him to join her, made him welcome, but the crowd she was with weren't Spanish-speaking, and he decided it would be too awkward. He'd made his apologies and continued along the high street, cursing himself.

'Life gets so full of the things we never did,' he said, as José slapped cologne onto his face.

After collecting Carlos and the late Señora Vine, he'd driven out to the house. It had been a fantastically sunny day, so sunny that Carlos was wearing sunglasses, which Manuel asked him to remove as they approached the house.

'You look like a gangster,' he'd told him.

Apart from the glasses, they were both dressed smartly; discreetly. They parked as arranged, between the house and the riverbed, and carried the coffin to a flat area of wild pasture. Tough, bright flowers grew among grass and dry goat droppings. People were arriving on foot and by car, dressed prettily as if for a picnic, and all were carrying flowers. Manuel had never seen anything like it. The two daughters were wearing dresses that Manuel imagined he recognised, summery and bright. They greeted the mourners, kissing them on both cheeks, taking the flowers and placing them in the grass around the coffin. The flowers varied widely, from the tidy wreaths of carnations that Manuel was used to seeing on such occasions, to displays of the kind he'd only previously seen at weddings: exotic arrangements piled high in Oasis. One woman, who arrived with five dogs in tow, was carrying armfuls of wildflowers from the mountains. There were posies of freesias and pansies, bunches of gladioli, individual stems of roses; rosemary and lavender, morning glory and hibiscus; there was even a dry arrangement of pomegranates. The offerings accumulated as more people arrived, until they surrounded the coffin in the shape of a heart, Señora Vine's head at the top, towards the Sierra Cabrera. Manuel and Carlos had stood at a distance from the proceedings, and Manuel had longed to be closer.

27

Canute

'Oh, my God. Look at that,' said Alison.

Bill looked over to where she stared. A building site rose out of the foothills as they descended from the mountain road. A semicircle of apartments was taking shape beneath the scaffolding. Identical units, meanly proportioned, clamouring for the sea view.

'That wasn't there before.'

This phrase became a mantra as they drove along the Mojácar sea front.

Bill couldn't share Alison's surprise, as he hadn't seen the place before, but he was disappointed by the number of bars with English names, like Snoopy's and Badger's; and the signs advertising Full English Breakfasts and Pool Maintenance. He'd imagined somewhere more authentic.

They stayed on the coast road with the sea to their right, beyond a wide promenade, palm trees planted as uniformly as lampposts. Between the beach bars and restaurants that lined the opposite side of the road, building work was rampant. Newly completed developments boasted their facilities on large hoardings. Above sea level, up in the mountains, diggers were busily slicing tops off the peaks like so many boiled eggs.

They reached a roundabout with an ornamental fountain and a complex system of signposts.

'That wasn't there before, either,' Alison said sullenly, as if there had been a conspiracy to make these changes just to spite her. As if, had she stayed here, she could have prevented it, Canute style. Up to

the left, Bill could see the old part of Mojácar village a couple of
miles away. It looked more authentic, more Moorish. It reminded
him of pictures he'd seen of Granada, only too pretty, too twee.

'Which way?' he asked.

'Carry straight on.'

The section of coast road from the roundabout was less developed. There was no promenade here, and the sea splashed untidily
onto rocks.

'This is what it looked like all the way along when we first came
here,' Alison said.

A few people walked on the beach. Someone threw a stick for a
dog. A couple sat in canvas chairs in front of a camper van, reading
newspapers, using the sea as their back garden.

They drove over a long bridge signposted 'Río Abajo'. Underneath, marshland and high grass met the sea.

'Oh, my God,' Alison said again as they reached the other side.
Trucks and machinery were strewn across the landscape, and were
dwarfed by it. Three cranes in primary colours stretched into the
sky. 'It's another fucking golf course. I'd heard they were planning to
develop, but I didn't believe it. Look at it!' Further along, a hotel
with a smoked-glass lobby had evidently just been completed. The
building was as uncompromising as an architect's impression; a
virtual hotel, without even the ubiquitous figures in the foreground
to humanise it. The gardens were still only faintly sketched, lines
drawn into the trenches of unyielding land. 'Oh, this is so sad.'

As they approached Garrucha, Alison directed Bill to the
harbour, and they parked by the fish market on the quay.

'Listen, why don't you grab a coffee while I go and find Mr
Martínez? I shan't be long.'

'OK. See you in that bar in half an hour or so,' he said, pointing
to a promising building on the waterfront.

Alison headed off towards the shops, and Bill felt relief to be in his own company. He walked along the harbour, smelling the fishy tang on the air. He was pleased to discover signs of a genuine community at last. Nets lay drying at the water's edge and, although the promenade above him was edged with an ornamental marble balustrade, the grey cement quay opposite had a ring of authenticity. Large container ships moored on the far side were being loaded with industrial-looking cargo. It would be some years yet before this became a cruise destination, he thought; Alison should find some comfort in that, at least.

28

Just a Pinch

She looks older, Manuel thought, as he rose from his desk to greet her.

'Good morning, Miss Vine. It is very good to see you.'

'I didn't realise you spoke English,' Alison said, shaking his hand.

'Only a little. I have been taking lessons. It is one year now.'

Alison paused. This was always tricky: should she continue in his English or her Spanish? They continued shaking hands a little longer than was comfortable.

'And your sister?' he asked, releasing her hand and letting his own fall to his side.

'Yes, she's very well, thank you.'

'She is not here with you?'

'No.'

Alison looked beyond Manuel Martínez to the calendar on the wall behind him. It was almost the same as the one that had been there when she'd first been in this office. She searched for something innocuous to say in either language that would explain why she was here without Hannah, but both languages failed her. She smiled and he smiled back. His eyes are just as I remember, she thought.

'Bueno,' he said, making the decision for her.

The rest of the visit was conducted in Spanish, although Alison's was so rusty that she kept her conversation mainly to nods and smiles. He had, he explained, not purchased an urn, but had kept the remains in a simple container as she had requested. He turned to a dark-green box on his desk, and paused. He touched the lid with the very tips of his fingers.

'These are they,' he said, reverting to English in deference to the box.

After such a long interlude, the physicality of Beth's remains had become abstracted in Alison's mind. She realised now that she'd had no idea what to expect. Beth's Ashes had become iconic, capital B capital A, and it was hard to equate them with this green box on Mr Martínez's desk. She had a desire to open them and check, but what was she looking for? How could she verify them?

'Do I need to sign for them?' was all she could think of to say.

'No, that is not necessary.'

'Right. Well. Thank you again for everything.'

'It was an honour,' Manuel replied. He passed the box to her and she took it from him, surprised at the weight of it. 'Do you have a bag?' he asked.

'Er, no.'

'Wait one moment, please.' Manuel went out through a door at the back of the office. Alison held Beth's remains in both hands, waiting for him to return. He came back into the office carrying a black nylon bag and shook it open. It was a brand-new rucksack. 'Here,' he said, 'use this. The box is perfectly secure.'

'Are you sure?' she asked. Not that she doubted that the box was secure; it was more 'Are you sure you want to give me this new rucksack?' and 'Are you sure about the protocol of putting final remains into this?'

Manuel's reply was unequivocal. 'Certainly. Please, take it.'

She realised she hadn't given any thought to the practicalities of walking through the streets of Garrucha holding this box in front of her, like one of the Three Kings, or of meeting Bill in a bar with it tucked under her arm. Maybe the rucksack was standard issue and came as part of the service from the crematorium, or was part of a promotion campaign, like mugs and Biros and baseball caps. Whatever the reason, she decided to be grateful for having a solution offered to her. Manuel held the opening of the rucksack wide, so that Alison could position the box flat in the bottom, and then secured the drawstring into a bow, flipping the cover over, and holding it out by the straps for Alison, like a waiter holding a coat. Put me in your pocket, Mike. Why did she think of that? Why now?

'Thank you very much,' she said, as she slipped the straps over her shoulders.

Manuel walked to the door and held it ajar as he stretched out his hand.

'Señora Alison, your mother was a wonderful woman,' he said.

She felt the tears brim up from her jaw, along her sinuses and behind her eyes. She still couldn't bear this, even now: the shock waves that Beth's death had caused – the people who had felt its effect and needed to share it with her – from the young man on the vegetable stall in the market to the goat herdsman in the valley. It wasn't surprising; she had been an exceptional woman; but each person's expression of sympathy brought her back to this place, as if it were yesterday.

'Yes,' she mumbled, smiling, trying to hold herself together. Strange how you try to smile to stop yourself crying, as if slamming the brakes on the tear ducts. There's a split second when it can tip either way. Alison's other defence was to think of something distracting to say, to shrug the emotion out of it. 'Oh, I meant to ask, how is your plant doing? The cutting of donkey's tail?'

Manuel's green eyes were moist; as if Alison's unshed tears had crossed the space between them, and welled up in his eyes instead.

'Very well, beautifully, thank you.'

'Oh, I am pleased. Mum would have liked that.'

Manuel watched her as she walked down the road and turned the corner towards the sea front. Closing the door, he checked his watch. It was almost lunchtime, a little early, but still. He locked the door, flipped the sign to Closed, and went through the back of the office into his house. He climbed the staircase and stepped out onto the roof terrace. It was a lovely day. He walked across to the place where the satellite dish had been mounted on a bracket. The bracket now supported a hanging basket. Dangling down among the pelargonium was the mint-green rope of succulent beads. Twice its length in eighteen months; it was indeed beautiful. He knew why. It had only been a pinch, he told himself. And Señora Vine would not have objected, he was sure.

29

Mojo

When Kim woke again it was early evening. The bed was itchy with their hair. She pulled her watch off the floor, checked the time and cursed.

'Shit. I'm late. You'll have to run me to the Cantina, Mick.' She rolled over to Mickey, shaking his shoulder, and stared at the back of his head. For a moment, she'd forgotten. 'Oh. Look what we've done.' She touched his scalp, amazed once more at the bumps and details she had uncovered.

Javier looked up as Kim rushed into the Cantina.

'Sorry I'm late, Javier.'

He stared at her. 'Hostia! What have you done?'

Kim touched her shorn head. 'Oh, it was an impulse. What d'you think?'

'You look like a tortillera, a lesbian. Why did you do that to yourself?'

'It's only hair, Javier; it'll grow back. Eventually.'

'Bueno. Well, come back when it has, then.'

He went through to the kitchen, the slatted saloon doors swinging to behind him.

Kim walked back along the paseo. It was still quite light, but the moon was rising out of the sea, swollen and yellow. She watched as it separated itself from the horizon and became round and whole, the sea burnished with its reflection. Her indignation dissolved under the sound of the waves; washed away on the tideless sea as it sloshed backwards and forwards, never going anywhere, but all the same transforming broken bottles into little gems, soothing tempers, making incidents incidental. She felt in her pocket for the little piece of glass, rubbing it between her finger and thumb. Across the road in Musica Musica, a man was singing along to the karaoke machine: 'Got my mojo working, baby.'

Mickey was at the table, rolling a spliff. In the corner of the room, next to the red dustpan and brush, was a heap of their hair fashioned into a nest; a couple of eggs in the hollow centre.

'Hello, baldy. I've just been fired. In fact, I've just been playing a supporting role in my own little Spaghetti Western.'

'Sorry I missed it.'

'Yeah, well, like you said, it was a crap job. I think he knows about the mobile.' She sat down next to him and took the unlit spliff that Mickey offered her. 'You've been busy, I see,' she said, lighting it and nodding towards the hair. 'Where did you find the eggs?'

'Fridge. I've changed the sheets, too.'

'My God, you're not going to get all domesticated on me, are you? Is that what happened to Samson, d'you think?'

'Maybe. Do you really not mind about the job?'

'Really. But I'm going to have to find something else pretty quickly if I want to keep this place.'

'I'll find something.'

'Oh? Like what?'

'I dunno.' He took the spliff from her and drew on it. 'We could do porn films together in Madrid.'

'Yeah, great idea, Mick.'

'No, think about it. We'd be getting paid for what we do anyhow. It'd be perfect. Money for old rope.'

'Charming. Know what? I think I'll stick to what I know.'

'Aw, where's your spirit of adventure?'

'I think maybe you shaved it off.'

'Oh, baby, I'm sorry. Do you regret letting me?'

'Hey, this is the Village of No Regrets, remember?'

Mickey stubbed out the joint, picked the helmet off the sofa and passed it to her.

'Come on, grab your jacket,' he said, standing up.

'Where are we going?'

'My secret. Trust me. I'm going to make it up to you. Restore your sense of adventure.'

Kim wrapped her arms round Mickey. They rode along the coast and turned left at the crossroads, up towards the village that perched on the mountain ahead of them, a jumble of white cubes flickering with lights. Mickey turned right before Mojácar, slowing down as a group of children stepped into the road. They were dressed in black capes and pointed hats.

'What's the date today?' Kim shouted in Mickey's ear.

'Dunno. Is it still October?'

'It must be Halloween. I'd forgotten.'

30

Spooky

Mexican tradition says that a person dies three times. A person's first death is when their body stops functioning and heart stops. The second is after physical death, when souls come back to Earth and no one can see them. And the third death is when no one remembers them.

Claudio Mendonca, *The Daily Illini*

'Did you and Ali used to do this with Nanna?'

Jo and Hannah were sat at the kitchen table, gouging out the innards of a pumpkin.

'You bet. Halloween was our favourite.'

'Better than Christmas?'

'Yep.'

'Better than birthdays?'

'I reckon.'

'What else did you used to do?'

'Well, it was usually turnips that we made into lanterns, and they ponged a bit. I don't think you could get pumpkins in our day. God, that makes me feel old. And we'd dress up as witches, of course. And we'd go round to visit our friends.'

Jo had her tongue between her teeth, concentrating on scooping out the stringy orange pulp with her spoon. The pile of discarded flesh was matted with seeds.

'Did Nanna dress up, too?'

'Absolutely. She was a very witchy lady.'

'Did you trick or treat?'

'No.'

'Why not?'

'That's new, and between you and me it's a bit American.'

Jo was going to do her first ever trick or treating that evening. Her friend across the road's dad had offered to supervise their little gang; make sure that they didn't get any razors in their sweets from sickos. Hannah had been nervous, but he assured her they'd just pop into a few houses of mutual friends. He'd be collecting Jo soon, and she had still to get changed into her costume.

'Right. Time to give him a face.'

Two diamond eyes, a triangular nose, and a sawtooth grin. Sawtooth. Hannah's Spanish was poor, but she remembered it was translated as '*sierra*'. She liked the economy of the language – how words doubled up, triggered links. She could picture the Sierra Cabrera, backdrop to their last Halloween with Beth. They had made a path of lanterns up to the house, and they had eaten pumpkin soup. Jo had been four then, a tiny witch. A witchette. Alison would be there again now. Without her. Hannah's choice. And soon Beth's ashes would be dissolving into the Mediterranean.

Hannah lit a night-light, put it inside the pumpkin, and replaced the lid. The stalk was cocked at a jaunty angle like a little hat. Stalks – umbilical cords which had once attached the fruit to the mother plant.

A feeling of ritual, of continuity, overwhelmed Hannah. She watched the flame mellow and fill the orange skull.

'We should put him on the windowsill before the others get here. He can ward off any evil spirits.'

'Can we go outside and see what he looks like?'

They stood in their back garden. It was only six o'clock, but it was already dark. The lantern grinned out at them from the kitchen. Hannah was determined to keep this tradition alive. Jo would have apple bobbing, a cape, a hat and a broomstick – the works: it was her birthright.

The moon was a day off full. It was just climbing over the shed. The sky was cloudless, and the air cold enough to see plumes of their breath.

Jo looked up at the stars. 'Which one is Nanna's?'

Sometimes, her daughter's intuition spooked Hannah. 'Gosh, I'm not sure.'

They both stood staring up at the sky.

31

SuperTurre

The building fever had spread to Turre. Even SuperTurre had got the bug; Alison hardly recognised it. In her absence, it had grown into its name. Once inside, the stock was reassuringly familiar. Bill followed her down the aisles, picking things up at random.

'Look,' he said, 'the bread's called Bimbo.'

'Yeah, I know.'

While Bill studied the labels on the dozen different brands of tequila, she selected vegetables with a sense of déjà vu. They were the same vegetables. The little artichokes, the shiny aubergines, the wild mushrooms.

Fat candles in red plastic wrappers and bunches of artificial flowers were stacked high by the check out.

'That's for tomorrow,' Alison explained as they walked across the car park. 'November 1st is when people spend the night in the cemetery.'

'Really? What for?'

'To keep the dead company. They take deckchairs and food, and the whole family camps out there for the night. It's quite a party. We can go, if you like.'

Alison put the shopping on the back seat of the car and Bill got in the driver's side.

'Where now?' he asked.

'To Mum's.'

Bill turned left into Turre high street.

'Change of plan. Pull in on the right,' Alison said.

She knew she was procrastinating. She hadn't returned to the house since then, since she and Hannah had combed through the contents directly after the funeral in an agony of indecision, numbly parcelling up their shared lives in bubble wrap, dividing their past as fairly as they could, and sending what they couldn't keep to a second-hand shop for animal welfare. They'd dreaded seeing Beth's possessions anywhere else, bumping into someone dressed in her clothes, but they'd been unable to put things in a bin: It was too impractical, too wasteful. Beth would have hated that. Beth, who'd hoarded. Waste not, want not.

The house had been rented out through an agency but had been empty the past few months, so it made sense to stay there. She still had a set of keys. She turned them over in her hand. She knew without looking which key opened what. But not yet. Not just yet.

Bill parked outside the Adelina and followed Alison into the bar. It was early and they were the only customers. They ordered two beers and chose a couple of tapas from the glass cabinet. Marinated anchovies and tortilla. They settled at the bar.

'Sorry. I just need some Dutch courage.'

'That's OK.'

'It's ridiculous really; we're so close. It's only ten minutes away. After all this time.'

'It's fine. Don't worry.'

Bill looked around. The beer taps dripped with a cool sweat of condensation. Behind the bar, a framed picture of a football team next to a poster of the Virgin and Child. A television mounted on the wall was showing a soap opera. It bellowed out, and Bill tried to guess what was happening. He lifted a slippery little anchovy out of the puddle of oil with his fork, onto a slice of bread

'These anchovies are glorious.'

'I know. It broke my heart when I came back to London, having

113

to pay real money for bad food with a drink. Andalucía is the last preserve of the free tapa.'

'Well, we've got our traditional free peanuts on the bar back home.'

'Exactly.'

Bill took a swig of beer. 'Did you know Turre is mentioned in the Disney mystery? It was the priest here who took the unnamed, smartly dressed Americans to see the records of the parish, apparently,' he said, mopping the last of the oil from the plate with the bread.

'It's weird you knowing stuff about here that I don't.'

'His relatives say that was when the pages disappeared. The last traces of baby Walt being a Mojácero – is that what they're called?'

'If you say so, Mr Expert All of a Sudden.'

'Do you fancy another? A sundowner?'

The sun was setting over Turre, birds whistled an ear-blasting trill from the trees outside. Inside, on the television, two actresses in loud clothes fought melodramatically over a man. Everything was noisier here, Bill thought.

32

K ♡ M

Kim and Mickey rode round the foothills of Mojácar, the sea to their right beyond the houses with their orchards of olives and oranges. They passed the football ground, and continued towards Turre. Mickey pulled over at SuperTurre. He fished in his jacket and pulled out his wallet, passing it to Kim.

'Here, get us something to drink. Your choice. And some snacks.'

SuperTurre was buzzing. Kim took a moment to acclimatise. She realised that she was starving, and tried to remember when she'd last eaten. No wonder Mickey called her 'Flaca'. She grabbed some bread and olives and cheese and a large bag of crisps, found the drinks section, and stood and deliberated. It was all so cheap.

The bike was parked in the far corner. Kim was fixing the carrier bag behind her seat with a bungee when Mickey joined her, passing her a black rucksack.

'Let's go,' he said, straddling the bike and turning the ignition.

Kim took the rucksack. 'Mickey? What's this?' she asked.

He didn't answer. She lifted it onto her back as they turned onto the road.

They drove out the other side of Turre. On the left, a lanky palm tree leaned into the road as if it were eavesdropping on the traffic. There was a giant jacaranda on the right that she'd seen in flower earlier in the summer; an unreal powder blue, like an old lady's blue rinse. They sped past men in cardigans and old ladies in black, and people coming out of the walled cemetery, carrying mops and buckets. Continuing on the straight open road, Mickey accelerated and Kim held onto him. The rucksack dug into the small of her back, and she adjusted the straps with one hand as they slowed down and turned left through a sandstone entrance. Kim caught sight of a signpost that read, 'Cortijo Grande'.

The road was tarmac but rough, and wound upwards into the mountains. Mickey swerved to avoid potholes. The moon was climbing over the mountains now, following Kim, and the daylight was beginning to fade fast. On either side of the road tough vegetation covered the earth sparsely; dry-looking bushes of gorse and herbs, and gnarled trees that looked as if they'd survived centuries of fire and drought. Tiny birds swarmed from the branches, rising like puffs of smoke as they drove by, and circling in the twilight. Mickey turned onto a track. The bike bounced on the uneven surface. Kim squeezed with her thighs. The rucksack knocked against her back. They dipped down into a gulley then up the other side, veering left past a gate and some large warehouses that Kim thought looked like an out of town superstore. Mickey slowed down and turned left, into a driveway. He turned the engine off and removed his helmet.

'We're here,' he said.

Kim dismounted and took off her helmet. She let the rucksack fall from her shoulders and dropped it by the bike. They were in a courtyard. Derelict buildings formed a horseshoe in front of her and to either side. Doors hung off their hinges, and graffiti covered the walls. At the centre of the courtyard was the dry plumbing of a disused fountain. Plants which must once have been carefully maintained sprawled over the ornamental circle of bricks. Without the noise of the engine, she could hear the birds. Their song ricocheted off the walls, filling the yawning silence of the place.

Mickey wandered off towards the buildings, and Kim ran to catch up. He was in one of the rooms, turning over some large canvases that were stacked against the wall. Dried-up tins of paint lay on the floor among empty beer bottles and cigarette ends, and the smell of turpentine clung on the air.

'What is this place?'

'Used to be an airport, once upon a time.'

Kim wandered through to the next room. There were wooden pallets and an old blanket on the floor. She walked over to the large square hole where a window had been, leaned on the deep sill, and looked out. A straight, flat road of cracked tarmac stretched the length of the mountain.

'Was that the airstrip?'

'Yep.'

'Who used it?'

'Rich people with their own planes. Expats who had houses built in this valley in the eighties. Not enough of them, it turned out.'

'Why? What happened?'

'It was a white elephant. They couldn't afford the maintenance. In the end, the only people using it were drug runners from Morocco. Come on.'

He took her hand and led her back into the courtyard, through a doorway on the other side. The room they entered must once have been a bar. The counter remained intact and, behind it, some empty shelves built into the wall where the bottles of spirits would have been kept. Kim tried to picture the room filled with rich expatriates and drug runners. She followed Mickey into a corridor that led to a stairwell, and climbed the narrow spiral staircase, letting go of his hand to hold the steel banister.

The flight tower was ten-sided; each wall a metre or so in width, and symmetrical like a giant musical box. It was constructed like a greenhouse, metal and glass from waist height to ceiling. It wasn't much larger than the greenhouse Kim's parents had in their garden, but that was where any similarities ended. She'd never been anywhere remotely like this. Some of the smoked-glass panels had been smashed; dates and initials, hearts and arrows written into the thick dust of the glass that remained. It was the kind of place that made you itch to leave your mark, to personalise it somehow. Her finger traced across a virgin pane: a K, a heart, an M.

Mickey rattled the handle of a metal door; it was locked. He walked around, assessing the other possibilities, took off his jacket and laid it across the sill of one of the broken panels. He levered himself up and climbed out onto a narrow platform that ran the circumference of the tower, girdled with a handrail. Kim followed. The view spread three hundred and sixty degrees. The mountains and valleys extended as far as she could make out in the dusk. She remembered long-forgotten geography classes, the teacher explaining mountain formations. Finally, it all made sense. She could picture the rivers that must have flowed millions of years ago in these aching spaces. It was stunning. Vast and alien, more like a moonscape than a landscape. The road they had ridden on from Turre was there in the distance, and she could make out the little Matchbox cars as they moved along towards the bridge at Los Gallardos, where they had first met. Everything was insubstantial in comparison to the earth: the pylons slung with their necklace of wires traced a delicate contour on the surface; the planting in the fields made patterns like icing forked across a chocolate fudge cake, the ostentatious white ranches with their marble columns and fenced-off land that tried, but made no impression on it.

'Do you have the booze?' Mickey asked.

'It's on the bike.'

He climbed back through the window. Kim could hear his footsteps as he went down the staircase and crunched across the courtyard. She tested the outside rail. It wobbled under her hand. Leaning her back against the tower, she pulled the Dymo gun from her pocket.

When Mickey returned he had the rucksack as well as the carrier bag. He dropped them through the window, climbed back out, fished in the carrier bag and pulled out a bottle.

'Nice choice, Flaca.'

'I was just being practical: no need for a bottle opener.'

Mickey twisted the cork out of the cava. Liquid fizzed out as the cork escaped into the sky, out of sight, and Mickey put his lips to the bottleneck, licking up the bubbles.

'What shall we toast?' he asked.

'Let's see. To joblessness and hairlessness.'

'To being bald as coots and broke.'

Mickey took a swig and passed the bottle to Kim. She lifted it over Mickey's head and poured. Just a drop. His skull shone. He took the bottle from her and copied. Kim felt the bubbles explode on the skin of her head, skin she'd never felt before. She turned to the glass pane behind her and surveyed their reflections. Two eggs. She touched Mickey's head, and hooked her hands behind his ears, pulling him towards her and kissing his lips.

'Thank you,' she said.

Mickey felt under her top, finding her nipples and twisting them like he was tuning a radio. She sucked his tongue and undid his flies. He fucked her from behind as she leaned on his jacket, smelling its smell, her head in the tower, her arse in the night. Afterwards, they ate crisp sandwiches and cheese, and fed each other green olives.

Kim needed to pee. She climbed back in through the window. It was dark now, and she had to touch the walls and feel her way into the room that led out into the courtyard. Once outside, the moonlight was bright enough to see by. She squatted down and peed onto the dry ground. The palm trees rattled in a gust of wind. She felt the cool air as it touched her damp skull.

33

Miss Polly

Miss Polly had a dolly who was sick, sick, sick,
So she called for a doctor to come quick, quick, quick . . .

Traditional

Hannah helped Jo with the cape. She'd spent the past hour stitching on silver stars and a crescent moon. Big tacking stitches. She watched as Jo did a twirl in front of the mirror. Her wavy black hair fell from beneath the black-brimmed witch's that they had made together in the time-honoured manner – sugar paper and card, foil and glue. Under the cape, she wore her black leotard and a long black skirt; and a necklace of plastic spiders that Jacques had made her. Her fingers were tipped with a set of long plastic fingernails, the only shop-bought bit of kit. She giggled and scratched at the air.

She looked fabulous. She had certainly inherited the Vine delight in dressing up. A fairy costume hung from the end of her bed, the pink gauze wings settled like a giant butterfly on her Barbie duvet. And she had a whole jar of magic wands on her dressing table.

It was a relief that she had moved on from her medical phase. The previous Christmas, she had begged them for a nurse's outfit. She'd played with all the medical instruments for hours at a time, bandaging up her teddies and dolls in a dolly hospital she installed on her bedroom window ledge – so they'd have a nice view. She'd been so interested in scabs and cuts and thermometers and stethoscopes that Hannah and Jacques had started to worry. But it wasn't surprising, really, when you considered. There had been a certain dovetailing in their worlds, Jo and her Nanna's; the potties and commodes, the little naps, Jo in a buggy, bumper to bumper with Beth in a wheelchair. When Beth had become extremely frail, Jo had taken it in her stride.

Hannah explained to her, 'Nanna has some tubes to help her breathe.'

Jo had thought for a second. 'Will I still be able to hug her?'

'Of course you will, my sweet pea,' Hannah had said, scooping her into her arms.

34

Ritual

Mickey was still outside on the platform. Kim saw his profile; backlit against the moon like one of those Victorian paper cut-outs. She stood by the stair rail and studied him a while. He was leaning against the broken pane, rummaging through the rucksack. Kim leaned on the window frame, and nuzzled her mouth against his neck. She rubbed the back of her head against the stubble on his chin, enjoying the sensation. Mickey didn't respond. He was holding something in front of him. Holding it the way you hold a present someone has given you; assessing it before tearing off the paper. Kim peered over his shoulder. The box was dark green, about the size of a large book.

'What have we here?' she said, putting her arms round his neck, pressing her body against his back. He eased the lid off, lifted the box closer to his face.

Kim reached round him. 'Let's see,' she said, stretching out one hand to take it from him.

She hadn't expected it to weigh so much. As Mickey let go, her wrist twisted, and the box fell, dropping between them, releasing a ghost of dust like an exhalation, sighing into the night, mixing with the air and floating away as the box thudded to the floor at Mickey's feet. It had landed on its side and Mickey stooped down to retrieve it. He used the lid to push the spilled contents back in as best he could. He pulled a lighter from his pocket and held it up to the label on the side of the box. Kim leaned over the window frame and watched. Watched Mickey as his expression changed. He looked very young as he read the words on the label in the light of the flame, mouthing them silently. They appeared to hold him in their spell until the lighter burned his fingers. He released his thumb from the gas, cursing. He remained where he was, crouched down on the narrow platform, the box at his side, and put his hands over his face. If I close my eyes, I'll become invisible, Kim thought.

'What is it, Mickey?'

'Shit, shit, shit.'

She could just about hear his words through his hands.

'Mickey?' What's happening?'

He turned his head to face her. 'Look, I was just trying to help. After the mobile . . . and your job. Shit. Oh, Christ. Shit, shit, *shit!*'

'For God's sake, what are you talking about?' Mickey looked out into the night, breathing hard. 'Mickey?'

He looked at her again, then at the box. He picked it up carefully, stood up and passed it to her through the window, as if he were serving her from behind a counter. As if they were playing shop.

'Look.'

Kim took the box from him. She peered at it, holding it up to the moonlight. There was a label on the side, a screen-printed triangle, a picture of a bird flying over a hill; three flowers. Beneath the picture, two lines of writing: 'Campos de Nijar, Tanatorio Crematorio.'

'What does this mean? I don't understand.'

'Well.' Mickey couldn't look at her. 'I'm not certain, but I think it's a crematorium.'

Kim stared at the word 'Crematorio.' 'These are someone's ashes?'

Mickey didn't answer. She stared at the box, then at Mickey, and finally up at the moon.

'Fuck, Mickey, what were you thinking?'

'I dunno. Oh, God, I dunno, Kim.'

123

He found a packet of cigarettes in his pocket and lit one. 'They're going to freak when they find out they're missing.'

'Who are? Whose bag is this? Where did you get it?'

'I just tried the boot when you were getting the stuff in the supermarket. It was open. I thought it might be something we could sell. I could sell. Help with the rent.'

'Oh, right,' Kim said quietly. 'Oh, I see. How thoughtful.' She walked to the opposite side of the tower. 'You fucking idiot. You pathetic, stupid, fuckwit loser.'

She ran out of words. She put the box on the floor, among the shards of broken glass and the cigarette butts, and groped her way back down the staircase. She picked her way by the moonlight across the courtyard, past the bike, following the route they'd taken when they'd ridden there. When everything had been different. For the first time, it occurred to her how isolated this place was, and how dependent she was on Mickey for getting back, and that she hardly knew him. Her ears throbbed with the rush of blood pulsing through her. For a moment she felt she was going to faint. The words on the label and Mickey's explanation sang in her head, repeating and dancing into a crazy nursery rhyme.

She arrived at the gate they'd passed, and walked towards the hangars that she'd thought looked like a superstore. A little further, she reached the point where the airstrip stretched left and right. She paced to the end of the runway, almost running. When she reached the end she turned round and started to walk to the other end. She heard Mickey calling her name. He caught up with her and walked alongside.

'It was stupid. I'm really, really sorry.'

Kim stopped. When she spoke her voice was foreign to her, strangled, and she heard it as if it came from a distance, the blood in her head was so loud.

'No, Mickey, this isn't like the mobile. This isn't a game; it's someone. It's the actual remains of a human being. It's awful.' She walked on in silence and reached the other end. The tarmac of the runway stopped in a straight line, like the finishing line of a school race. Beyond it, the bushes and trees gave way to the edge of the plateau. Beyond was nothing. 'Sorry to who, anyway? It's not me you've scattered. It's not my husband or wife or child you've lost. What the fuck did you think you were doing? And don't talk about helping me. I've never asked you to share, contribute even.'

'I know.'

Kim turned and continued pacing. Mickey followed her.

'You're going to have to return it.'

Mickey stopped walking and looked at her. 'Half of it's missing, Kim. And anyway I don't know where they are now.'

'You must remember what the car looked like. Think. Colour, make, registration. Surely you look at the cars you steal from?' Her voice was clipped. She measured the words, concentrating on remaining calm.

'Grey. A two-door something,' Mickey almost whispered.

'Come on, you'll need to do better than that.'

'It had the car-hire company sticker in the back window. That was what made me. I thought tourists.'

'Made you?' Kim hissed. She started walking again. 'Well, that's something.' The moon cast a silvery light on the runway. 'We're going to have to replace the missing ashes. There's still some in there, we'll have to see what they're like and add some.'

'OK.'

Mickey was biting his nail, staring at the ground. Kim watched him. She wasn't used to this. He was usually so self-assured that she was able to drift along with his schemes. She knew that things had just altered between them. It was palpable, as if the change in her perception of Mickey had actually made him change. It was new territory for them both.

125

'Look, I've got this friend in London, Gordon,' she said, walking over to him. 'He's a homoeopath.' Mickey was blank. Kim carried on, 'He told me this stuff about potency. What he said – how homoeopathy worked, he explained – was that you only need a tiny bit of the ingredient. The more diluted it is, the stronger it becomes. I can't remember how it worked, but the way he explained it, it made sense. We've still got some of the ashes. So long as there are still some there, it'll still count.'

'What will?'

Kim spoke to him as if she were speaking to an idiot. 'Whatever it was they were planning to do before you came along. As long as we can find the car, we have a chance.' She turned abruptly and started walking towards the bike. 'Get the stuff. If we're going to do this we need to get cracking.' Mickey remained where he was. Kim turned her head towards him, still walking. 'Come on.'

Mickey still didn't move.

'Listen. You're right,' he said. 'It was me who fucked up. You don't have to do this.'

Kim stopped. She walked back to face him. 'It's not you I'm doing this for. Don't you understand? I couldn't live with the idea that I'd been a part of this and not tried to change things – at least tried.'

Mickey looked into her eyes. He was young and stupid and Kim was suddenly aware of it.

'I'm really sorry, Kim. Whatever you say, I'll try it.'

'Come on then,' she said.

Kim put her hand into the box, tried to touch the ashes in the bottom, and withdrew it.

'I can't believe I'm doing this.'

She tried again. As her hand touched the surface, she felt a charge of energy. She didn't know if it was her own anxiety or what, but it was so powerful she couldn't pretend it hadn't happened. She took a little of the powder between her fingers. It reminded her of making pastry. Rub between fingers until the mixture resembles breadcrumbs. She repeated the action, closing her eyes this time, trying to analyse what it felt like, this substance that had been someone.

'Shells,' she said, 'Here, you try.'

'I can't.'

'Yes you can. Here.' She passed Mickey the box. He put it on the ground. He looked at her.

'Go on,' she said.

Mickey reached into the box. As he did, a shrill tune rang out a familiar jingle. Mickey jumped up as if he was on fire. He pulled the mobile out of his pocket and hurled it into the bushes. It carried on ringing. They stared at the place where the noise rang out. It stopped.

'Jesus fucking Christ,' he said.

35

Loft

Hannah groped around in the loft with her torch, trying not to breathe in the fibreglass, careful only to stand on the grid of rafters. Some day, this would be their study, or a sound studio for Jacques, or a teenage den for Jo. Some day. But right now it was where they stored things they wanted out of the way, or things whose fate was yet to be decided. Jacques called it Purgatory.

The beam of the torch hit the two tea-chests of stuff from Beth's house. Hannah had paid a fortune to have them shipped over from Spain, and she still wasn't ready to delve. She didn't trust herself. It wasn't time yet. She believed that whatever she chose to bin would be the wrong thing. Take the photographs. She had started to go through them, but it was an impossible task. Not only did every single image emerge thick with significance, dragging her backwards, it was also the business of selection. It wasn't a simple matter of keeping the good, in-focus ones, or the happy ones where they all looked their best. Who was she to edit history? Who was to say that the exact opposite pile didn't have more of a claim, showing the true stories that she was terrified she'd forget without the visual aids, the memory flash cards? And that was just the photos. She knew that deep within the boxes were bundles of letters bulging with shared past. She could almost hear them breathing. No. Not yet.

Here was what she'd been looking for, a large, navy blue canvas holdall. She dropped it down through the square of the trapdoor. It thudded onto the hall landing, and she climbed back down the ladder. She couldn't explain why the sight of five Harry Potter wizards dressed identically in shop-bought costumes had made her flip out like that. All she knew was that there were only two people who would understand how Wrong it was – Beth and Alison.

'Dad! Guess what?' Jo ran out to meet Jacques as he came up the front path, her cape flapping and the silver stars catching the light from the porch.

'Hello, my favourite witchy witch. How was the tricking and the treating?'

'It's trick or treating,' she said, jumping into his arms and wrapping her legs round him. 'We're flying tonight.'

'Oho? Where to, my pickled onion? Are we travelling by broomstick?'

'Mum's got tickets and everything. We're flying to Nanna's house. You're looking after Molly and Polly.'

Jo put one arm round Jacques's neck, and with her free hand took off her hat, putting it on his head. He stepped sideways into the house with Jo still attached. Hannah was kneeling in the hall, zipping up the canvas bag.

'What's happening?' he asked, lifting Jo to the ground and taking off the hat.

Jo ran off into the kitchen.

Hannah looked up at him. 'I couldn't not go,' she said, 'I've been online, and there's a flight to Murcia tonight. If I hire a car, we'll be there in time to catch Ali.'

'Are you sure?'

'I've never been so sure.'

36

House

A room is still a room
Even when there's nothin' there but gloom.
Hal David,
'A House is not a Home'

It was dark when they finally got to the house. They parked out at
the front and carried in the bags of shopping. Alison led the way up
the path that she'd covered in chunks of marble collected from the
quarry, but had never got round to concreting into place; past the
bush whose real name they'd never known, but which they called the
popcorn tree because its yellow flowers smelt of Butterkist popcorn
when it rained. The jasmine and the honeysuckle were rampant, and
had come loose from the trellis that Alison had hammered into the
archway. She brushed past them, releasing the sad smell. All this she
could divine in the moonlight without even looking.

She walked over the patio that she and Beth had bordered with a
mosaic one hot summer before her illness; little stones and pieces of
smooth glass made into fishes, hearts and flowers.

'Here we are, Casa Luna,' she said, dropping the bags by her feet.

The wooden doorframe had got more rickety. She felt her way
along to where she knew the lights were and switched them on. The
smell was all wrong; she didn't recognise it. It wasn't a bad smell, just
the smell of an empty house. She busied herself with looking
around; doing a mental inventory, noting what wasn't there more
than what was.

Bill followed her in. 'Where shall I put the shopping?'

'Oh, sorry, the kitchen's through here. I'll give you a tour in a bit.' She shivered. 'You forget how cold it is indoors here when the sun goes down. We should build a fire.'

'Look,' Bill said, 'why don't I cook for us while you make a fire?'

'Are you sure?'

'Of course. You know me; I love cooking. I'll work out where everything is.'

'OK, great. Thanks. I'll see what wood there is.'

She slid open the French windows, remembering the familiar 'shh' sound they made, and went outside. There was a pile of wood where it always was, stacked against the wall, covered with tarpaulin. She piled logs into her arms. So long as she had things to do, she'd be OK. The moon was high over the Sierra Cabrera and Alison stood still, cradling the wood. The mountains always made her think of a rough blanket thrown over a pile of rubble, smoothing out any sharp lines. They were covered with tufts which she knew were bushes of rosemary and lavender, wild thyme and gorse. She knew the smell of the mountain range, like aftershave, she knew its feel between her fingers and under foot, the loose rocks and the red earth. But from a distance it was this old, felted blanket. The same trees clung to the summit, like a herd of animals frozen in the headlight of the moon. Somewhere out there, a dog was barking, and its bark came echoing back. Alison felt like howling, too. She used to sometimes, when the moon was full. She thought about Bill and stopped herself. They were both being a bit strange, she thought, a bit too polite. But then it was a strange situation.

There was an old newspaper and some packing card in the basket near the fireplace. Alison sat on the same little stool and started twisting the pages of newspaper and knotting them loosely. She ripped the card into lengths.

*   *   *

131

Two years ago. Beth is lying on the settee, watching her tearing paper.

'There used to be a lad lived on our road. Simple, he was. Always playing with himself. We all used to collect paper for him to rip. So long as he had paper, he'd not fiddle with himself.'

They are playing Scrabble, listening to Dionne Warwick.

'A chair is still a chair/Even when there's no one sittin' there.'

That song really annoyed Beth. 'Of course a chair is still a chair.'

She preferred 'Do You Know the Way to San José?'. One day, years ago, they drove to the San José in Almería, near where they made the Spaghetti Westerns. For a lark, they stopped the car by a road sign that said 'San Jose', and took photos of each other puzzling over a map. Alison didn't even need the photo, it was so clear.

She balanced the skinnier logs on the paper and card, and struck a match, watching the blue flame lick the card, and feeling the heat as the newspaper caught.

Bill came through from the kitchen with a bottle of wine and two glasses, and placed them on the low table. The table that Beth had had shipped over when she moved here twenty years ago, the table that Alison had lain underneath when she was small. When she was Jo's age.

'You finding your way around the kitchen OK?'

'Well, I've found the bottle opener, which is the main thing. Everything's under control.'

'Good. I've already started thinking in Bacharach lyrics, and it's not even late yet.'

He sat down on the chair, poured wine into the glasses and handed one to her.

'What shall we drink to?' he asked.

'To Hal and Burt.'

'Hal and Burt,' Bill said, clinking her glass. 'Which is your favourite?'

'Between Bacharach and David?'

'No, which of the songs?'

'Oh, easy. "Say a Little Prayer". Aretha, not Dionne.'

'I think mine has to be Cilla doing "Alfie".'

'You're full of surprises.'

'Or Isaac Hayes's "Walk on By".'

'Oh yes. And what about Shirley Bassey's "One Less Bell to Answer"?'

'"One less egg to fry". Did you know Burt Bacharach used to wash out Marlene Dietrich's underwear?'

'No, I can't say I did.'

Bill went to the kitchen and returned with a dish piled high with fat green beans still in their pods. Abas. Alison shelled one of them, throwing the husk into the fire and eating the five pale green beans.

Beth is harvesting the sweet peas she planted in spring. She's too weak to collect them from the stems that tangle through the garden, so Alison brings them over to her and she sits with a colander full, cracking the dry pods open and running her thumb along the slit. The seeds are like peppercorn. They patter down into the basin like hail.

When Beth died, Hannah and Alison sent her harvest of sweet-pea seeds to her friends and family around the world. Alison ate the abas thinking of Beth's sweet peas growing in America and Ireland, Denmark and Scotland, Birmingham and Brighton. Butterfly petals of pink and white clinging to more indigenous plants; wrapping green tendrils round trellises, sending the scent of talcum powder across the globe.

'If you don't pick them, they won't flower.'

133

37

Fig Tree

Down in the valley, in the dry riverbed that wound between the mountains, fringed with palms and bushes of oleander, Kim and Mickey poked around in the ashes under a fig tree. Breezeblocks that must have served as seating for an impromptu barbeque circled the tree trunk.

Mickey had felt in the box and had thought of this place, where he'd seen families picnicking earlier in the summer, resting in the shade of the tree. They'd taken the bike the mile or so down from the airport.

'We're lucky the moon's so bright,' he said.

'I don't feel there's much lucky about what we're doing,' Kim said. She sat on one of the breezeblocks, pulling her feet up and hugging her knees. 'I'm sure there must be snakes out here.'

Mickey found an old paella pan of black speckled metal and knelt at the edge of the barbeque remains, scooping the ashes and sifting them through his hands like a gold digger. He dropped some bits back into the pan. There were some bones, maybe rabbit or chicken, that still had traces of flesh attached.

'We could burn stuff,' he said, walking away to the bushes, collecting some sticks.

Birds hooted and dogs howled, playing with the echoes they created as the sounds bounced from the mountains and returned as another dog, another bird. It was cold now, and Kim wrapped her arms round herself. She missed her hair, its warmth, and put her helmet back on.

Mickey came back and dumped the sticks, went to the bike and returned with the carrier bag of leftovers from their picnic. He removed the paper from the cheese and the wrapper from the remains of their bread, crumpled them, and poked them under the wood. He knelt down and held his lighter to the paper. It took greedily.

'Bingo,' he said.

He fanned the flames carefully. Kim got up and started to collect more wood. There was plenty. It had hardly rained for all the time she'd been there, and the bushes seemed to drop their outer branches as they dried, growing new shoots from their centres. Looking at this place, you could almost believe the story of Moses and the burning bush, she thought; it was a tinderbox.

When she came back to the fig tree, the fire was burning less tentatively. She dropped her armful of wood at Mickey's side. She had heard that it was bad luck for two people to tend a fire; it could lead to quarrels, she recalled from some deep recess, God knows where. A bit late for that, she thought as she held her hands to the fire.

'Have you ever been to a cremation?' she asked.

She realised she knew almost nothing about Mickey. She suspected he was probably from a pretty well-off family; he had the disregard for things that came from having been able to take them for granted.

Mickey reached for the pan with his selection of bones, and pushed it into the centre of the fire. 'Yeah. My uncle's.'

'What was it like?'

The bones started to sizzle and give off a faint smell of meat.

'Not very emotional. You're sitting there in the crematorium, and there's the coffin at the front with the vicar, and then he presses a button, and that's it.'

'What happens?'

'This red curtain opens automatically, like in a cinema, and the coffin slides in, and the curtain closes again. It was all a bit James Bond.'

He walked off towards the riverbed. Kim looked at the trunk of the fig tree in front of her. It was silvery white, knobbled with ancient gnarls like knuckles and knees and elbows. Above her in the

135

branches she saw the ripe fruit nestling in the large hands of leaves. She stood on the breezeblock and reached up. The figs were heavy and pendulous as testicles. Kim cupped one in her hand, feeling its weight before twisting it free. The skin was thin and the fruit as sweet and dense as mincemeat. She looked in the carrier bag to see what they had left, broke off a chunk of bread and pushed it onto a stick, holding it over the fire. When it was toasted, she wedged a lump of cheese into it. It tasted great. She took off the crash helmet, feeling a little warmer with the fire going and the food inside her. There were some cans of beer, and she opened one, watching Mickey as he scrabbled in the earth, picking up things and studying them, keeping some and throwing the rest over his shoulder. His head caught the moonlight. She was impressed by his dedication, even if he was a fucking idiot. She walked over to him.

'Found anything?'

'Yeah, there are these really chalky stones, look.'

He passed Kim a lump. She squatted down and picked up a piece of grey slate, trying the stone out on it. It left a mark.

'If we could smash them up small enough,' she said. 'We need a pestle and mortar or something.'

She tried balancing the stone on the slate and sandwiching another piece on top. She jumped on the pile, lifted the slate and looked. The chalk had slipped from between the stones. She thought for a while.

'Have you got socks on?' she asked.

'Why?'

'Take one off.'

Mickey sat on the ground and removed his boot. He pulled off a black sock and handed it to her. She put the pebble in the sock and tried again with the slate sandwich. It worked.

'Brilliant,' she said, collecting more of the chalky stones and dropping them into the sock.

38

Electric

Alison had forgotten both how good a cook Bill was, and how much she loved being fed. They ate from the dinner service she'd used when she cooked for Beth. Wreaths of dark green ceramic leaves framed botanical illustrations of fruit and vegetables. Maybe the plate that Bill presented her with now, piled high with baby artichokes that they dipped in butter and ate with their fingers, was the same one that Beth had eaten from on the day she died. Strawberry jam smeared on white bread; the only thing she'd fancied. And the dish filled with frilly skirted wild mushrooms in oil and garlic, parsley and lemon juice was possibly the one that Alison had made Beth's porridge in each morning, decorating it with a heart of chopped dried apricots to sweeten it. Other meals superimposed themselves on the crisp little lettuce hearts chopped into wedges, the green olives and bread, the thin slices of aubergine blackened to surrender on the pan, the salad of tomato and red onion and perfectly ripe avocado.

But it didn't take away from the food. As she ate from the plates and drank wine from the recycled green glass with its twisted stem, and watched the fire and talked with Bill, she accepted this overlaying as a kind of communion, and she was surprised to find that she wasn't as sad as she'd prepared herself to be. She threw the chewed artichoke leaves into the fire and watched them sizzle.

It is New Year's Eve. Beth and Alison are sitting by the fire, playing Scrabble. Beth has just got a bonus of fifty and a triple word score for 'urinated'. They turn off the music and switch on the television to see the arrival of the New Year. Clocks are striking twelve. People in party dresses and dinner suits are letting off party poppers, opening champagne, shouting and embracing. 'Feliz Año Nuevo!' the presenters shout.

Beth and Alison hug.

'Happy New Year, Mama.'

'Happy New Year, love.'

Instead of resolutions, Alison suggests they write down the things they don't want to carry into the virgin year; things they'd rather be rid of. They tear paper from the Scrabble score pad. They have a pen each. They begin tentatively at first, but then with a real sense of urgency, writing and folding and throwing the screwed-up pieces of paper into the fire. Watching, as the little pieces of bad last year – the fear and sadness and anger, the out-of-controlness and unfairness of it all, the why me? and why now?, the hospitals and doctors and appointments and tests and results, the not being explained to and not under-standing – as all their demons are committed to the flames, and they watch them and are warmed by them as they are turned to ash.

Bill declined Alison's offer to help. He returned to the kitchen, and she could hear him opening cupboards and drawers. It was strange being a guest in her own house. She could recognise the geography of the kitchen through Bill's movements. He was looking in the cupboard by the sink, then opening the cutlery drawer, then banging something on the work surface, but she couldn't work out what. She got up and put some more wood on the fire, then looked through the cassettes on the shelf, found one of Nat King Cole singing in Spanish that they'd picked up in a petrol station one time, years ago, and put it on the old ghetto blaster.

'Quizás, Quizás, Quizás.'

Nat had never spoken Spanish; he'd learned the sounds phone-tically. She listened to his perfect diction, his extraordinary voice that put you at your ease. You knew he was never going to strain or struggle with a note. He could soar and dip and you were safe in his hands. And yet he died of cancer in his forties. She'd seen a documentary about him, which made her feel that all that calmness – that ease – had been what had eaten him up inside. The price he paid for sounding so carefree. That was always the way with cancer, even more so in alternative treatment. Not only did you have this hideous illness, but also it was your own fault: you hadn't managed your anger, or expressed your grief sufficiently. You'd suppressed stuff, and this was the result. What a double whammy. Nat crooned on, his cigarettes no doubt in his immaculate suit pocket, his cells already probably making war on themselves, Nat doing his best, always doing his best.

Bill crossed the room, switched off the light, returned to the kitchen and reappeared with a tray. On it, a bottle of cava, two fluted glasses, and two tiny lantern heads of hollowed-out pomegranates. They flickered with the night-lights he'd placed inside them; their tiny smiles not much larger than nail clippings, their eyes the diameter of pencils. He carried the tray to the low wooden table. Between the two little heads was a mound of pomegranate flesh; gobbets of translucent red, honeycombed cells with a little black seed encased in each.

Alison clapped her hands. 'Oh! I love Halloween.'

'I know.'

Bill opened the bottle carefully, with a tea towel over the neck so that the cork released with a muffled belch. He tipped the glasses as he poured, so that the bubbles behaved themselves, just rising to the rim before subsiding and settling into the pale yellow. He passed a glass to Alison.

'Happy Halloween.'

'Happy Halloween.'

They clinked glasses and the fizz rose up and they drank.

'Spoons – I forgot the spoons.' said Bill, standing up.

'The first time we had pomegranates,' said Alison when he came back, 'we ate them with a pin. It took for ever. Do you remember that? When garlic was really exotic? Seems incredible now. Can you remember the first time you ate things?'

Bill passed her a spoon. 'I can remember my first peach, my first mango, my first yoghurt – one of those chocolate ones with a layer of real chocolate on top.'

'Oh, yes. And Walnut Whips and Kunzel cakes. Life was so exciting then, wasn't it? When every experience was new.'

'I like to believe – at least when it comes to food – that each time is a first.'

'That's why you're a great cook.'

'Thanks. I remember going to my first posh restaurant and having half an avocado. I think the choice of starters was grapefruit juice, avocado, or prawn cocktail. Quite retro now.'

'Who were you with?'

'Mum, Dad and some business associates they were entertaining, I imagine. I remember the food more than the people. Dad would have had a steak tartare, I expect, Mum a mixed grill, and I had trout with almonds. All very seventies.'

'You hardly ever talk about your dad.'

Bill spooned a little heap of the pomegranate cells into his mouth and crunched the seeds.

'Not everyone's like you,' he said, taking a drink from his glass and then refilling it.

'What do you mean?'

He looked at her. 'Well, you find talking easy, and I find listening to you easy. That's probably why we get on.'

'But I'd like to know more about you. It's not that I don't want to listen; that's not altogether fair.'

'I don't find talking about it easy. I envy you that.'

'Well, try. What was he like?'

Bill stared into the fire. 'He wasn't an easy man. I didn't get on with him like you got on with your mum. We weren't what you'd call friends.'

'Yeah. I was really lucky, I know.'

Bill was silent. He swilled the cava round his glass and watched the flames.

'What is it?' Alison asked.

'Nothing. I'm just being touchy.'

'What d'you mean?'

He didn't answer.

'What?' she asked him.

'Well, it's just the way we work. It's hard to change, but . . .' He paused. 'OK, I'll say it. You ask me about my dad, and without even realising you bring the conversation immediately back to you. The thing is, you don't even know you're doing it.'

Alison said nothing. The Nat King Cole cassette finished and made a loud chugging noise before clunking to Off, but she didn't want to get up and turn it over. She wound back over their conversation to try to see where they'd started to go astray. Bill was draining the last of the cava into his glass.

'I'm sorry, Bill. I was just trying to empathise. I guess I'm not as good at it as you are, but I do really want to hear what it was like for you. I didn't mean to take over.' Bill stared into his glass. 'Please, Bill. Try again, and I'll try and be a better listener.'

He turned to the fire again and directed his voice there, as if he was telling the flames.

'When he was dying, I sat with him in the hospital. It was just me and him. And he did this thing. This uncharacteristic thing. He touched the hair on the back of my head. He never normally touched me; he wasn't that kind of a dad. But he touched my head, and it felt like this rush of electricity.'

Alison watched him. It might have been five minutes or fifty before she leaned over and touched the back of his head. Bill didn't move. She began to stroke his hair softly, feeling it under her fingertips, gently touching, from his neck to his ears. She felt him let go.

39

Sweets

'La Muerte' is 'the bald one' of the Days of the Dead. You see La Muerte in baked goods and sugar candies – in 'calaveras de azucar' – as it is widely known that the Dead love sugar.

www.globalgourmet.com

The air steward leaned over Jo, holding out a small basket of boiled sweets.

'Would you like one of these for take off, young lady?' Jo looked up at him. 'They help stop your ears popping.' Jo looked at Hannah, who nodded, and then back at the steward, smiling. 'Tell you what,' he said, 'take two. One for each ear.'

Jo selected two of the red ones. 'Thank you,' she said.

'My pleasure. Enjoy your flight, although looks to me like you're a regular flyer – did you fancy giving your broomstick the night off for good behaviour?'

Jo giggled. She still had on her black witch's cape over her tracksuit; she'd insisted.

'Can I eat this now?' she asked Hannah.

'Sure.'

Despite the sweets, the take-off hurt Jo's ears; it always did, and as Hannah tried to keep her distracted, and did everything she could think of to relieve her pain, she began to worry whether this had been such a good idea after all.

It was this transit that was the killer – the leaving of her defined world and the launching into another, through Passport Control and Customs, passing through some kind of time portal into a place where things were unsettled again. Her passport had been twice altered: the person to notify in case of an emergency amended, her daughter's details appended. And yet the same face appeared inside the cover, benignly oblivious.

The times she'd made this same journey over the years. From the first trips, when it was a matter of grabbing a couple of weeks off work and having a holiday in the sunshine; her bag crammed with Marks & Spencer's tea bags and other treats that Beth would have sent for on a list – maybe a book she'd read a review of, a slab of Lancashire cheese, and a couple of glossy magazines. Even then, the return home to Beth's had been a regression to something un-resolved: the fact that it was set in another country only served to magnify it. The hellos and goodbyes were always so much more intense; the time together put into a stronger relief.

When she was pregnant, everything entered a state of flux, and after Jo's birth – lugging all the paraphernalia of bottles and buggy, nappies and changing mat – they moved along a notch, with Jo now the daughter. Only they didn't really move along. In transit, Hannah still went from mother to daughter.

And then came the trip when Beth hadn't been waiting at the other side of the barrier, straining to catch the first glimpse of her. The time after the phone call, when she'd dropped everything and rushed out on the first flight she could find. From her home to airport, airport to hospital.

Every time we say goodbye I die a little.

She realised now what it had felt like. The years of continual rupturing had been like an eternal rehearsal for the real thing.

Jo had the window seat, and even though it was dark she peered out. Her reflection superimposed itself on the night sky; wisps of clouds drifting through her features. When the meal arrived, she systematically worked her way through the little portions of food in the moulded plastic tray – through novelty more than hunger. It was all like a doll's tea party, with the plastic-wrapped paper napkin, and the tiny sachets of salt and pepper and sugar. She peeled the foil from her serving of chicken and rice, and forked up every last mouthful before opening the tiny containers of butter and cheese to go with the bread roll and the packet of crackers. She dipped her white plastic spoon into the white plastic dish of fruit salad, even eating the maraschino cherry that floated in the syrup like a traffic light among the yellow fog of pale grapefruit and pear. She ate with relish things that she normally didn't like. As though her taste buds were also in transit. Hannah picked at her food; she hadn't the heart for it. Jo turned to her, holding up a foil-wrapped piece of chocolate.

'Nanna can eat this now, can't she?'

'Sorry, Jo, what did you say?'

'Now that she's in the sky, out there.'

She pointed to the window, and Hannah understood.

Beth's diet had been one of the things that had concerned Jo most. All the sacrifices of sweets and cakes had bothered her more than the visits to hospital and increasing fragility had seemed to. Beth had shared the special treats of natural fruit chews and cereal bars that any visitors from places better endowed with health-food stores were asked to bring out; treats she stashed in her bedside drawer. Jo knew where to look for them, and Beth had made into a ritual the Nannaly business of producing them for her.

After Beth died, Jo had asked Hannah if she'd be able to eat sweets again, now she was in the sky. It had been terribly important. She had needed the reassurance that she certainly could. Hannah had forgotten. She looked out of the window.

'Yes, I expect she can.'

'I wish we could give her this piece,' said Jo.

'So do I,' said Hannah.

40

Loss Adjuster

There is only so much wine
That you can drink in one lifetime,
But it will never be enough
To save you from the bottom of your glass.
The Handsome Family,
'So Much Wine'

'How many bottles did we buy, for God's sake?' Alison asked as Bill uncorked another red wine.

'Oh, a few.'

He filled their glasses and helped himself to a handful of pistachio nuts. The fire was blazing, and a compilation tape of sixties pop was playing on the ghetto blaster. It was very late, but as neither of them wore a watch, and as the clock on the mantelpiece had been saying five past three since they arrived, they had no way of knowing how very late. All they had to measure time by was the number of logs the fire had consumed, the times one or the other of them had got up to use the loo or change the tape, and the number of empty bottles they'd accumulated – three wine and one cava so far. Alison was stretched the length of the settee. She'd undone the waistband of her jeans, still full after their marathon supper. Bill sat in the armchair by the fire, his legs propped up on Alison's fire-making stool.

'What was the worst thing anyone said to you after your dad died?'

145

'Let's see,' he said, throwing shells into the fire. 'I know. "It must be such a relief."'

'Oh, yes. I mean, who for? You might think it; a part of you at least, secretly and guiltily, but how dare anyone else say it.'

'And "He's in a better place now." Six foot under; shoulder to shoulder with two people he'd never met. That was rich.'

'Of course, he was buried, wasn't he? What was that like?'

'Ridiculous. It wasn't what he'd have wanted at all, but Mother insisted. She insisted about everything, chose the graveyard – near her place – the plot, the kind of gravestone, even what it says.'

'What does it say?'

'Oh, dates of death and birth, or the other way round, and then some crap about great hubby and daddy, sadly missed, et cetera, et cetera.'

'I had real grave envy for a while. I used to wish I had somewhere to visit Mum.'

'So why was she cremated?'

'Her choice. I think maybe if she'd have died in England, and we could have got her a nice plot in the Lake District . . . but it's not an option here. You don't go in the ground; they put you in these drawers. She dreaded being put in one of those.' Alison sipped her wine, remembering. 'We went to someone's funeral here, and after the coffin was slid into the hole we all stood around in the midday sun, watching as two workmen in overalls slapped plaster over the opening. It was quite mesmerising.'

'Sounds like an episode of *Home Front*. To be honest, I don't feel a grave's much comfort, if that's any comfort. Maybe if I'd been more involved in the choices, or if I believed that's what he'd wanted. I just used to think of his nails and hair still growing, like . . . who was it? Christina Rossetti? No, Lizzie Siddal.'

'Oh, God.'

Alison and Bill fell into a silence for a while. Alison remembered how Beth's hair had become so strong and healthy as her illness had progressed. Thick and grey and lustrous. Her nails, too. They'd been stronger than ever. They seemed to flourish as she got weaker and weaker. Maybe there was a clue in that, something that could be part of a cure in the future. When she heard news of breakthrough treatments now, it broke her heart.

On the tape the Moody Blues sang 'Go Now'.

Thumping piano intro; 'We've already said goodbye . . .'

Alison felt herself getting teary. It was the wine and the exhaustion and the emotion, all of it catching up with her, but she didn't want to move. Didn't want to go and sleep in her old bed, didn't want to be left alone. She knew that if she tried to stand up the room would spin. What had they been talking about? How had it ended with nails? And she remembered.

' "So what are you going to do now?" ' she said. 'Someone actually asked me that at the funeral.'

Bill smiled, 'Some people just don't think – or they think so much that anything they try to say comes out wrong. Like "At least it was swift" or "At least he didn't suffer much." '

Alison nodded. She was almost too tired to speak. 'What would you have wanted people to say?' she asked.

'I don't know. Nothing, really. Or nothing I know. I guess it's possible someone could have said something and it would have been the right thing, but I can't tell you what that would have been.'

'I know what you mean. I think I just wanted to feel I could weep and be held. I think that's still how I feel.'

The song continued.

> Well, you'd better go now,
> Go now, go now, go now . . .

They fell back into silence. It wasn't an uncomfortable silence, just one that neither trusted themself with. They were ripe for melancholy, and it was too dangerous.

Bill cracked first. 'What's the first thing you remember saying goodbye to?'

Alison thought a while. 'I know, I know: it was the TV screen.'

'You what?'

'Yeah, I know. It must have been around the time Mum and Dad split up, though I don't remember saying any big goodbyes to him, which is interesting. I was three and I used to go to this nursery at a big house nearby. The same time each day we'd sit on the floor in front of the big old television and we'd watch *Andy Pandy* on *Watch with Mother*. Do you remember at the end, they sang "Time to go Home", all the puppets hands flopping up and down?'

'"Andy and Teddy are waving goodbye, goodbye,"' Bill sang, doing the floppy arm action.

'That's the one. Well, afterwards we'd all troop out, but I'd hang back. The TV would have been switched off, but with those old tellies it took ages for the picture to fade. I'd watch the screen till there was just this star of white left in the centre, and I'd kiss this belly button of static, feel it tingle on my lips.'

'So you've always been a bit weird, then.'

'Fuck you.'

'I suppose mine was the first tooth I lost.'

'Ah, that doesn't count, 'cos you get compensation.'

'The tooth fairy. What do you think's the going rate for teeth nowadays?'

'I don't know. Jo's still got all hers, I think. Must be at least a pound with inflation. If you think about it, losing teeth should be nature's way of giving us our first taste of losing, and we've gone and invented this bloody fairy to sugar the pill. They're like fucking loss adjusters. If your Mr Disney hadn't come along, we'd have had to invent him, too.'

'OK, if I can't have my tooth, my next one was a garden. I used to go into work with my dad sometimes on Saturdays. He'd be in the office and I'd just wander around. That was when I first had a go on a typewriter, I'd try and make pictures of Christmas trees using the x key.'

'A promising writer even then.'

'Ha ha. Well, there was this garden at the back of his offices. It was really magical, all overgrown and mysterious. I spent hours there. Looking back, Dad probably wanted me out of the way so he could get on the phone to one of his girlfriends. Then one Saturday, as I was thumping out another Christmas tree, he said if I wanted to go and play in the garden it would be my last chance, 'cos it wouldn't be there next time I came.' Bill stopped and picked up another handful of pistachio nuts. 'I was really shocked. I couldn't imagine letting anyone destroy something so beautiful. I went out and walked every inch of it, trying to commit it to memory. In fact, I pretty well did. I can still remember it really clearly.'

'What happened to it?'

'He'd sold it to the offices next door. It was a car park next time I saw it.'

'Bloody hell, Joni. Didn't you write a song about that?'

Bill threw a pistachio at her. It caught her on the nose. 'Ow!'

'Christ, I'm trying share my most intimate thoughts with you and what thanks do I get?'

Alison looked at him, not sure if he was being serious again, and he started to laugh.

'"Paved paradise, put up a parking lot." How does it go?' he asked, pelting her with nuts.

41

Replenished

As the moon sank behind the mountains, leaving a sky crammed with stars, Kim and Mickey worked like a Stone Age couple, foraging and burning and pounding. By the time the sky had begun to pale to slate grey, before the birds began, they had created their reproduction of the missing remains.

Mickey started up the bike. The noise surprised him, dragged him back to a reality that had been suspended for the length of the night. Kim sat behind him with the replenished box in the rucksack on her back. They had left the place almost exactly as they'd found it. They set off back down the dirt track, towards the road out of the valley, past a row of houses obscured from view by a bank of hedges. When they'd arrived, Kim hadn't noticed them in the darkness, and she was surprised to discover civilisation so near where they'd been.

A few seconds later, Mickey stopped. He turned off the engine and stared.

'What's wrong?' Kim asked.

'There is a God after all,' he said. In front of the end house, in the rough track, was a silver-grey Peugeot. 'That's it. That's the car.'

'No!'

'It is,' he whispered. 'Look: the sticker I told you about.'

Kim got off the bike and waited while he walked over to the car. 'He returned to the bike. 'It's the same one, I'm sure. Look, I'll push the bike onto the road. Wait there while I try the boot.'

Kim watched as Mickey quietly opened the unlocked boot, replaced the rucksack and shut the boot again. He tiptoed back to her. It was that easy.

42

Oasis

They are at the hospital for a second day when the flowers arrive. An elaborate arrangement fussily displayed in Oasis, cascading from a wicker basket. Alison reads Beth the note.

'They're so beautiful,' Beth says. 'I wish I hadn't had to go through this to be given them.'

After watching a talent competition on television – young girls with ringlets performing pasa dobles; little boys playing outsize guitars; big women sitting with their legs apart, clapping, and shouting 'Anda!' – and after they've eaten what they can of the extraordinarily unsuitable hospital food – York ham and tinned vegetables – they try to sleep. Upstairs it sounds like they're having a party. The sharp clicking of high heels on marble floors, the strong smell of Ducados wafting in from the corridor.

Earlier, Alison had been out for a walk. Not far – not possible to go far: the hospital cut off on an island of ring roads, the sea visible on the horizon but impossible to reach. She walked past the polythene-covered greenhouses of tomatoes, and smelled the chemicals that hung in the air. Her presence caused the dogs tied up in the fields to bark. She crossed the road and found a café. It was small and noisy and clean. She asked for a beer. The other punters were lorry drivers, drinking shots of brandy with their coffees. The old woman who served her was curious. Alison explained she was at the hospital with her mother.

The woman nodded. 'And the rest of your family? Your brothers and sisters?'

'One, a sister; she's coming soon.'

The woman shook her head, looked her in the eyes, sadly. 'Only one?'

As they try to sleep under hospital sheets, their heads on slippery hospital pillows, a low light at the foot of the beds, Beth looks at the flowers.

'Can you do something with them? I feel like I'm in a morgue.'

43

Delay

Alison opened her eyes cautiously and saw the purple and brown fabric of Beth's settee. She knew it like she knew her own name, but it took her a few seconds to place. Her cheek was pressed against a small, hard object, which she discovered was a pistachio shell. She held it between her fingers and studied it as if it held all the answers. She could hear a loud gurgling coming from the kitchen, and as she sat up her head spun and her temples pounded.

'Oh, God,' she groaned, putting her head in her hands and closing her eyes again. All she could think of was water. She desperately needed water. Buckets full. Swimming pools full.

'Good morning.' Bill popped his head round from the kitchen.

Alison raised her head carefully. He was holding a tea towel in one hand and a glass in the other. He looked fine.

'What is that noise?' she asked, her tongue thick and her voice deeper than she expected.

Bill stopped polishing the glass and listened. The gurgling was replaced by a whooshing. 'The dishwasher. We're on final rinse,' he said.

'Christ. How long have you been up?' Alison eased herself up and walked through to the kitchen.

'A couple of hours.'

She opened the fridge and took out a plastic bottle, drinking the water straight from it. The weight of the bottle was immense. She put it down, noticing that her hands were shaking, and groaned again.

'We left everything in the car last night, do you realise?' Bill said.

154

Alison squinted at him, but he was standing in front of the window and the light hurt her eyes. She shielded them with her hand.

'No.'

'It's OK. I went out this morning and brought everything in.'

'Wasn't it even locked?'

Bill shook his head.

A sudden wave of nausea washed over her. 'Mum's ashes?'

Bill nodded. 'They're there,' he said, waving the tea towel towards the hall.

The rucksack was on the hall table, their bags on the floor. Alison looked in the rucksack. The box was there. She removed it and held it, shaking her head. 'I can't believe I did that.'

'We were pretty pissed.'

'You can say that again.' She put the box back on the table and touched the lid. 'Haven't you even got a hangover?' she asked, walking back to the kitchen.

'Took some Solpadeine last night before I went to sleep and drank about a gallon of water. I feel quite good, actually.'

'Christ.' She peered at him. He did look sickeningly perky. 'You haven't got a couple spare, have you?'

Bill handed her the packet. 'Help yourself.'

'You're a star.' She poured herself a glass of water, using both hands to hold the bottle steady, and dropped two white tablets into it, swilling them round and watching them dissolve. The sight of them effervescing and gradually disintegrating made her feel queasy. 'Where did you sleep?'

'The room at the end – was that all right?'

Alison looked to the door at the end of the corridor. It was Beth's room. Beth had died in that bed.

'Of course. Did you sleep OK?'

'Fine. You conked out and I didn't want to wake you. Do you fancy some breakfast?' He was constructing a sandwich with what looked like the leftovers from last night. Alison watched as he drizzled olive oil over the bread.

'What are you like? Let's see if I can keep this down.' She tipped her glass towards him and started to sip from it gingerly. 'Ugh. Then I'm going to need at least a pot of tea before I can think about food. But first I need a shower.'

She walked over to the stuff that Bill had brought in and unzipped her holdall, tipping the contents onto the cold stone floor and rummaging through for her toilet bag. Her mobile phone fell out and cracked against the floor. She picked it up and switched it on to see if it was broken. The envelope icon was flashing. It took her a while to remember how it worked, but eventually she managed to access her messages. At first it looked like a random selection of letters, and she cursed texting, the language for people younger than her, which read as if dictated by someone who was choking. She squinted at the black liquid crystal shapes on the tiny grey screen: 'DNT DO NYTHNG YET! H + J ON THR WAY. W8! J'.

'Oh my God!'

'What?'

'It's from Jacques. Hannah's coming. I wonder when he sent this? I haven't switched the phone back on since the flight.'

'She's coming here?' Bill asked through a mouthful of bread.

'Apparently. With Jo, too, I think. At least, I'm presuming that J is Jo and not Jacques. I don't think Jo can text yet. Oh, Jesus, my head.'

She pulled a chair out from the table, the noise as it scraped on the floor amplifying inside her head, and gently lowered herself into it, cradling the mobile in her hands, half expecting the message to change, or the mobile to morph into a creature that would spring away and scurry out of the house like some textbook symptom of DTs. It didn't; she shook her head in disbelief.

'I need a shower,' she said again, picking her toilet bag from the floor and heading for the bathroom.

44

Murcia

'What's Spanish for bed?'

'Cama.'

'What's Spanish for curtains?'

'Sorry, I don't know.'

Jo walked around the room at the hostal, picking objects at random, while Hannah dressed. They'd arrived in Murcia at two in the morning, and Hannah had carried her sleeping child out to the taxi rank, trusting the driver to take them to the address she'd found on a website and scribbled on a piece of paper. It was exactly as the site had described it: clean, quiet, no frills.

'Come on, Jo, let's get you dressed now.'

'I know some Spanish you'll remember,' Hannah said to Jo's reflection as she brushed her hair in front of the mirror. 'Hola, guapa.'

'Oh yes, I know that. It's in my head now. I've found it. What does it mean? I know. "Hello".'

'It means "Hello, gorgeous."'

'Yes. I remember now.'

'Not surprising, the number of times people said it to you.'

'What else did they say?'

'Oh, all sorts, but wherever I went with you they gave you sweets. We're lucky you've any teeth left, the number of lollipops you had.' Hannah slipped an elastic band round the end of Jo's sleek plait. 'OK, that's you done, guapa.'

Hannah paid the bill, and she and Jo left the hostal with their holdall, and found a bar for some breakfast on their way to the bus station. Jacques had persuaded Hannah not to hire a car. Alison and Bill could meet them off the bus, and she'd be more relaxed for not driving. She couldn't believe that the word 'relaxed' would ever be used in connection with this, but there she was. It was Jo's normalising influence at work again.

She ordered coffee for her and orange juice for Jo, and great boats of white toast smeared with the pulp of tomatoes and drizzled with olive oil. Hannah would never think of eating this for breakfast at home, but here it seemed more natural than marmalade.

Everything about Spain delighted Jo; she was on holiday, and her mood was contagious. She loved the napkin dispensers on the tables, and the straws that came with everything. She'd been thrilled by the large porcelain toilet and the bidet in their hostal bathroom.

'For washing dolls.' she'd said, turning on the taps, where C didn't stand for cold, but for 'caliente', which meant 'hot'.

'Well, that too, I guess,' Hannah said.

45

Time to Kill

Alison had to walk into the middle of the meadow beyond the house to get a signal. As she stood there, looking at the scorched ground, waiting for Jacques to pick up, she realised she was standing on the exact spot where Beth's coffin had been placed. For a second, she could see the crowd of people who had gathered on that morning. She put the phone in the back pocket of her shorts and looked over to the house, realising she felt foolish having to tell Bill about this change of events. Apart from anything else, it made her feel as if she'd been melodramatic, dragging Bill all this way – for what? She walked back slowly, past the log pile and the pink oleander at the side of the house, her feet loud on the gravel. Today was the kind of day when she'd have to do everything slowly.

'Well, I got hold of Jacques,' she said, tramping up the stairs to the roof terrace where Bill lay on a plastic sunbed, an open book on Disney balanced on his face. 'It's all true; they're on their way. He said she had a last-minute change of heart. She phoned him this morning, and they're getting the bus from Murcia.' Alison spoke to the book; the cover portrait of Disney replacing Bill's own features, only too small. He looked creepy, the iconic moustachioed head leering from Bill's neck.

Bill lifted the book, holding it above his face to shade his eyes. 'Well, that's good, isn't it?'

Alison wiped her brow. The alcohol was making its getaway from every pore. She knew that it was partly her hangover and the heat that made her feel crotchety and unreasonable, and that Bill was

159

right – he more than anyone had heard her drone on about how it was all down to her, how unsupported she felt. Yet she didn't feel happy. She felt belligerent, reluctant to give up the higher moral ground, and strangely robbed of her status. Unlike Hannah, she had neither partner nor child, nor even the kind of job that prevented her from investing her energy (too much of it?) in this. Hannah was stealing her limelight, swanning over like this at the eleventh hour, and it pissed her off. No sooner had she given houseroom to these thoughts than she felt guilty for them. She didn't trust herself to say anything to Bill, aware of how pathetic she sounded. She felt guilty for feeling belligerent, mean for being so petty, and angry for being made to go through this mangle of stupid, childish emotions. All this hummed around her head as the sweat trickled down her back. She drew a breath and opened her mouth to speak. 'Christ. It's so hot.'

'What time will the bus get here?'

'I phoned the station. They said it'll be in Vera at five. We'll have to go and collect them from there. It's half an hour from here, tops. I guess it's going to be tomorrow before we can do the ashes.'

Alison realised something else. That she resented having to change her plans. Spending so much time on her own had made her pretty inflexible. She floundered without an agenda. Had looking after Beth been good for Beth or good for her?

'Which leaves us,' said Bill, looking at his watch, 'the best part of five hours.'

'What d'you want to do?' Alison asked.

'Well, it appears we need to remain sober, so . . . I don't know . . . show me the sights?'

46

Cessna

The plane is apparently a Cessna. Beth and Alison sit next to each other in the tiny cabin, the air full of August heat. They've come directly from El Cid's, a beach bar, and are wearing only bikinis under their printed cotton wraps. Alison is maybe twenty and Beth not yet fifty. Mother and daughter; handsome women, both. Too tall and too fair ever to be mistaken for Spanish. Alison's hair is long and blond and unruly. The sun has brought out a scattering of freckles across her nose and on her shoulders. Her feet are bare, and there is still sand between her toes. Beth's thick chestnut hair is cut sharply into her neck. She wears a pair of tortoiseshell-framed sunglasses, and although from choice she drives barefoot she put on a pair of leather sandals when she arrived at the airport in Cortijo Grande. In the two seats facing them are the men: Rupert and someone whose name they're not sure of. Something German – Hans, maybe. A Londoner called Jed is in the front, the cockpit. He's a cabby but he's just got his flying licence, apparently. He turns a key in the ignition as if the plane were a hackney cab. Like *Chitty Chitty Bang Bang*. There are no seatbelts, and there's nobody running through any safety drill. They begin to move, scorched scenery passing horizontally through the thick plastic windows as if it were painted on flats; the speed makes it hard to judge what's still and what's moving. Jed manoeuvres the plane to the far end of the runway, turns it round, and they begin to move forward, gathering speed in a surprisingly short time. Seconds. The runway disappears; the ground separates from the wheels. They feel the lurch in their stomachs, and they are in the sky.

'Wow!' says Alison, 'What a view!'

The lime-green golf course fills the valley like a fitted carpet, decorated with a pattern of orange groves. Water sprinklers whisk the light on its surface. Large villas with kidney-shaped pools, square pools, oblong pools and circular pools edge the greens and the fairways. All this water does nothing to quench the dryness of the surrounding valley, which coughs cracked red earth and raw rock in the August heat.

They soar higher and cruise over the ridge of the mountain, the small dark blot of their shadow creasing on its summit, and suddenly, there's the sea. The sea where Alison had been swimming half an hour ago, when she met Rupert. He'd introduced himself to her in the waist-deep water. He was a record producer, he said. He had an aeroplane, he said. Did she want to fly with him?

'Can my mum come, too?' she asked him.

'Come on, it'll be an adventure,' she convinced Beth.

Weatherwise it's such a lovely day.

Beth had driven them, Alison in the passenger seat, Rupert and Jed the cabby in the back. The German man (Otto?) had been at the bar in the airport, waiting; drinking beer from a pint glass.

The deep sea is jade, paling to turquoise in the shallows, and where it breaks on the shore is laced like a doily. The beach ends as a roughly torn edge along the ruler-sharp road. The tops of the straw beach umbrellas outside the bar, where Beth had been lying, reading a book by Margaret Atwood, make a uniform pattern in the sand, like a blister packet of pills.

They circle back, away from the sea that is still on Alison's skin, and the beach that is still between her toes, and she looks down at the airport, the glass flight tower at its corner, and the tiny runway that stretches like an ironing board the length of the plateau, and they prepare to land.

'What an experience. You see, Mum? Aren't you glad I persuaded you?' Alison says, as the plane swoops down.

The wheels are almost on the ground, but there is no runway left ahead. Jed has misjudged it, and he yanks the controls. The plane lifts skywards again, and they circle, and no one breathes, and Jed levels out, makes a second attempt. If anything, it's worse this time. Ahead of them, red rock is within touching distance, forcing itself into sharp focus. No one speaks. Jed sweats. Alison watches the back of his neck, watches the salty rivulets leaking from his short ginger hair, trickling down his sunburned neck, momentarily enlarging his freckles before soaking into the collar of his Fred Perry, turning it a darker green. Rupert attempts to light a cigarette that he has taken from his pocket, and Beth screams at him, 'Don't you dare light that!'

Rupert puts the unlit cigarette back in the packet, holds the packet like a small Bible between his hands.

At the third attempt, the airstrip seems to have become smaller, impossibly small. No sooner is it there than there's none of it left, and the mountains are hurtling closer and closer, and then at the last possible second the plane has risen up again, just in time.

Without having to say anything, certain facts have become apparent:

Jed has lost his nerve.

Daylight is fading fast.

No one has been informed that they are in the sky.

There is not sufficient fuel or daylight to reach any other place safely.

'My God. What did you do?' Bill asked.

'Held tight. I don't think I understood how dangerous it was till afterwards. At the time it was just . . . happening. You were there in the second, willing the plane down safely. We made it on the seventh attempt. Rupert got out first, and we scrambled out behind him. Mum headed straight for the toilet in the airport, and Rupert said something like "Hey, isn't it great to be alive?" And it was.'

'I dare say, but there have to be easier ways of feeling how lucky you are to be alive.'

'Sure, but you can see the attraction. The rush you get. Like scary fairground rides and drugs.'

'And sex.'

'Oh yes. And sex.' Alison walked along the runway. 'Mum was furious. Not with me, but with herself. It was a kind of Laurel and Hardy moment: "Another fine fix you've got me into." She'd remembered a film, she told me, where people survived a plane crash in some remote place and ended up eating each other, and she'd thought how ill prepared we were to survive, that I didn't even have shoes on. She was able to think about the what next even then.' Alison picked a stem of rosemary from a bush at the edge of the runway, rubbed it between her fingers and smelled it. 'Mainly, though, she was staggered that she'd gone along with one of my crazy plans.' She absently pushed the sprig of rosemary into her pocket. 'But then she always did.'

'So who were these strangers you trusted your lives with?'

'Fuck knows. Drug runners, probably. There were no checks at the airport – well, you could hardly call it an airport, really. Look at it.' She gestured towards the ramshackle buildings perched above the crusty, cracked airstrip where they stood. 'And you could get from Morocco or Algeria in a couple of hours. Mum was right: it was an amazingly stupid thing to do. I don't know how they got to whereever it was they were headed; I can't imagine Jed flew them. Afterwards I imagined hailing a cab in London, and there would be Jed.'

'Christ, I wouldn't have got in if it were.'

'Do you want to take a look at the airport?'

'Sure.'

'We can leave the car here.'

The car was parked at the other end of the runway. Bill followed Alison up a track that led to the old airport buildings. He saw a green lizard scuttle through the dry grass. It was midday and there wasn't a cloud in the sky. He felt light-headed with the heat. Alison led the way across a neglected courtyard, past abandoned rooms littered with junk.

'I haven't been here for years,' she said. 'I think it's been squatted since then.'

Bill hoped she wasn't going to switch to travel-guide mode again. She always wittered on when she was anxious.

'This was the bar,' she said, her voice bouncing off the walls in the derelict room. Like a man in the desert seeing an oasis, Bill could almost taste the cold beer that used to be served here. He could murder one right now. This had to be the most parched place he'd ever been. 'We should've at least brought some water,' Alison said, and he saw that she was as much in need of a drink as he was, and remembered how much he liked her, and why they were here.

'Is this the way up to flight tower?' he asked, pointing to the stairwell. He started climbing the stairs.

'Yeah. Careful; I don't know how safe it is.'

He was already disappearing up the spiral staircase. When he reached the top, she heard him let out a long whistle.

'Fucking hell.'

Alison smiled. She climbed up after him. 'Thought you'd appreciate it.'

'What a view. What a waste. God, this would make the most amazing club.' He kicked at the crap that littered the floor; a champagne bottle rolled against the wall. 'You certainly get a better class of squatter out here.'

'Well, given the choice, where would you rather sleep rough, here or down the Embankment?'

'Yeah, but you wouldn't sell many copies of *The Big Issue* out here,' Bill said, lifting himself onto a window ledge and climbing out onto the platform. He cupped his hands round his mouth and yelled. The sound travelled out over the dry land and disappeared into silence. It was so quiet. The cars he could see on the road in the distance were out of earshot, and all he could hear was the noise of insects and birds, and the papery sound of the dry leaves as they rustled in the infinitesimal breeze. He breathed in the warm air and released the stale air from the very bottom of his lungs. He turned to Alison who was still inside, on the other side of the glass panels that were coated with red dust. She had her back to him. On his side of the window he noticed some black strips of plastic; inch-long pieces of Dymo, each containing a single word and stuck randomly over the surface of the glass. 'GRACIOUS', 'SPACIOUS', 'SALACIOUS', 'FE-LATIOUS', 'DELICIOUS', 'CAPRICIOUS'.

He picked underneath the corner of 'SALACIOUS' with his thumbnail, peeled it off and stuck it in his wallet. He turned again to the planes of red earth, the deep, dry riverbed and the patchwork of fields beyond, and then climbed back in through the window.

'This is an extraordinary place. Now I can see what attracted your mum to it. This makes sense.'

'Yeah. She loved it. I wish you'd come out before, when she was well. You could have taken it in turns with the cooking and played Scrabble with us.'

'The cooking bit sounds great, but I'd pass on the Scrabble.'

'When she got ill, people would say to her, "Don't you want to be at home?" As if she'd prefer to be in a centrally heated bunker rather than here.' She leaned on the sill and shook her head.

'Don't you think about moving out here sometimes?' Bill asked. 'You could work with email, surely?'

Alison took in the three hundred and sixty degrees of view, from Turre to Los Gallardos and over the valley, to the peaks of the Sierra Cabrera.

'Nah, it's too sad,' she said, heading back down the stairs.

Back on the airstrip, Bill opened the car door. The temperature inside was insufferable. He turned the keys in the ignition and activated the electric windows, letting the hot breeze waft in. He switched on the radio. A man's voice shouted in fast, impenetrable Spanish, and he leaned over to twiddle the dial. A tango emerged through the ether and he fine-tuned until it was almost crackle-free. He turned the volume as loud as it went and got out of the car again. Alison was picking wild flowers at the edge of the runway. She looked over to him as she heard the music, and smiled.

'Care to dance?' he asked, walking towards her. She stood up, the bunch of weeds in her hand, and laughed.

'I can't do joined-up dancing,' she said, 'and I always lead. Comes from Mum teaching us.'

Bill shimmied over, took her hand in his, and grabbed her waist. 'Just follow,' he said.

Alison put the stem of a poppy between her teeth, threw her head back and let herself be led. Bill was a good dancer. He guided her to the centre of the runway and dipped her low, his hand supporting her as she leaned back, the poppy still between her teeth. He raised her again and spun her round, and they half walked, half tangoed cheek-to-cheek towards the car, the volume of the accordion increasing as they got closer. The song ended and Bill dipped Alison to the ground with a flourish, her hair brushing the tarmac. The flower had lost most of its petals, and Alison stood up, removing the stem from her teeth and shouting 'Olé!' as she flung it into the air. The red petals trailed like drops of blood along the runway behind them.

'What's the time?' Alison asked.

'Nearly four,' Bill replied. 'Just time for a driving lesson.'

'Oh, please, no. Tangos are one thing, driving is something else.'

'Why?'

'It just is. I can't explain it.'

'What's to fear?'

'Trust me, I can't.'

'No, Al, trust me, you can. You've got to believe you can.'

Alison snorted. 'Look, Bill, I'm not Tinker Bell, you're not fucking Peter Pan. I'm shit scared of driving. End of story.'

'Please will you at least try? I'll be with you; nothing terrible's going to happen. Please?'

Alison ignored him. She rolled an elastic band off her wrist and dragged her hair back from her face, securing it in a tight ponytail. She looked about ten, Bill thought.

'We've half an hour,' he said. 'Let me show you the basics.'

She eventually looked at him.

'Truly, it'll be fine.' He held out the car keys to her, 'Just have a little go. It's the perfect place – a long road, no other cars.'

'Sure, and a fucking huge drop either end, and no one knowing we're here.'

'It's not like I'm suggesting we fly a plane. Compared to that, this is a breeze. Trust me.' He dangled the keys between them.

Alison thought a while then took the keys from him. 'Ten minutes, and if I don't like it, we'll stop, OK?'

'OK.'

She opened the door on the driver's side and lowered herself in, reaching for the seatbelt.

47

Coach

Jo had never been on such a long bus journey. She went on buses with her dad in Brighton sometimes, and with her mum if it was summertime, because it took so long to find a place to park the car. She liked the buses in Brighton. When they went home, the bus stop was right next to the Pavilion, which was the most beautiful building Jo had ever seen: a great big golden onion. And the bus stop by their house had a bar that was really good for swinging on while they waited for the bus to come. This wasn't actually a bus; it was a coach. Her mum said the difference between a bus and a coach is that coaches have toilets. They need to have toilets because they go much longer journeys, so you can't always hang on.

Jo looked out of the window. Outside were things that she felt she'd seen in a dream. She couldn't remember everything about being in Spain. She'd been four, her mum said. She didn't even go to school or write or anything then. They had lots of photos of when she was in Spain, so sometimes she wasn't sure if she remembered or if she remembered the stories that went with the photos. She tried to think of all the things she could remember: Nanna, blue eyes, a drawer full of sweets, a doll called Naughty Baby with purple and green clothes, plants like green mittens, Nanna's dog Jess, watering the garden with her own watering can, picking flowers, jumping in the waves, pink plastic shoes, goats with bells round their necks, collecting sticks to make fires in Nanna's house, Nanna with tubes to help her breathe, a paddling pool, a plastic hand on a stick for hitting flies.

She didn't think she remembered seeing the old ladies, much older than Nanna, who all wore black. Or the men with really big tummies like the ones she'd seen when they were having breakfast that morning. Or the policemen. As her mum had pushed lots of coins into the phone and talked to her dad, Jo had watched the people at the bus station. She'd seen two policemen with green uniforms and sunglasses and guns. She'd never actually seen anyone with a gun before, and she couldn't wait to tell her friends when she was back at school. Lots more people smoked here, as well. Even the policemen were smoking, and they didn't use ashtrays, they just dropped their cigarettes on the floor. She'd seen them do it in the place where they were having breakfast, too. They dropped their cigarettes and their serviettes all over the floor. If she dropped anything on the floor, her mum made her go back and pick it up and put it in a bin, or if there wasn't a bin, hold on to it until there was. The only things she was allowed to drop if they were in the countryside were apple cores. They would feed the ground, and the seeds would grow, so it was actually like planting trees, and not dropping rubbish at all.

She liked saying 'actually'. She knew how to spell it. When she said it to her dad he rolled his eyes and told her she was too clever by half, and she asked him half what and he rolled his eyes again, making her laugh. She wished he was here with them now, but he had to stay and feed Molly and Polly, and he'd promised he'd come and meet them at the airport when they went home, so that was OK.

Her mum had explained why they were in Spain; it was to throw Nanna's ashes in the sea. She wasn't sure why or how Nanna was ashes, or what the difference was between throwing other things in the sea (which was wrong) and throwing Nanna in the sea (which her mum and Al wanted to do, so it meant it must be OK). When her mum had been Jo's age, Nanna had been her mum. She'd seen the photos. So did that mean that when her mum was old like Nanna, she, Jo would have to put her in the sea as well? Most of the friends in her class still had all their nannas and grampses. Her friend Ruby, whose nanna was also dead, had a place near a church, a cemetery where she went at the weekends and put flowers for her.

At the end of their garden at home they had a compost bin. Jo was a bit scared of it, because it was warm even when it was cold outside. You could feel if you put your hands near it, like it was alive. And it smelled really strange. It was full of old bits of vegetables and the loose grass that smelled lovely after the lawn had been cut. Her dad said that when everything at the bottom had been there for a very long time it changed into something that was good for making the flowers grow. Food made her grow, and the bits of food they didn't want to eat, like the peelings from the potatoes and the floppy leaves on lettuces, became just the sort of food the garden liked.

Hannah put her arm round Jo, stroking the hair at her temple, the way she remembered her own mum doing. She was aware of Jo fighting to keep her eyes open, not wanting to miss a thing, but the rhythm of the coach and the unremitting emptiness of the scenery won out, and Hannah felt the weight of her sleeping child as she nuzzled into her.

She'd never been to America, but imagined it would be a little like this. Or Mexico. Not driving for once, she was able to look through the coach window as the scenery sped by. There was such a lot of space between one town and the next; the kind of space there wasn't room for in England. She wondered how long it would be before the towns expanded and reached each other, blurred into each other. The land was so arid, so barren; how could it ever be tamed? Although the places that were now inhabited must have been as unyielding once. They passed a clutch of white houses with their own water tanks, dusty back yards, red peppers and washing hung out to dry. Then gaping space, then a large, modern furniture store with a handwritten sign, 'Muebles', just a couple of cars parked in front.

The driver was playing loud Spanish pop music, which no one seemed to be listening to or to mind. Jo certainly had no problem sleeping through it. Hannah envied Jo her ability to sleep through noise. It must be something she got from her dad, because Hannah needed a whole series of conditions to be met before she could relax enough to sleep: silence, a proper bed, darkness. Around her, other passengers dozed, chatted or looked out of the window. A couple of young lads sat near the back in the smoking section. Hannah had watched them as they joined the coach a couple of stops back. They must have been about seventeen and were dressed in full army uniform; doing their military service, she guessed. They still had acne. She couldn't imagine what it must feel like, sending your children off like that. She couldn't even bear to think of Jo leaving home.

Andalucía was still so different from the rest of Spain, she thought, despite the smart, wide motorways like the one they were driving along now, which sliced through the landscape, leaving buildings from a different era orphaned on the roadside. It was a difference that had been much more marked when Beth first moved here twenty years back, when the roads were still circuitous, and no one spoke English, and young girls were chaperoned. But at its heart, it was still wild.

Over the years of visiting Beth, as Hannah had grown from teenager to adult, so had Mojácar. She'd seen their local bar install satellite TV; the waiters standing open-mouthed, polishing glasses and watching Madonna blaspheme; transfixed. She'd experienced at first hand the transition of language as her bad Spanish was superseded by the same waiters' swiftly improving English. She'd seen the supermarkets adjust their stock to include Heinz beans and PG Tips. But even if Mojácar had moved with the times, you didn't have to go far to realise that under the skin Andalucía hadn't changed much.

Sometimes she wished that Beth hadn't lived here, even though it had always been an exotic place to come and visit. They could always have gone on holiday somewhere like this if they'd wanted to. Why hadn't she lived round the corner, within easy babysitting reach? Unplanned, just popping in reach? Why hadn't she been at the end of a phone – one of her 'friends and family' numbers – so they could have spoken every day, cheaply and easily, with nothing in particular to say? Instead, their phone calls had been over-whelmingly concerned with time, cost and distance; racing through their news. She remembered that split second delay in transmission, either blurring the ends of their words into each other's or causing unnatural silences in their anticipation. Always remembering too late some little thing she'd wanted to ask her, or realising too late that the catch in her voice had been a clue and she'd missed it. Always feeling sadder after putting the phone down.

And why hadn't she lived to be as old as the two old women with their black cardigans and bandy legs who'd sat at the front of the coach and had down climbed the steps at this latest stop? It was hardly a village even, just a bend in the road with a small bar and little else. The driver handed them their trolleys and baskets from the storage below. Hannah watched him through the window as he smoked his cigarette, unrushed. He shared a joke with a man outside the bar. The coach engine was still running, and the pop music escaped from the open door, following the two old women who walked off into the rusty, dusty landscape of caves and lazy cats.

'Un beso de la flaca,' the song went.

Hannah wished Beth had lived to be their age; had lived to walk into the distance, wheeling a trolley of vegetables, serenaded by wisps of pop music.

Ah, she thought, as Jacques would say, 'If wishes were horses.'

48

Flan

Oh you'll never go to heaven
In a biscuit tin
Coz a biscuit tin's
Got biscuits in.
Traditional

Bill was the first to spot them as the coach pulled into Vera. He saw
Jo through the window, and she stared straight at him and smiled.
He'd met her before, of course, but not recently. He and Alison had
been to Brighton a few times for day trips and met Hannah, Jo and
Jacques for fish and chips on the pier and walks along the sea front
as Jo had progressed from buggy to bike to roller skates. But it
wasn't so much a matter of recognising her as knowing her. Alison's
niece, Hannah's daughter, Beth's granddaughter; Jo. He wasn't sure
what this reunion was going to be like, and he couldn't pretend to be
looking forward to it, although he felt surprisingly happy at seeing
Jo. From leaving the airstrip to reaching the bus station, Alison's
increasing introspection had been palpable. She'd given directions,
but even her voice had altered. And she kept doing that thing. That
scraping her hair back thing, undoing her ponytail, pulling the hair
tightly off her face and refastening it with an elastic band. She did it
as unconsciously as a smoker reaches for a cigarette.

They hadn't made any plans as such, although Alison had said that
it would be good if she and Hannah had a chance to talk without
interruption. Bill wasn't sure if she'd meant interruption from him or

Jo or both, but he was more than happy to spend some time on his own with Jo if the opportunity arose, judging the company of an overtired child to be infinitely preferable to stressed-out grown-ups.

They were the last off the coach, Jo jumping from the platform ahead of Hannah. Alison went over to greet them, kissed Hannah on the cheek and bent down to hug Jo. Bill watched Alison's shoulders relax in her niece's embrace.

'You got Jacques's message.' Hannah said as Alison stood up, still holding Jo's hand. 'Thank God. We're not too late?'

'No. You're fine. You haven't missed a thing.'

'Hi, Bill,' Hannah said, kissing his cheek, too.

'I'm doing a sponsored swim,' Jo told Bill as he helped with their holdall and started towards the car.

'Are you?'

'Yes. Will you sponsor me?'

'Hang on, Jo, give Bill a chance,' Hannah said.

'What's it in aid of?' Bill asked.

'It's for our school pool fund. Did your school have its own pool?'

'No. I wish it had.'

'Will you sponsor me, then?'

'Jo,' Hannah and Alison said in unison, both giving the little word an extra syllable.

Jo looked at Bill and raised her eyebrows; Bill smiled and gave her a conspiratorial, eyes to the heavens look.

'Are you hungry?' Alison asked.

'Actually, now you ask, I'm starving,' Hannah said. 'We just had a snack in the café we stopped at, and it's hours since breakfast.'

'We thought maybe we'd have something in Garrucha.'

It was the first Bill had heard of it.

'Sounds great.'

'Where's Garrucha?' Jo asked.

'It's not far. It's by the sea.'

'Can we go swimming?'

'Oh, I doubt it. It's a bit too cold for that, and besides it's getting late.'

Hannah's words sounded phoney even to her; it was still hot, even though it was five o'clock, and the sun was still shining, making it feel much earlier. Compared to Brighton, this was positively high summer. No one chose to contradict her, though, as Bill unlocked the car and packed the bags into the boot.

'Do you want to drive?' he asked Hannah, offering her the keys.

'I'd rather not, if you don't mind. I'd like to get my bearings a bit first.'

'Sure,' Bill said, getting into the driver's seat.

'Al, why can't you drive?' Jo asked.

Bill winced and concentrated on reversing out of the parking spot.

'I never got round to it. But I had a go today, didn't I Bill?'

'Yup.'

'Really? Where?' Hannah asked, twisting round in the passenger seat and looking from Bill to Alison.

It was interesting, Bill thought, the way Alison had made straight for the back seat. Never had he known such a clear case of back-seat driving.

'Out on the old airstrip.'

'In Cortijo Grande?'

'Yeah. I went up and down it and I did all the gear changes, and I lived to tell the tale.'

'All the gears?'

'Well, I got up to second and I did reverse.'

'That's great,' Hannah said, and she sounded as if she really meant it.

Outside the fish restaurant in Garrucha harbour, round a table covered with a thick white linen cloth, everyone chose their favourite dish. Bill wanted to try the whitebait, but the little fishy eyes unsettled Jo, who wanted calamari, even though she didn't know what it was, and chips, which she did. Hannah plumped for the spinach tortilla and Alison asked for berenjenas, deep-fried slices of aubergine, because she wanted Bill to try them and work out how to cook them. The huge plate of salad studded with olives and crowned with a star of slippery tinned asparagus was placed in the centre of the table, and after Hannah dressed it in oil and vinegar they all pitched in.

In between forkfuls of food from the shared plates, they clarified the important details on their collective agenda. They would all stay at the house that night and would do the ash scattering the next day. Bill and Alison would take Jo and Hannah back to Murcia the day after next, before catching their own flight from Almería later that night. Sometime between now and then, Bill would hopefully fit in some Disney research, and Jo would do her best to secure herself a swim in the sea. Once all that had been decided, everyone appeared to mellow, reassured by having a plan, and pleasantly soporific from the meal.

'Who's for pud?' Bill asked.

'Not me – that was perfect,' Hannah said. 'A coffee would be great, though.'

'How about you, Alison?'

'No room, thanks. I'm full up.'

Bill had quickly adopted the role of ordering, not because he was the only man but because he was the person most interested in food. Besides, it gave him something to do. Dealing with so many members of the Vine family at once was easier with a strategy.

'Can't you even squeeze in a little flan?' he coaxed Alison.

'I can't,' she whined, rubbing her stomach.

'Course you can, Malcolm,' Hannah said.

Alison flinched, but so imperceptibly – so internally – that she didn't think anyone noticed. Hannah's response had been a knee-jerk reaction, she knew; the way as kids they'd shouted 'Crackerjack!' at the television when they got given the cue. She hadn't been able to help herself. And, as ever, Alison knew the best way to handle it was not to draw attention to it.

'Malcolm? Who's Malcolm?' Jo asked.

'Oh, it's just a joke,' Hannah said. 'It's what me and Nanna used to call Al.'

Alison looked at the table. She couldn't believe it. It was going on to the next generation. Now Jo would call her that, too.

'How about you, Jo? Will you join me? I'm going to have the flan,' Bill said, not dropping a beat. Bless him, Alison thought.

'What's flan?'

'It's . . . How do you explain flan? Like crème brûlée, only Spanish.' Jo looked at him blankly. 'It's like egg custard and burned sugar.'

'Yuck.' Jo pulled a face.

'I'll take that as a No, then, OK, how about an ice cream?'

'Can I, Mum?' Jo asked.

'Are you sure you've room for one?' Hannah asked. Jo nodded. 'OK, if you're sure.'

Bill wandered off to find a waiter, and Jo's eyes followed him, swooning.

'Al?' she asked.

'Yes?' she replied, copying the inflection.

'Is Bill your boyfriend?'

'Jo, that's not any of your business,' Hannah cut in.

'Is he?' she asked again, leaning in to Alison, touching her bracelet.

'Well, he's my friend and he's a boy,' she replied, perfectly aware of what an annoying answer it was.

'But do you kiss him?' Jo twisted the bracelet round on Alison's wrist.

'Jo!' Hannah hissed.

Alison raised her eyebrows at Jo and grinned. Jo grinned back.

'Do you?' she asked again, encouragingly.

Alison shook her head and saw the disappointment in her niece's face, just as Bill returned to the table. He looked at the three of them. Hannah busied herself, using the side of her hand to collect breadcrumbs from the tablecloth; Alison gave him a wink, and Jo stared at him.

'What did I miss?' he asked.

Alison and Jo looked at each other. 'Nothing,' Jo said, in her fluty, grown-up voice, in a way that meant 'Something.'

'What's the Disney connection, Bill?' Hannah asked.

'That's what I'd like to know,' Bill said, a spoonful of flan held in suspended animation, wobbling slightly.

'What do you mean?'

Bill swallowed the yellow pudding, the sharp caramel cutting through the eggy sweetness. 'I mean, is there one?'

'People here seem to think so. They're always going on about it. Have you got a theory?'

Bill considered his empty spoon. 'I have absolutely nothing.' he said, scraping the last slippery remains from the ramekin dish. 'Although, looking around, Mojácar looks like it could have come out of a Disney fantasy. Those fairytale buildings up in the village.'

Alison let out a dry laugh. 'Only now they've turned it into Disneyland.'

'Yes,' said Hannah, 'they've really been busy, haven't they?'

'Wait till you see what they've done along from here,' Alison said.

'Wasn't there some story that Disney got himself frozen?' Hannah asked.

'Mm, but there's no truth in it as far as I can make out. He was cremated.' Bill hadn't meant to bring the conversation around to cremation. He blundered on, trying to cover his tracks. 'I wonder how that rumour got started. It's like an urban myth.'

'Hannah, do you remember when we saw *Bambi*?' Alison asked. 'The egg you tried to hatch?'

'Mum tried to hatch an egg?' Jo looked from Alison to Hannah. 'Did you, Mum?'

'Yep. I kept it in a biscuit tin.'

'You do remember it, then?' said Alison. 'I wasn't sure whether I'd made it up.'

'Yes, I do.' Hannah stirred her coffee. 'I honestly thought it would hatch.' She lifted the cup to her lips. 'I really believed it.' She took a sip. It was hotter than she'd expected and she jolted the cup, spilling coffee on the cloth. She took some tissues from the napkin dispenser and blotted.

'What happened to it?' Jo asked.

Hannah seemed absorbed in the tissues as they took the stain. 'Did it hatch, Mum?'

'Sorry, sweetheart, did what what?'

Jo tutted and rolled her eyes up to the sky, and Hannah saw Jacques's face superimposed on hers. 'The egg. Did the egg hatch?'

Hannah smiled slowly, picked up the wet napkins and dropped them onto her saucer.

'Do you know, I can't remember,' she lied.

Walking around the marina after their meal, Jo read out the names of the boats. '*Sea Legs, The Captain's Table, La Sirena Feliz*. What does that mean?'

'The happy mermaid,' Alison said.

Jo continued, struggling with the Spanish names and shouting out the English ones when she spotted them. '*Happy Hours, Fantasea, Reel Time, Luna Sea.*'

'These puns are awful,' Alison said. 'Imagine shelling out all that money to sail about on a floating pun.'

'*Sea Dancer, Miss Behavin', Escape, Giddy Herm* . . . *Herm* . . . how do you say that?' she asked Bill, who was next to her.

'Hermaphrodite,' he said.

'What's that?'

'Er, it's like someone who's not boy or girl,' he replied, carefully. Jo thought for a moment. 'So which toilet do they use?' she asked.

'Great question. Don't know,' Bill answered, smiling at her.

Jo carried on, '*Giddy Hermaphrodite, Lazy Daisy, Caroline Two.*'

'I wonder what happened to *Caroline One?*' Hannah said.

'Maybe she sank,' Bill offered.

'That's like the *True Love,*' Alison said. 'When Grace asks Bing what he's going to name his next boat, and he says the *True Love Two.* "My, but she was yar." I love that expression. What does it mean?'

'Was it Grace and Bing or Katharine and Cary?' Hannah asked.

'Don't know. Maybe it was the same line in both films.'

'That's the only film I can think of where the remake is as good as the original.'

'No, *The Philadelphia Story*'s better. When Hepburn says to Sinatra, "Put me in your pocket, Mike." I love that line, too.'

'Stewart,' Bill said

'What?'

'James Stewart was Mike in *Philadelphia Story.* It was Sinatra in *High Society.*'

'Oh, you're right.'

'Isn't it strange the way we have to name everything?' Hannah said. 'Boats, beach huts, houses, stars . . .'

'If I had a boat, I'd call it *Jo's Boat.*'

'Good for you, Jo,' Alison said.

Further along, away from the jaunty weekend sailing boats and speedboats were the fishing vessels, their large wooden hulls like giant Brazil nut shells, buffered from the edge of the dock with dirty orange fenders. A man sat on the quay, mending a net that was spread out to dry, tufts of emerald seaweed clinging to the rope. Hannah took Jo's hand and steered her away as she was about to walk on it. The fisherman looked up, unsmiling. In the distance a cargo ship moved slowly towards the jetty, where ash-coloured mounds were heaped like giant molehills. The sea wall, the boat and the mounds were all muted grey against the deep blue of the sea.

'It's nice to see it's still a working port,' Bill said. 'What do those boats transport from here?'

'I'm not sure what it is,' Alison replied. 'Sand or cement or something.'

'Apart from the fishing it's about the first sign I've seen of real, indigenous life; some industry that's not pretty, not for the benefit of the tourists.'

'Yeah. It used to be a mining area – tin, I think – but now it's fucking Ulf's leather works, ice cream parlours, and golf, golf and more fucking golf.'

'Alison, language,' Hannah said, nodding towards Jo, who had run off ahead of them.

'Sorry, Hannah,' Alison said, then she laughed. 'Mind you, Jo's been cursing like a good 'un for years.'

'What do you mean?'

'Don't you remember "Bastard"?' Alison accentuated the word, the 'b' exploding and the rest escaping in a hiss.

Hannah laughed and repeated, 'Bastard.'

'What's this?' Bill asked.

'When she was really little she'd patrol Mum's house wielding this fly swat – do you remember it?'

'Yes,' Alison said. 'A blue plastic hand on a stick.'

'Well, I don't know where she'd heard it,' Hannah said, looking at Alison.

'Can't imagine,' Alison said.

'But one day Mum had some visitors, the type who speak more Swahili than Spanish. Then Jo appeared with the swat, looking like a little dolly. She lunged at a fly with it, muttering, "Bastard."' Hannah laughed as she remembered. 'It was unmistakable. Mum was mortified.'

Her voice trailed off. As soon as the word came out, she regretted it, and her own discomfort was mirrored in Bill's face as his grin collapsed into a polite smile. Mortified. Not embarrassed, or horrified; mortified. She remembered a friend of Beth's who visited her in hospital, talked about this and that, about anything and everything except illness, cancer or death. Then, saying her good-byes, walking out to the car park with Hannah, fishing for a tissue in her handbag, her bright, brave expression slipping, Hannah remembered this woman blowing her nose and saying, 'I love your mum to death.' And she recalled the woman's face colouring as the word fell into the silent space, echoing around them, chasing in and out of the parked cars, the ambulances and asphalt. The minefield that language became. Sick to death. Bored to death. Done to death. Deadline. And the more self-consciously you tried to tiptoe through the innocuous phrases, the more they tripped you up. She remembered that Jo had said 'tender hooks' instead of 'tenterhooks', and she thought that was what it had been like. She had – they had all – been permanently on tender hooks.

'Mum, look! *Mulan!*'

Hannah looked up as Jo came running back to join them, pointing to a poster on the wall that led from the harbour to the promenade. They all walked over to it. The poster showed a girl looking back over her shoulder under a curtain of thick black hair. Below were the words 'Cine Garrucha', the dates and times.

'It's on today,' Alison read.

'Can we go, Mum?' Jo asked.

'Haven't you already seen it?' Alison asked her.

'Only a few hundred times,' Hannah said. 'She's got the video, haven't you?' Jo nodded. 'And guess who plays the male lead? Only Donny Osmond.'

'It's brilliant, Al. Can we go?'

'It'll be in Spanish.'

'I don't mind.'

'It starts at seven. What's the time now?' She looked at her watch. 'Quarter to.'

'I've not seen *Mulan*,' Bill said.

They all turned to him.

'Do you want to?' Alison asked.

'Sure.'

'Well, how about the two of you going?'

Bill asked Jo, 'Is that OK with you?'

Jo nodded. 'Can we? Please?' She held Hannah's arm, pulling it. Hannah looked at Bill, who shrugged. He was more than happy to go, in fact. Not only as research; to sit down somewhere and relax for a couple of hours was an inviting prospect.

'You're sure?' Hannah asked.

'Yes. I'd love to.'

The cinema was three roads up from the sea front. Bill leaned against the counter of the ticket booth, a hatch in the wall that opened onto the street, and pushed his money across.

'Well, have a good time, you two,' Hannah said, squatting down to give Jo a kiss. 'Enjoy.'

'We shall,' said Bill, giving Jo her ticket, and Hannah watched as they joined the others filing through the brass-trimmed doors. They entered the foyer, an old-fashioned room that must once have been plush; with vinyl chairs and a popcorn machine at the far end. 'Popcorn?' Bill asked Jo, heading towards the sales point and recognising the girl operating the machine as the one who had sold him their tickets.

Jo's rambling commentary and Bill's buffering effect were only fully appreciated once Alison and Hannah had walked back to the harbour without them. Alison felt they needed to clear the air, but wasn't sure what it was she needed to say, or what she wanted to hear said. It was a vague, niggling sensation, like a dream that's so vivid on waking, then, trying to summon it again, you discover it's vanished. And the harder you concentrate, the more stubbornly it eludes you.

'Hopefully Jo'll be spark out by the time we get to Mum's. It's been a long day for her.'

'It's been a long day full stop,' Alison said, thinking about the house. Mum's. Would it always be Mum's? Even after it was sold?

They passed the garage where Señor Martínez had taken Alison all that time ago, when Beth's death had still been in its research stage. A lifetime ago. She thought about telling Hannah about her meeting with him yesterday; his sweetness and his gift of the rucksack, but she hadn't the energy. Her hangover had entered a new phase, after the wine with their meal and the seeming end-lessness of the day. Now she felt drowsy and emotional, slow and heavy, and would have dearly loved to take a nap.

What have you lost?

I have lost a few billion brain cells.

All at once she felt shame flooding through her for not taking better care of the ashes last night. She realised she couldn't tell Hannah what she'd done. It was a sister thing, having her actions measured and wordlessly judged by this internal yardstick. Not that it was very likely that any harm would have come from leaving them in the unlocked car overnight, but she just knew Hannah would never have been so reckless.

'So where shall we go?' Hannah asked, breaking into Alison's thoughts, making her start.

'Wherever you fancy. We've at least an hour.'

'Wow, that was a stroke of luck.'

'What?'

'The film.'

'Oh. Yes.'

They carried on down the narrow side street, the shadows from the buildings making it feel much cooler than it had been outside in the harbour. Alison wished she'd thought to bring another layer. A woman passed them, carrying a large bunch of carnations, yellow and red and pink.

'Is it some kind of fiesta today?' Hannah asked.

'Don't know. Why?'

'On the bus, we kept passing people with flowers.'

Alison stopped and turned to her. 'Of course. It's Todos Santos, All Saints – or is it All Souls? You remember? When everyone spends the night with their dead? They'll be on their way to the cemeteries. I forgot. They were cleaning SuperTurre out of candles last night. Do you want to go?'

'Where? SuperTurre?'

'No, the cemetery. You've got the car keys?'

'Yes, but the cemetery?'

'It'll be nice.'

'Nice?'

'Come on.'

'Well, I suppose it'd be good to get used to driving on the right without Jo in the car.'

'Just a quick look. Then we can have tapas in Turre.'

Hannah looked at her. 'You really want to?'

'Yes.'

'All right.'

49

Mulan

'This is the bit when Mulan has to go and visit the matchmaker,' Jo hissed in Bill's ear, 'but she's not ladylike enough, so the matchmaker says she's a disgrace.'

Bill listened to Jo's commentary as he watched the screen. The movements of the old woman's mouth bore no relation to the torrent of Spanish that poured out. Just as well he had Jo to fill him in, although the action was pretty self-explanatory. And just as well the other cinemagoers weren't the arsey kind who shushed you for talking. There was a continuous murmur all around them as people chatted, and the film rolled along regardless. The cinema was half full, which surprised Bill, as he'd assumed that video would have killed it off in such a small town. They'd chosen seats bang in the centre, where Bill preferred to sit, as, it turned out, did Jo. When he leaned towards her to hear what she said, Jo's breath tickled his ear and enveloped him in the smell of salty popcorn.

Bill realised that he was enjoying himself immensely. The fifties decor of the lobby was continued through into the auditorium: the soft, balding velvet seats; the little enamel plaques with their seat numbers – 16 and 17 – screwed into the chairs in front. A frieze of celluloid sprockets unfurled round the tops of the walls, the theme repeated in the lights that had been dimmed imperceptibly until they had found themselves in a thick darkness made delicious by the knowledge that outside it was still daylight. The screen itself was set back behind an ornate proscenium arch. A couple of rows in front, Bill saw the backlit silhouette of a young boy sitting between his parents. He had short black hair, and his ears stuck out exactly on a level with the back of the chair. Bill tried to imagine a young Walt Disney, one who had stayed on in Spain and not emigrated to America – if indeed he'd really been born here. Would he still have been a filmmaker? Bill wondered. And, if so, what would the world be like if Walt Disney had grown up Spanish? Or if he hadn't become a filmmaker but had died in the civil war, or run a bar, or become a fisherman or a mayor, then what? Would someone else have filled the space?

Bill returned his attention to the screen, wondering as he watched the rotund matchmaker's bottom catch fire, and heard the laughter bloom around him in the darkness. Jo was humming along to a song, as the ghosts of the ancestors came to life and gave orders. She hummed tunelessly, absorbed in the story that she already knew by heart. Bill watched her from the corner of his eye, not wanting her to become self-conscious, but enchanted by her involvement. He tried to recall feeling like that; so absolutely in the moment, and he couldn't remember when it had been. Maybe he'd managed it for a few moments watching Wimbledon. He wondered at what age you lost that ability. Adults spent years trying to regain it, lying in flotation tanks immersed in salty water listening to whale music, or taking shedloads of drugs. Or flying in small aeroplanes with incompetent pilots, he thought, remembering the airstrip. But all Jo needed was the dark cinema, the familiar story and a bag of salty popcorn. Lucky Jo.

As the film progressed, Bill could see why Jo was such a fan of Mulan. She was a spunky heroine who used her brain; a far cry from the insidious Ariel. When Mulan cut off her hair to disguise herself as a boy, Jo had whispered to Bill that she'd cut off her Barbie's hair, even though she knew it wouldn't grow back, which impressed him no end. Mulan was singing again, looking at her reflection refracted through a kaleidoscope of mirrors – which must have been a bugger to animate. He leaned towards Jo to hear the words in English. She sang over the top of the Spanish in her thin, funny voice; her words dovetailing with the movements of the mouth on the screen more neatly than the Spanish lyrics.

The song was all about never passing for a perfect daughter, and how if her family saw what she was really like it would break their heart.

That could be the song of a closet dyke, he thought, chuckling to himself. He remembered a late-night showing of *West Side Story* at the Ritzy with Sam, where the back row of Brixton lesbians had sung along with Rita Moreno's Anita: 'One of your own kind, stick with your own kind,' changing the song for him for ever. But thinking about Mulan, was it possible to find redemption or fulfilment through being dutiful? It seemed an outmoded concept. And then he thought of Alison.

50

Todos Santos

An ambulance is a special van to carry people who are ill to hospital . . .
The windows of the ambulance are made of special dark glass. People
inside the ambulance can see out, but no one can see in.

The Nurse, Ladybird Books

The sun was at its lowest point as they drove inland from Garrucha;
the dangerous, blinding light that it throws out just before setting.
Hannah had to borrow Alison's sunglasses to see the road. Beth's
tortoiseshell Ray-Bans. Alison glanced over and saw Beth in her
sister's profile, in her thick, chestnut hair, and in her bare feet
pressed on the pedals. She'd forgotten Hannah did that, too.

They are in the ambulance, Alison and Beth, on their way to
Hospital Virgen del Mar – Virgin of the Sea. Neither of them has
ever been inside an ambulance before. Neither can believe they're in
one now. Beth lies on the stretcher, a tank sending oxygen into the
pipes that feed into her nostrils. The device strapped to her face
looks like the free headphones they give out on aeroplanes. Alison
sits by her side, looking through the windows in the back at the view
that has already passed them.

   She is going to have to initiate it. The conversation she's been
dreading. She had hoped Beth would do this for her. But she had
known that she wouldn't.

   'We've never discussed details, Mum. We haven't had to until
now. But I don't even know if you want to be buried or cremated.'

Beth avoids her eyes, picks at the blanket that covers her. 'I suppose I'll have to go in one of those drawers.'

Her blue eyes meeting Alison's, challenging her to disagree.

'Not if you don't want to.'

Cars already lined the road either side of the cemetery gates, so they parked in the makeshift car park on the plot of land nearby, beneath a development of ugly new townhouses. As they got out and locked up, they heard the bark of a tethered dog echoing in the still air. They walked down to the road and joined the others making their way inside. Old people dressed in black were carrying flowers; their grandchildren with fold-up beach chairs as if on their way to a barbeque. The walls surrounding the cemetery had been recently whitewashed, and the cemetery itself was looking immaculate, the trees pruned, the ground swept and a new-looking marble footpath intersecting the plots. Hannah stopped at the entrance and looked around. In every direction groups of people were settling down, arranging flowers, lighting candles and opening hampers of food. A woman wearing an apron over her black dress filled a vase from a standpipe. A wire bin spilled over with flowers that still appeared to be perfectly good; a sky-blue statuette of an angel with a chipped wing lay abandoned next to it.

'Are you sure about this? I feel like we're intruding.' Hannah spoke in a whisper.

'We could be visiting relatives as far as anyone else knows.'

'But we're not, are we?'

'No, but we could be.'

Alison led the way past a family, a man in his sixties, two younger women and a teenage girl. They sat in striped canvas chairs in front of a plot decked with gladioli; the fat red night-lights on the floor already lit. They unwrapped sandwiches and poured drinks from a large flask, oblivious of Hannah and Alison, who walked on between two rows of graves that were stacked high, like library shelves.

191

'Mum knew she didn't want this,' Alison said, stopping and looking at the front of one of them.

Like all the others, it was about two feet square with a glass front. Behind it, a recess for the words and dates and picture. A hand-tinted sepia photograph had frozen the deceased, a middle-aged woman, in half profile, for ever looking seriously into the middle distance. Two stem vases were attached to the wall, flanking the grave with two tightly budded yellow roses. Alison stepped back. The grave was sandwiched between one below and another on top. There were maybe thirty rows along each aisle. She looked along the aisle, calculated: three times thirty is ninety. How many aisles? How many altogether? She looked beyond the cemetery walls to the new houses. They looked like a parody of the graves; meanly spaced, cramped together. They walked on, stopping occasionally to look at a photograph or read an inscription, hardly needing to translate what were generic words of solace; attempts at expressing the inexpressible. They noted the names, some of which they recognised, and they shuddered at the photographs of infants, the heartbreaking angels and sad silk flowers.

'You know, Jo's friend Freya's mum came round the other day,' Hannah said. 'While the girls were playing we had a coffee, and she told me she believed her dead father was a butterfly. Literally. She seemed to find that consoling. I can't imagine Mum as anything so simple. How could someone as profound as Mum become anything as . . . well . . . simple?'

Alison listened to Hannah's hushed voice. She didn't want to reassure her. She didn't want to be strong and logical. To be Malcolm.

They made their way between groups of people clustered round the red night-lights, the power of their little flames intensifying as dusk fell, the perfume of the flowers more pungent in the early-evening air. Birds sang thinly and brightly in the avenues of cedar trees that edged the pathways.

'What made you change your mind, Hannah?' Alison asked, not stopping the thought as it bubbled up from her solar plexus and out of her mouth.

Hannah breathed in the heady air, a mixture of candle wax and waxy lilies, and sighed. 'It just seemed inconceivable not to. I think I'd always been unable to prepare for coming rather than actually coming, if that makes any sense at all. When it came down to it, I realised I had to be here.'

She looked at Alison, who studied the marble pathway.

'Thanks for waiting,' Hannah said.

'It's OK,' Alison replied, and she realised that was what she'd wanted to hear.

They arrive at the hospital and Beth is immediately wheeled through to Intensive Care. Alison finds the doctor, explains. Please don't make her stay. She wants to die at home. He nods, and Alison walks through to the canteen, queues at the self-service counter, and pushes a tray along, past baby octopus in red sauce and other food that looks too medical to eat in a hospital. She thinks about the sanitised fare that English hospitals provide, hermetically sealed sandwiches, baguettes with inconspicuous fillings, and she feels out of her depth. She orders a beer. On the television fixed to the wall above a cigarette machine Jane Seymour is starring in a dubbed episode of *Doctora Quinn, Mujer Medicina*.

'Remember Doctora Quinn?' Alison asked, as their beers were served in the garden outside the bar on Turre high street.

Hannah smiled. 'Mujer Medicina. What a role model we had. If only it had been like that in real life.' She sipped the beer, then she laughed out loud, 'Do you remember when I had the aromatherapy oil burning in Mum's bedroom? When the nurse came, she had a fit.'

'Oh God, I'd forgotten. We could've blown ourselves up. An oxygen tank and a naked flame. Very clever.'

'And I was thinking, How nice, some soothing lavender oil.' Hannah shook her head in disbelief. 'We could all have been incinerated. Cremated there and then.'

'We were so stupid.'

'We were so stressed. I can't believe now what we coped with, the intensity of it.'

'No.'

They sipped their beer in silence.

'I think the thing about the butterfly is this,' Alison said, tracing a figure of eight with her finger in a drop of beer on the table. 'It's the transformation. From caterpillar to butterfly. They seem unconnected, but they're part of a process.'

'But you don't believe Mum's a butterfly?'

'No, but I don't think she's a box of ashes, either.'

'Then why's it so important that we scatter the ashes if they're not her?'

'I suppose I need to keep our promise to her.' She looked up from the table to Hannah. 'It's something practical; I'm OK so long as I'm doing something practical. It's a ritual. And,' she continued, 'I don't feel as if I can move on till it's done.'

'I'm the opposite. I feel it's the only bit of her we have left. When we scatter her ashes, there'll be nothing.'

'You don't really think that?'

'A part of me does, yes. I mean . . . Oh, I don't know. Don't you wish we had something tangible? Somewhere to visit, even take a picnic?

'Sometimes I do, yes.'

'I felt jealous of those people in the cemetery.'

'I know.'

'But that wasn't what Mum wanted.'

'No.'

51

Tears

Jo woke up when Bill turned the engine off. The valley was silent, and the moon was already high over the mountain, illuminating the garden with a cool, blue light.

'Where are we?'

'We're here. Nanna's house. Come on, sleepyhead, let's get inside and ready for bed.'

Hannah carried her from the car and Bill and Alison got the bags from the boot. The sensor triggered the security light as they walked up the path, blinding them with its glare. Alison followed them to the door and unlocked. Hannah put Jo down. She was unsteady on her feet, and leaned against her while Alison opened the door.

'Let's just get your teeth brushed, and then say goodnight to everyone and straight to bed,' Hannah said.

Jo walked inside, bleary eyed, and followed Hannah towards the bathroom.

'Where's Jess?' she asked as Hannah found their toothbrushes and squeezed some paste onto Jo's.

'She doesn't live here any more, don't you remember? We found some nice people to look after her, people who really love her.'

Jo's face crumpled. It happened in slow motion, the way the tears oozed from her eyes and started to fall, fat and salty. Then the wail began, like an air-raid siren, starting quietly and low, then increasing in volume as the note soared, her mouth opening to a fully formed howl.

'I want Jess!'

'I know you do, precious,' Hannah said, scooping her close and burying her face in her hair, toothpaste in one hand, brush in the other.

'Tears before bedtime,' Bill said to Alison, picking up a bottle of wine. 'And that's just the grown-ups.'

He pulled the cork neatly from the bottle. Alison was kneeling down, clearing out the ashes from last night's fire.

'So, what's with Malcolm?' he asked.

Alison looked up at him and sighed. 'Oh, God. It's this name I've been lumbered with for about thirty years now. I hate it.'

She swept the ashes up into a sheet of newspaper. 'It was an advert, do you remember? I think Thora Hird was the mum? Her dopey son complained about feeling ill or something, said he couldn't go to work. She said, '"Course you can, Malcolm."'

'I know it. Wasn't it for Vick's Sinex?'

'Fuck knows. Yes, I think so. Anyway, it's just been a catchphrase with Mum and Hannah. If I said, "I can't," they'd say, '"Course you can, Malcolm." It's stupid.'

'Why does it bother you?'

'I don't know.' She sat back on her heels. 'It was about me being the strong one after Dad left. I don't know why – I mean, I was the youngest – but it always felt like my role to be the coper, the Malcolm. Whenever I did something strong, like open a stiff lid on a jar, or carry a heavy bag, they'd call me Malc.' She started crumpling newspaper into the grate. 'I know it was done affectionately, but I suppose it pissed me off that I couldn't be Alison and strong.'

'Malc got all the credit.'

'Yes. As if the strong part of me couldn't be female.' She snapped twigs into pieces, building a wigwam over the paper. 'I just learned – as you do – that when they saw how it riled me they teased me, so I tried to ignore it.'

'Here you go.' Bill handed her a glass of red wine.

'Thanks.' She knocked back a mouthful. 'Jo wants to know why you're not my boyfriend.'

'That's easy,' he replied. 'I'd never be able to date anyone called Malcolm.'

'Ha fucking ha.'

52

Australia

'Come on, let's go,' Beth says.

'Where to, Mum?'

'On the plane. To Australia.'

She smiles; skin pulled taut over newly accentuated cheekbones, eyes burning grey-blue.

'OK. Let's get our seatbelts on, then.'

'No, don't joke. I mean it. Let's go now.'

'OK, Mum. Let's go.'

Alison has finished her vigil. Now it is Hannah's turn to sit with Beth, to monitor the changes in her breathing, the steady stream of air insinuating through the plastic tubes into her nose and rasping from her mouth. Her turn to prop her up on white cotton pillows, to stroke her head with a damp flannel and to administer the morphine.

No one could have predicted this final tenacity. A day ago it had seemed that any second it would all be over. The telephone has been silent, nobody daring to intrude, not wanting to hear what they're expecting to be told; nor to be the first to offer condolences. Now, after a long night of four-hour shifts, of snatched, dreamless catnaps, it seems as if this will never end. They have worked their way through all the cassettes they'd prepared; the Kol Nidrei and Mozart, Pachelbel's Canon and Kathleen Ferrier. The soothing and the lulling and the significant. All the dignified, tidy endings. And now it is truly unbearable. Alison walks out into the riverbed, not caring if she misses the final breath.

We've already said
Goodbye.

They've used up their supplies of intensity, and if they aren't careful they will become hysterical. Giggly. They might gibber.

And then, when they've about given up expecting, it is the moment. And still Beth fights against it.

'Come on, Mum. Can you see the sea? Dive. Please, dive.'

Alison opened her eyes and felt her heart pounding, her cheeks wet with tears. She lay still and looked at the ceiling for a matter of seconds, then leaped out of bed and searched for her watch. Seven o'clock. How had she slept so late? She had to get cracking, put the Essiac on to boil, prepare the coffee solution for the enema. Why had Beth not pressed the bell, the Ding Dong Avon Calling electric doorbell they'd rigged from her bedside to the corridor?

And then she remembered. Beth was dead. Alison sat on the edge of her bed, her feet on the cold stone floor, feeling the blood pulsing in her ears like the roar of the sea, and made herself take deep, steady breaths. A tap on the bedroom door.

'Hello?' she said, the sound of her own voice surprising her. The door opened slowly and Jo entered carrying a mug of tea with both hands, concentrating on not spilling it.

'What a nice surprise. Good morning.'

'Good morning.'

Jo passed the cup carefully, not looking at Alison until it had been safely received.

'Thanks, Jo. What a treat, tea in bed. Did you sleep OK?'

'Yes, but then I woke up and I forgot where I was.'

'That's funny, so did I. Is everyone else up?'

'No, Mum's still asleep. Bill was in the kitchen, so I went to see him.'

Alison got back into bed and put the mug on the windowsill. She plumped up her white cotton pillows and pulled back the duvet, patting the space next to her. Jo kicked off her red slippers and climbed in, her loose hair tumbling down over her pyjama top and spreading out over the pillow. Her face was still soft with sleep and her breath sweet and milky.

'Do you know where Bill slept?' Jo whispered to her. 'In Nanna's bed.'

Alison sipped her tea, Jo's cold toes snuggled under her legs. She could hear Bill in the kitchen; smell the homely smell of toast. Sharp morning sunshine poured like lemon juice through the gap in the curtains. And she remembered why they were all here.

Making herself a cup of camomile tea, Hannah had said goodnight to Bill and Alison, too tired to talk any more. When she'd crept into their bedroom, Jo's breath had been deep and rhythmic. She was curled up on her side, her face squashed against Old Ted's, outlined in the grey moonlight. Undressing quietly, Hannah climbed into bed, hearing the familiar squeak of the mattress springs beneath her. It was the bed she always slept in, although Jo had progressed from her travel cot to sharing Hannah's bed and now finally her own single bed, the bedside table separating them. Tonight she would have liked Jo to crawl in beside her; would have welcomed the elbows in her back, wouldn't even have minded being cramped against the wall; needing the comfort the way Jo needed Old Ted. It was a long time since she'd slept without Jacques, and the single bed made her acutely conscious of his absence. Lonely, restless and infantilised. She tried to use the rhythm of Jo's breath as a metronome and to slip into its tempo, but her exhaustion was beyond sleep. Her mind raced on, refusing to wind down and allow the tiredness to carry her off, words buzzing inside her head like mosquitoes. Bastards.

Making lists usually helped. It was something she'd got from

Beth. Hardly a day had gone by when she hadn't written one, on the back of an envelope, or on the bright white card that came with a new pair of tights. Not just shopping lists, but questions to remember to ask the oncologist, or people she owed letters to, or how much money she'd spent, and what on. It gave her a feeling of being in control in some small way. It made the unmanageable manageable. Hannah turned from her side onto her back, the mattress uncomfortably hollowed into a shape she didn't fit, and thought of all the brand names she'd seen on mattresses, the woven labels sewn onto the patterned fabric: Slumberland, Sleepeezee, Silent Night, Rest Assured. There was something so intimate about the old mattresses that people abandoned, lolloping by bins like old drunks; or dumped in skips or on bonfires, their stains and dents revealing more about their old owners than you could read in their palms. More than it was decent to know. She thought about Beth's bed. Bill would sleep in it tonight, she supposed. There was no way she'd ever be able to. Rest Assured. Rest in Peace. Hannah thought about the cemetery, the shrill birdsong that had reached a crescendo as the sun sank in the sky, the families and the flowers. And she remembered what Alison had said about butterflies, about transformations. Caterpillar to butterfly. Water to ice. Grapes to wine. Wine to blood. Rock to sand. Wheat to flour. Flour to bread. Bread to shit. Poppies to morphine. Pumpkin to carriage. Mice to horses. Frogs into princes. And she remembered the faces in the photographs. One had been of a tiny baby, little plaster cherubs holding artificial blue carnations either side of the portrait. She had tried not to look. When Jo was a baby, Hannah used to hover over her, checking her breathing, terrified. The words 'cot death' and 'meningitis' would be thrumming inside her head, but she would not permit them to surface, superstitiously imagining that if she uttered them, she would be invoking them.

Thinking about the times she'd nursed Jo through fevers, she suddenly saw herself aged seven, standing naked on the pink ottoman in the bathroom, her skin smeared chalky white as Beth smothered her in calamine lotion. It was when she'd had chicken pox. She remembered Beth singing 'Spotty Muldoon', and how soothing the cold lotion had been on her feverish skin. What were all the other songs she used to sing, first to her, then to Alison, and finally to Jo? 'Daddy Wouldn't Buy Me a Bow Wow'. 'How Much is that Doggy in the Window? Woof Woof'. Why had so many of them featured dogs? she wondered, trying to evoke Beth's voice, high and sweet and smiling. Then she heard it. But it wasn't the song she wanted to remember, and yet the more she tried not to listen, to block it out with some other tune, the more clearly it filled her head. Beth singing, her voice laughing as she acted out the lyrics. High and sweet and smiling.

> There was an old woman who swallowed a cow
> I don't know how she swallowed a cow
> She swallowed a cow to catch the goat
> She opened her mouth and it went down her throat
> She swallowed the goat to catch the dog
> Oh, what a hog to swallow a dog!
> She swallowed the dog to catch the cat
> Imagine that! She swallowed a cat.
> She swallowed the cat to catch the bird
> How absurd to swallow a bird
> She swallowed the bird to catch the spider
> That wiggled and wiggled and jiggled inside her
> She swallowed the spider to catch the fly,
> I don't know why she swallowed a fly –
> Perhaps she'll die!
> There was an old woman who swallowed a horse.
> She's dead, of course!

53

Manacar

It was agreed. Bill would spend the morning digging around for Disney clues. He drove the car as far as Rico's, a beach bar that Alison had thought might be a good place to get some local opinions, and a pleasant enough spot to pass some time anyway. They'd join him there later. He said bye, gave the car keys to Hannah, and disappeared down the steps past a Mexican restaurant, through a garden of cactus and mimosa and bougainvillea, towards the palm-covered roof of the bar below. Alison could hear music floating up, glasses chinking, a deep bass laugh. Bill would be fine.

Hannah took over the driving from there, with Alison in the passenger seat and Jo in the back. Alison held the box of Beth's ashes on her lap. She'd taken it out of the rucksack, wanting Beth to share this last journey. All three of them were dressed smartly, and looked more like they were on their way to a party than to the beach. Jo's hair had been brushed and braided, and she wore a pale lilac dress. A long necklace of large wooden beads she'd found in the house that morning hung from her neck down to her waist. She had a book of flower stickers on her lap, and had started to peel them from the page and fix them to the car window. Hannah and Alison were both wearing dresses that had been Beth's: Alison's long, pale blue silk; Hannah's cream linen. Some people were shocked when they said they wore their dead mother's clothes – not that they put it like that, but they might as well have done. To Hannah and Alison it seemed perfectly natural. They'd never discussed it, but for both of them it was a way of keeping her close – not in any morbid way but in celebration of her. And besides, Beth would have wanted it. They'd always shared their clothes, all three of them, and she'd have hated to see hers go to waste.

Once off the main road, they followed the track past the sand-coloured ruins daubed with graffiti almost as old – a smiley face spray-painted in blue; an arrow which signposted a beach bar and had outlived the bar itself, and the initials of a political party, remnants of a campaign long since fought. After passing the Moorish tower with foot-thick walls on the sea's edge, they turned right, following the contours of the mountain. There was no way of reaching Manacar but this narrow track chiselled out of the mountain with a sheer drop of sea to their left. Hannah dropped down to second gear, then first, and they inched their way in silence, praying not to meet anything coming the other way.

No one spoke.

Jo knew instinctively not to; she even stopped fixing the stickers to the back of Hannah's seat. There had been a building that was like a giant sandcastle, and she had wanted to say so to Mum and Al, but she knew it wasn't a good moment. She looked out at the sea, which was sparkling, and she watched as it lapped prettily against the rocks below them. A man was fishing from one of them. She saw his line far out where the sea was bright, spangling blue, and she imagined Molly and Polly swimming in the sea. It was a beautiful day.

Hannah was concentrating on the road, avoiding the rubble that crumbled from the mountain face, while staying clear of the sheer drop.

Alison was miles away, thinking about all the other times they'd made this journey. For summer picnics with Beth driving barefoot, the windows wound down, the sea breeze blowing through, and a cassette playing sunny music.

They'd turn it down to concentrate when they got onto this

section of the road. They weren't playing any music today. A shame. She remembered how much stuff they used to pack. A ridiculous amount, really. The blue plastic cold-box would be filled with goodies – more by far than anyone else appeared to bring. Some people would just have a bottle of water and an apple. Not them. For Beth, food and drink were an expression of love, and she had so much love to express – cold-boxfuls. There would be water, of course, but also a few beers – or a bottle of champagne if it were any kind of occasion. Snuggling among the cold sweat of the freezer bricks would be a fresh loaf of bread, a slab of Manchego cheese, tomatoes on the vine, and plenty of fruit. Slices of obscenely sweet chilled melon, still-crunchy pears that oozed juice, a fat bunch of perfectly ripe grapes, and Beth's favourite, strawberries. Then there was the rest of the stuff. First, there was the essential beach umbrella that needed levering through the pebbles to stop it wheeling away across the beach and impaling someone. Once that was safely in place, they'd have some shade to unpack everything else. The fold-up, stumpy-legged green plastic chairs that they cooled off in, suspended slightly above the shallow sea, and a raffia mat each; suntan lotion they smeared on each other's backs and shoulders, hats and sunglasses, books and magazines and the essential Travel Scrabble that they'd play later in the afternoon, swimming between turns. Sometimes they brought a lilo, or flippers and snorkels. In July and August, the sheer effort of unpacking the car was enough to leave them dripping with sweat, and they fell into the sea as soon as they'd stripped.

Manacar wasn't the official naturist beach, which was an un-appealing area a few kilometres north in Vera, a playa naturista for the die-hards, with no features beyond an endless expanse of grey gritty sand and a clutch of peeping toms. They were easy to recognise; they had white bums. They were the ones who slipped off their trunks at the boundary – a sort of clothes Customs delineated by a low fence – to walk along and leer, sloping into the sea when they got an erection. Beth and the girls weren't lifestyle naturists; they just enjoyed the feeling of sun on their skin, and of swimming naked. And the beach at Manacar was so beautiful. A secluded bay of clearest sea surrounded by cool, shady rocks at the base of the two mountains, with a ledge of rock to one side, a series of inlets to the other, and a beach of smooth pebbles in between. Even in the height of the season it was never crowded; it was too hard to reach and offered no amenities. People who came here, the regulars with their berry-brown bottoms, were always respectful and set up camp a reasonable distance from anyone else; they were a community of like-minded sun worshippers, not exhibitionists. The few times when a family arrived who kept their swimming costumes on, the whole dynamic of the beach changed; it was palpable. Manacar wasn't immune from creeps, either, and Beth had always been careful not to be the last car to leave. It was a pretty isolated place if they were to break down, and anyway women without men accompanying them had always to be vigilant, sensible, alert. It was an unspoken code that Hannah and Alison had grown up accepting.

They passed Torre Pirulico, an ancient tower perched above the sea, framing a perfect Mediterranean vista through its arch of stones. It was a real picture postcard of a view if you dared take your eyes off the road to see it. In fact, you could buy cards in Mojácar with that exact view. Alison always imagined a set of inverted commas around it. From there the road widened and wound inland, around the base of the mountain that led to Manacar. Hannah and Alison both sighed deeply, as if they'd been holding their breath the last mile.

'Are we there yet?' Jo asked, pushing her head between the two front seats for a better look.

'Just about,' Alison replied.

54

Rico's

The beach bar was reached from a path of gently descending steps that wound between mimosa trees. It was beautifully built, a complicated geometric dome of metal supporting the covering of cane rushing, creating cool, dappled shade. Something orchestral played through an expensive-looking stereo, not loud but pleasantly audible along with the rustling of the palm trees beyond the bar and the sound of the waves breaking in the distance.

There was only one other person there when Bill arrived. A man in his sixties with cropped white hair sat at a table, reading his newspaper and sipping a glass of white wine. Waiting for someone to serve him, Bill saw a sign behind the counter: 'Surf by the Surf'. He looked around and saw a couple of computers at the other end of the bar, with a view beyond the screens out to the sea. What a fantastically civilised way to live, he thought as he ordered a café con leche from the guy with wispy grey hair who had appeared through a beaded curtain from a room behind the bar.

'Is it OK if I use your computer?' Bill asked him when he brought the coffee over.

'Sure. I'll set it up for you.' He spoke gently and had a languorous American accent that made Bill think of Beach Boys songs and Californian surfers. He wore a faded blue T-shirt and long khaki shorts. 'Write down the time you log on. It's two hundred pesetas for ten minutes.'

After he'd checked his email, Bill went to Google and typed in 'Cryogenics'. It was something he knew hardly anything about, but

Hannah had reminded him yesterday when she'd asked. The word had come up time and again; just about everyone he'd mentioned to that he was researching Disney had asked the same thing: didn't he get himself frozen? It would be amazing if it were true; the ultimate Snow White scenario, the animator in suspended animation. But his research had proved categorically that Disney had been cremated two days after his death from cancer. In fact, the death certificate said cause of death had been not cancer but 'cardiac arrest'. Bill wondered if there were any cause of death other than that your heart just stops beating?

He skimmed through the sites that came up on his search while he drank his coffee, and randomly clicked on one that mentioned stem cells.

'Give Your Whole Family Genetic Insurance!' the home page pronounced. He read on, past the scientific-looking illustrations, fascinated. Cryogenics was, it appeared, alive and kicking. So to speak. You could send the fresh umbilical cord of your baby to this company, where they'd store it cryogenically and charge you rent on it each year. If the child ever needed a transplant, they'd pop it in the post and Bob's your uncle! A perfect match, even a possible match for same-parent siblings, and a good chance of a match – say, about twenty-five per cent – for parents. Bill thought about umbilical cords and their trace, belly buttons. It was extraordinary to think of the scrap of flesh that once connected mother and child. Sam had told him that some of the women she photographed did these ritual burials of their newborn's umbilical cords, under trees or rose bushes. He tried to imagine his mother burying his; her well-manicured nails digging a hole, her heels sinking in the grass of her tidy lawn. Sam's belly button was beautiful, tiny and deep and slightly oval.

As he drained his cup and logged off, another man arrived at the bar. His left arm was missing, the smooth stump protruding from his shirt sleeve like the end of a rolling pin. He had a leather satchel strapped across his chest, which he opened now with his good arm as the two other men went over and chatted with him in Spanish. The guy who had been reading the paper checked some tickets against a sheet of paper that the one-armed man showed him, then gave out a deep laugh and tore them up, dropping the pieces into an ashtray. Bill realised that the one-armed guy must be selling lottery tickets. Alison had told him that in Spain the lottery specifically employed disabled people; people who'd had bad luck, he mused, as he wrote his name and the time he'd been online in the spiral-bound notepad next to the mouse mat. I'm with them, he thought, taking his empty cup back to the bar. You takes your chances and you hopes for the best. Life's a fucking lottery and you can't get any guarantees, not on anything.

The American was refilling the other guy's glass of wine and serving him a triangle of tortilla, which looked very good, so Bill ordered the same and took it to a table that looked out across the sea. The bar was on a level with the new-looking promenade, the tarmac walkway and cycling lane that stretched all the way from the Hotel Indalo to the riding school he'd seen a kilometre or so away. A couple walked past. They were unmistakably British, their faces red from too much sun or beer or both. They descended the steps that led from the promenade to the beach, where empty beach beds and rush-covered umbrellas were organised in tidy rows, and a net for volleyball was stretched taut across the sand. It was hard to believe that it was November. The sea sparkled with bright sunlight. Only three days to Bonfire Night. Incredible. Bill drank his wine and ate his tortilla, thinking about umbilical cords, and wondering how Alison and Hannah and Jo were getting on.

Rhododendrons

Marianina! Marianina!
Come, O come, and turn us into foam.
Traditional

Theirs was the only car as they parked on the flat area facing the bay. Hannah turned off the engine and unstrapped her seatbelt. Alison got out, placed the box of ashes on the roof and pulled her seat forward to let Jo out of the back.

'Well, here we are,' Hannah said, too brightly. She opened the boot. 'Not too far, Jo,' she shouted as Jo set off towards the sea, pebbles clicking underfoot as she ran. Alison helped Hannah with the blue cold-box. They took the handle, lifted it between them and set off.

'Have you got Mum?' Hannah asked.

Alison stared at her uncomprehending for a second, then stopped, slapped her forehead, looked at Hannah and laughed.

'God, I don't believe I almost did that,' she said, retrieving the box from the roof of the car.

Hannah smiled, shaking her head. 'Do you remember the time we nearly lost you in that National Trust garden? Where was it? Hampton Court?'

'I think so.'

'Mum went spare. We were searching for you for ages. You must have been about three and you were wearing a pink raincoat, and all the pink rhododendrons were in flower. Do you remember?'

'I remember her telling me,' Alison said, finding the familiarity of the tale comforting.

'You were absolutely fine. You'd just been wandering about, perfectly unaware that you were lost. I think of that now when I'm out with Jo and she disappears from sight.'

They crunched over the pebbles, the cold-box swinging between them, the box tucked under Alison's arm, till they reached the sea. The beach was sandier here, a coarse sand of broken shells. Jo had already taken off her sandals and was walking backwards, using a stick to draw a long, wavy line where the water lapped the shore. They put the cold-box down and looked around. A gentle wind from the sea fluttered their dresses. It took the edge off what was an amazingly hot day for the second of November.

'So what now?' Hannah asked.

'You know what we're about to do is technically illegal?' Alison said, looking at the box she held. 'You're not supposed to just scatter human remains willy-nilly.'

'Well, who's to know?' Hannah said. She watched Jo tripping along the beach, picking up stones as she went. 'You know, I see her in Jo every now and then. Her gestures. Even the things she says; it's spooky sometimes.'

'I can see that,' Alison said, suddenly remembering the bicycle outside the ice rink, the dynamo creating light long after the cycling had ceased.

Jo came over, the hem of her dress darkened with seawater.

'Are we going to put Nanna in the sea now?' she asked.

'Yes, sweetheart,' Hannah said, touching her shoulder lightly.

'Can I see her?'

Hannah and Alison looked at each other. Alison handed the box to Hannah, who took it in both hands and was perfectly still. The breeze ruffled her hair.

'Mum?' Jo waited. Hannah knelt down on the sand and stared at the box.

Jo squatted down beside her. 'Is that really Nanna?'

'Yes. It is. Well, it's her remains. Her ashes. The really important part of her is already free.'

'Can I touch them?' Jo asked

Hannah looked at Alison, who had knelt down the other side of her.

'If you like, sure,' Alison replied, taking the lid from the box.

Jo put her hand inside, and touched the ashes while her mother and her aunt watched. The breeze blew hair across her face, and carried some of the ashes across the beach.

'Why are we putting her in the sea?'

'Well, because that was what she wanted. She loved it here,' Hannah said.

Alison heard the crack in her voice and saw the tears filling her eyes.

'And it means that if we want to be close to her,' Alison continued, 'we can go to the seaside and feel that she's near. All water connects. It gathers in clouds and falls as rain and fills the seas and rivers. So no matter which sea we're near – Brighton or here or anywhere else – we can always be close to her.'

Jo looked down at the ashes that she sifted through her hand, and then at the two of them, and smiled. 'I thought she was a star.'

'She is. She's in our hearts, so she's wherever we feel her to be.'

'So are we going to put her in the sea now?'

'I guess so. That's why we're here.' Alison took her sandals off and walked to the water's edge. 'Except I'm not sure how we're going to do it. They'll just blow straight back from here.'

Hannah followed. The sea wasn't rough, but there was a definite wind coming towards them.

'What are we going to do, then?'

Alison looked around. On the right of the bay, a shelf of rock hung over the sea. It was deep enough at the farthest point to dive from. She'd climbed it a thousand times, knew all the footholds, and knew that on the other side was a blowhole, a small cave hollowed out by the action of the sea that constantly bottlenecked in, to be spat out again with tremendous force. It was a wonderful way of cooling off in summer.

'We could climb up there,' she said.

'Are you serious?' Hannah asked.

Alison nodded.

'We'd get soaked.'

'We could strip off.'

'It's pretty dangerous for Jo.'

'Not if we're careful. There's two of us – one could hold her hand all the while.'

Jo listened. 'I'm a really good swimmer, Al.'

'She is,' said Hannah.

'So?'

Alison waited while Hannah thought.

'Oh, come on, let's do it,' she said finally.

The three of them took off their dresses and folded them with their underwear and shoes. Out of the cold-box they took a carrier bag containing the bar of chocolate and the punnet of strawberries that Hannah and Jo had bought that morning, and the bunch of flowers and herbs they had picked from Beth's garden. Late roses, rosemary, jasmine, oleander, honeysuckle, bougainvillea and marguerites. They put the box of ashes in there, too, and walked together over to the rock. It was deceptively hard to climb, the surface shiny smooth to waist height.

Alison swung a leg into the foot-hole and pulled herself up. When she was sitting on the ledge Hannah passed her the bag and then lifted Jo up to her. Alison pulled her onto her lap.

'OK, Jo, now you've got to be really careful. Sit here a minute and hold this.'

Jo sat leaning against the wall of the mountain, naked and cross-legged and grinning, with the bag on her lap. Alison took Hannah's arm and heaved her up onto the ledge beside them. Their naked skin touched, and they felt the cool stone underneath them.

'I just pray nobody turns up now,' Hannah said.

They looked out and watched the sea for a while as they caught their breath. They watched a fat green wave roll in, accumulating a line of white froth like the curls of butter in fancy restaurants, gathering force as it swelled towards them and hit the blowhole. A second later the blowhole spat it out again, soaking them. They all squealed at the shock of cold water; the surprise of it. Jo was still holding the bag tight and laughing, her face wet with splashes of the sea.

'Look at us,' Hannah said. 'We look like a whole family of mermaids.'

Jo giggled, delighted to be here, naked with two naked women. Alison stood up slowly and got her balance, then sat back down, shaking her head.

'It's pretty slippery. How are we going to do this?'

'Well,' Hannah suggested, 'if we wait for the next big wave and release everything from here, the sea will carry it out again, won't it?'

'OK. Let's get everything ready.'

As the next wave coursed towards them, on the count of three Jo, Hannah and Alison let fall the chocolate, the strawberries, the flowers and the ashes into the undertow as it sucked at the sea, pulling in its strength before it crashed into the blowhole. This time they were prepared for the splashback. Hannah and Alison watched, shiny wet, each holding a hand of Jo's as the flowers floated out into the sea, swaying to and fro on smaller waves, dispersing to the far side of the bay and out into the deep jade Mediterranean.

Alison, Jo and then Hannah slid down from the rock with the empty carrier bag and the empty green box, the breeze cool on their sea-splashed skin. The waves rolled gently onto the shore, and they stood for a while looking out to the horizon.

It was Jo who finally broke the silence. 'Can we go for a swim now?'

'That sounds like a great idea,' Alison said.

'Did we bring any towels?' Hannah asked.

'Er, no. Damn, that was a bit of an oversight. But we can't get much wetter than we already are.'

'True,' Hannah said. 'Come on, then.'

She ran in, splashing through the waves, shrieking as the cold rose to her waist, and then dived under. Jo and Alison followed, holding hands, until the water reached to Jo's armpits. They began to swim, staying parallel to the shore with Alison between Jo and the horizon.

Hannah swam beyond the waves to where the sea was calmer. She dived under again, only this time with her eyes open. The sea was beautifully clean; she could see right down to the seabed where shoals of small black fish darted in complicated, jerky formation. Purple sea urchins clung to the rocks, and seaweed swayed in slow motion. Coming up for air, she turned over to float on her back, allowing herself to be supported, her arms spread wide, her hair swaying like the seaweed. She closed her eyes for a moment, feeling the sun through her eyelids, hearing the waves and the clicking of pebbles in her head, weightless. Her skin was the thinnest membrane between her warm blood and the cold seawater that held her safely, cradled her, lapped over her.

'Rest in peace, Mum,' she said. She turned to the shore, and began swimming towards her sister and her daughter.

Jo and Alison stood in the shallows, watching the waves like seasoned surfers, and squealing as they jumped over them or were smacked by them, their legs and stomachs stinging with the impact. They caught one on the point of collapse, letting it hurtle them onto the shore, where they lay like a pair of seals, basking in the brilliant whiteness of the foam. They slid back and forth as the waves tugged at them, the foam breaking down into lace. Mum is in this water, Alison kept thinking, Mum is dissolved like a stock cube, seasoning the sea, this sea that is full of life, that is energising me. She grinned at the thought. Whenever I swim in the sea, Mum will be there with me.

When they eventually got out, they squeezed the water from their hair, and jumped about, shaking like dogs to throw off the seawater, which left salty traces as it dried on their skin. Hannah used her knickers to mop Jo dry.

'Mum! Those are your knickers!' she shrieked, and Hannah laughed with her.

She pressed her face against Jo's wet tummy and planted a kiss on her belly button. Jo wriggled and squealed as Hannah wrestled her down onto the beach. They lay there, feeling the hard, sun-warmed pebbles pressed against their skin. Hannah closed her eyes and breathed in the smell of wet seaweed. She felt the sun warming her from above, the stones from below. She heard the crunch of footsteps, and looked up to see Alison.

'We should celebrate,' she said. She squatted down next to them, opened the cold-box and pulled out a second punnet of strawberries, a bottle of cava and three glasses.

'Champagne!' Jo said, helping herself to a strawberry.

Hannah and Alison looked at each other and laughed.

'Get you, madam,' Alison said

'I can have a little taste, can't I, Al?'

'That's up to your mum. I've got some orange juice to mix it with.'

'Well, just this once, seeing as it's such a special occasion.'

Hannah and Jo held the glasses as Alison poured the orange juice. She picked up the bottle and prised the cork between her thumbs. It released with a *pop!* and flew into the sea – they could see it bobbing about on a wave.

'Now Nanna would definitely approve of that!' Hannah said.

'Look! There's one of our flowers,' Jo said, pointing.

A rose drifted on the movement of the sea, the pink petals gradually becoming waterlogged. It floated towards them, and then disappeared under the tug of the next wave, lost from sight but still there, somewhere.

Alison topped the glasses of orange juice up with the champagne, causing them to froth up thickly before they settled. She took one of the glasses from Hannah and held it up.

'To Mum, Nanna, Beth.'

'To Mum, Nanna, Beth.'

They chinked glasses and solemnly sipped the orange fizz.

'And to the three mermaids,' Hannah said.

'The three mermaids.'

They helped themselves to strawberries, pulling the stalks free and tossing them into the sea.

'Can I keep this?' Jo asked, picking up the box that had held Beth's ashes.

'If you like,' Alison said. 'What are you going to use it for?'

'To keep things in.' She read the words on the side. 'What does "Tanatorio" mean?'

'"Parlour", I think; it's the place where Nanna was taken when she died, where they prepared her for the funeral.' She selected a perfect strawberry from the punnet. The stalk came away cleanly, and she twirled it between her finger and thumb.

'Why are they parlours, I wonder?' Hannah said, her mouth full of strawberry. 'There's beauty parlours, dog parlours, massage parlours, funeral parlours, parlour games. Why is that?'

'I don't know,' Alison answered, watching Jo, who walked along the seashore collecting shells and pebbles and placing them in the green box.

56

Duende

She liked his tears so much that she put out her beautiful finger and let them run over it.

J. M. Barrie, *Peter Pan*

Bill stretched out on the beach bed. He'd been right about the American guy's accent. Originally from California, Rico had been in Mojácar since the sixties. He'd been one of the first to move here when it was a hippy haven, and knew all there was to know about the place.

The bar had filled up towards midday, and Bill found himself a table and sat reading his Disney book. Most of the lunchtime clientele appeared to be English-speaking. There were a few obvious tourists; ones whose new-looking holiday clothes still had the suitcase creases. But mainly they were people who staked a territorial claim on the place with their more casual dress and their familiarity with one another. There was a table of older ladies; the kind of women who Bill imagined played a lot of bridge. Women whose husbands played golf, and who cooked coronation chicken at their dinner parties, and had someone Spanish in to clean once a week. They talked in loud voices about nothing in particular while they shared seafood paella and a bottle of wine. One of them kept taking titbits from her plate and feeding them to her pug-faced dog.

An attractive young couple with shaved heads came up from the beach, arms round each other. She was barefoot and carried a pair of trainers in her hand; he was wearing a black leather jacket. They walked up to the bar and ordered beers, which they drank straight from the bottle. The guy in the leather jacket rolled a joint and passed it to the young guy with a goatee who was behind the bar now. He dried his hands on a dishcloth, took a toke and passed it to the girl. She drew on it, and the leather-jacket guy put his hand down the back of her jeans. Bill couldn't help watching as the guy stroked her arse.

The music had changed to some old R and B, and Bill expected the ladies to complain, but they seemed perfectly happy. They weren't even perturbed by the middle-aged man who strode down the path wearing a Native American headdress. He walked over to them and raised his hand in salute.

'How,' he said.

The ladies answered him politely with a chorus of Hows and continued with their chatter. Tiny birds hopped onto their table and pecked at the crumbs of bread left from their lunch. Van Morrison growled from the speakers. The How man greeted each person in the bar, including Bill, who nodded politely in response. He then sat at a table in the corner, took off the feathered headdress, ordered a coffee and pulled out the *New York Times*.

Bill had given up even the pretence of reading by now; he was finding the bar far too entertaining. He went to the bar to order another wine. A man came and sat on the stool next to him. 'You're so fine, my brown-eyed girl,' he sang, banging his fist against the bar, not quite in time. He had straggly blond hair and could have been anything from sixty to a very rough forty. He wore cowboy boots under his jeans, and a denim jacket over a filthy T-shirt. A cut on his forehead was caked in dry blood. He pulled a crumpled packet of cigarettes from his jacket, and prised one out. He had difficulty connecting the flame of his lighter to the tip of the bent cigarette, but eventually succeeded, sucked on it and started to cough.

'See him?' He nudged Bill, pointing to the couple.

Bill didn't answer.

'MV3646GW,' he said. 'Her?' He nodded towards one of the ladies, the one with the pug on her lap. 'AL99870, yellow Volvo.'

The woman looked up, surprised, as if she'd heard someone call her name. The man looked at Bill, triumphant, gripping the bar as he swayed backwards, then lost his balance and fell to the floor, swearing. The bar stool fell on top of him. Bill offered his hand, but the man struggled to his feet, ignoring Bill. He picked up his cigarette and walked away, banging into tables. He crossed the promenade, and went down the steps to the beach, still shouting numbers and letters.

Bill picked the stool from the floor and heard the swish of the bead curtain behind the bar.

'Don't mind him; he's Johnny Numbers.' It was the American guy who'd served him the coffee. Bill saw the wry smile on a face leathery with lines, the eyes a watery blue. 'Photographic memory. Did you want another wine?'

'Er, yes, please, and some olives.'

'OK. I'll bring them over.'

Back at his table, Bill watched Johnny Numbers kicking at the waves. He was still shouting, but the words were lost to the sea.

When the American brought Bill's wine and olives over, he noticed the Disney book, and started a conversation. Was Bill here on holiday, had he been to Mojácar before, what had brought him here? Bill told him about his research, and the guy's face lit up. He introduced himself as Rico, the owner of the bar.

'Come to my office. I've something to show you.'

He led Bill out of the bar, through a maze of potted cacti, to an amphitheatre; the broad white steps progressing in arcs, a stage at the base with the sea its backdrop. At the top of the steps was a long, glass-fronted bar, to the side of which was Rico's office. He pulled a key from his shorts and unlocked the thick wooden door.

The room was dark after the sunshine, and full of clutter. It was hot in there, too, and smelled of old dogs. A strawberry iMac on the desk in the corner looked hopelessly futuristic among the piles of junk, stacks of paperwork and lumps of driftwood. The light from the screensaver illuminated motes of dust. Rico picked things off a couple of chairs and threw them onto a coffee table, gesturing for Bill to have a seat. As he did, Bill saw the dog sleeping under the table. It was enormous, the size of a small pony. Its outstretched paws were like the ornate wooden carvings on the legs of old furniture. A thick drip of spittle hung from the wet black gums as it snored. Rico picked up a pouch of tobacco and found some Rizlas; he sank into the other chair and nodded towards three photographs on the wall.

'Take a look at those. See if you can tell me which two people are related.'

Bill walked over to get a closer look, and the dog raised its head, rumbling as if clearing its throat before barking.

'Don't mind Simba – he's a pussy cat,' Rico said, stroking Simba with the end of his sandaled foot as he licked papers together. The dog's head slumped back down.

Bill looked at the three men in the photos. One was familiar – it was practically the same picture of Disney as the one on the cover of his book. The other two were as different from each other as two faces could be: one looked like Disney and one didn't. Bill had pointed to the obvious pair, knowing he was about to hear the punchline to a well-rehearsed joke.

'Aha,' Rico said, smiling as he rolled the joint between his fingers. 'That's what you'd think, wouldn't you? But oh no, the guy who is Disney's fucking double is Gines Carillo, a doctor from Mojácar. The guy who looks like he's got a stick up his ass, that's Elias

Disney, so-called Dad. In truth, he adopted the bastard child of Carillo and a washerwoman. A kid called José Guirao, aka Walt Disney.'

Rico sealed the fat joint with a flourish. Bill had been surprised at the passion in his soft voice.

They shared the joint, and Rico told Bill Mojácar's own fairytale. He told the story of the eccentric doctor, the beautiful young laundress and the scandal. A poor miner had been forced to marry the laundress and emigrate with her and her bastard son to America. Rico was adamant: *Carillo* was the father – *had* to be. Here was a man who built a castle topped with crazy towers; a folly he named 'Duende' – 'Spirit of Inspiration'. He built his own theatre, staged magical plays, even created an orchestra of local children. Their music poured out into the narrow streets and flowed down to the public fountains, where women like the beautiful Isabel Zamora washed their clothes. There were blood relatives, Rico said, willing to take DNA tests, to prove beyond a shadow of a doubt.

Bill looked up at the chinks of light that pierced the beach umbrella, wondering why he didn't feel more pleased with himself. This was the story he'd come here for, wasn't it? Words swam in his head; the joint had been strong on top of the wine. If you believe in fairies, clap your hands, he thought. What could you ever prove without a shadow of a doubt? Would DNA convince him that he was his father's son? Maybe an X-ray of his liver might. His mother's son? He felt his belly button, pushed his finger into it; this ruptured artery that he took on faith had once been a direct line to his mother. He'd read that at the earliest production of *Peter Pan*, J. M. Barrie had paid someone to start the clapping, not trusting that the audience would clap spontaneously. But they had. He remembered Jo singing along with Mulan; her belief in the world the film had created; the magic it had woven. And he thought of Johnny

Numbers and the bald couple and the 'How' man and the lottery man and the pug-faced dog and Simba. Mojácar was a Never Never Land; somewhere people didn't have to grow up, didn't have to return from after two weeks' holiday – maybe didn't have anywhere to return to. Mojácar's Lost Boys. Disney could very well have been born here, but what did it matter? If you believe in fairies, clap your hands, he thought again, sitting up and looking out to sea. If you believe in Mojácar, clap your hands.

*   *   *

'Well, look who it is! Long time no see,' Rico said, leaning across the bar to kiss Alison on both cheeks.

'Hi, Rico,' Alison said. 'And look who I've brought with me.' Jo looked up from Alison's side across the bar to Rico, suddenly shy.

'Is that your little niece? Can it be the same person, so tall and grown-up?'

'You remember Rico, don't you, Jo?' Alison said. Jo smiled noncommittally.

'I know who you will remember,' Rico said, pointing to an oversized dog basket in the corner of the bar. Simba snored gently, his slack mouth lolloping over one paw.

'Simba!' Jo said, running over to stroke his back. Simba opened his eyes, repositioned his head across his other paw, and closed his eyes again, allowing himself to be stroked.

Hannah came down the steps and saw Jo with the dog. 'Careful, Jo, be gentle. Hi, Rico,' she said, taking the bar stool next to Alison's.

'Wow. The whole Vine clan. How long are you all here for?'

'Oh, it's just a flying visit this time. We're leaving again in the morning.'

She supposed they were the whole Vine clan now, but it was strange to hear it said like that. It was strange to be back here, too, sitting in the same place. The little respites from caring, calling in for a coffee as she and Alison changed shifts, trying to snatch some normal time with Jo and Jacques, conscious that everyone else here was carefree, and feeling like a spectre at the feast. The last time she'd been here had been the day after Beth died, when she had received all their condolences, their small kisses planted on her cheeks. She remembered she'd had to ask what the correct Spanish was, how to say it in the correct tense, recent past: 'My mother has died.' It had been really important that she said it right. 'Se ha muerto mi madre,' she remembered.

'We're looking for a friend of ours. We're supposed to be meeting him here,' Alison explained. 'Tall, dark hair, about my age? We dropped him off here this morning.'

'You mean Bill? So it's you guys that he came with?'

'You've met him, then?'

'Sure. I think he's down there.' Rico pointed to the beach.

Alison crossed the promenade and leaned over the wall, looking down to the beach. It was his feet she saw first, poking out from under a beach umbrella. She walked down the steps and went over to where he lay, fast asleep on a beach bed. As she watched him, his face completely relaxed, the Disney book lying open in the sand, she realised it was the first time that she'd seen him asleep. She bent over and kissed his cheek.

He opened his eyes. 'What was that for?'

'Oh, I don't know. Just felt like it.'

'How did it go?' he asked.

Alison smiled and sat down on the edge of his beach bed. 'Really, really well.' Pushing her feet into the sand, she looked at him and added, 'Thanks.'

'What for?'

'Being my mate. Putting up with me. Coming to Mojácar with me.'

'Yeah. Mojácar. What a strange place this is. You wouldn't believe the people I've met.'

'I gather you've met Rico.'

'I certainly have,' he said, stretching his arms behind his head.

'You didn't tell me about his Disney theories.'

'I didn't know he had any.'

'And some.'

'Great. So, you got what you needed?'

Bill thought for a moment.

'Yes. I got what I needed.'

57

Klaxon

'You sure about this, Flaca?' Mickey asked as they walked from the bar, through the gardens at Rico's, arm in arm.

Kim had left without saying goodbye to anyone. She hated all that; they'd all forget her by this time next week, anyway, or by next month, tops. Mojácar was like watercress; if it became damaged it grew back, mended seamlessly.

'Yes, I am. Now feels like the right time.'

The bike was parked outside the Cantina. Mickey picked up their helmets, handing one to Kim.

'You know I'd drive you to Alicante?'

'What, with my suitcase strapped on the back of the bike?'

'OK, I'll come on the bus with you.'

Kim was surprised to hear Mickey sounding so clingy, and herself so determined. She kissed him. 'Thanks, but I'd just rather say goodbye to you here. I want to remember you as part of Mojácar, not at some bus station or the airport.'

'It's because of the ashes, isn't it?' Mickey said, kicking the bike stand free.

'Isn't what?'

He revved the engine. It purred. Kim loved that sound.

'Your not wanting to stay.'

She thought about it, fastening her chinstrap. When they'd returned to the beach after replacing the ashes, the sun had been just rising. It was stunning, molten gold dripping on the pale sea, seeping into it. It had been so beautiful; Kim had felt like crying. They'd fallen into bed, sleeping deeply for the rest of the day. When she woke up late that evening, it had been decided: it was time to go. Simple as that.

'I don't know,' she said, getting on the bike behind him. 'I don't think so. Maybe.'

They rode out of Mojácar along the coast road, turning off at the tower and following the track to Manacar. Kim wanted to spend her last hours there, on the empty beach, alone with Mickey. She held his waist as they bumped over the uneven surface of the track, the mountains to her right, the sea to her left and Mickey here in front, his back pressed against her. She looked at the back of his beautiful neck, feeling disbelief that she could choose to go. But she knew she would.

The track wound inland round the foothills, past the irrigated gardens carved in a series of steps up the reluctant surface of the mountain. A complicated system of hoses trickled a steady flow of water onto shrubs and trees that really had no place there. They were the gardens belonging to the white villa that perched on the top of the mountain with views across the sea, Kim imagined, to Africa. She'd heard a story about the house. Whether or not it was true, she couldn't tell; Mojácar was so full of stories. It had its own folklore of scandal and intrigues and overindulgences. This one was about the couple who had made their fortune selling dog food. They'd built their dream castle here at Manacar, but instead of living happily ever after, he'd met someone half his age and asked for a divorce. She'd incarcerated herself up there, Rapunzel-like, buggered if she was going to let down her hair. When he returned to try to reason with her, she pelted him with tins of dog food. Kim imagined her like some medieval warrior; saw the tins rolling down the hill, bumping down the irrigated steps of red earth. What was it about the story that made her know it was time to leave, she wondered. A part of her felt like the trees and shrubs on that mountain, as if she'd been here under false pretences. But more than that, it was about the belligerence of clinging to something after it had ceased to give pleasure. Mojácar had made Kim happy, it had made her very happy, and so had Mickey. But she knew that neither Mickey nor Mojácar could continue to do that. They hadn't changed; she had. She wasn't sure how or why, she just felt it in her bones. Party's over. Time to go.

The beach was deserted, as she'd hoped it would be, and when Mickey turned off the engine there was just the sound of the sea. They walked down to the water. A bedraggled flower drifted to the shore, its soggy petals clumped together.

'I could come over to London if you like,' Mickey said.

Kim smiled. She couldn't picture it; Mickey in London, the two of them in some flat, or sitting upstairs on a bus together, looking at the view, not speaking.

'You'd hate it. I'd hate it for you.'

'Stay here with me, then. I'll change, I'll get a job.'

Kim put her fingers on his lips. 'C'mon, Mick. No regrets, remember?'

Mickey pulled her to him, ran his fingers from the top of her head, as if anointing her. Kim remembered a game she used to love when she was little. You close your eyes and someone pretends to break an egg on your head. They tap your skull and then they drag their fingers down, and you believe – you really believe – that it's the egg trickling down, tickling and gooey. Mickey placed his hands over her ears, covering them so that she heard the sea inside her head. He followed the nape of her neck, the line of her jaw, lifted her chin up to his face, and kissed her mouth.

As they pulled off their clothes they studied each other's bodies, taking in each crease, each freckle and dimple, every hair and scar. They tasted each other, drinking in the scents, tracing each curve and crevice, mapping their flesh like blind cartographers, committing each other to memory. They fell down on the shore, the wet pebbles bruising as the sea licked them.

At the exact moment when Kim let out a deep moan, they heard an ear-splitting sound, like a foghorn. They stopped moving. They looked at each other, then out to sea. Kim was suddenly aware that her skin burned with grazes from the pebbles. Mickey's cock slid out of her as he propped himself up on his arms and scanned the horizon.

'Up there, look.' Kim lay on her back and pointed above her.

Mickey's eyes followed. 'What the fuck?'

They could just about make her out. On top of the mountain, near the white house, a woman holding a pair of binoculars to her face and firing a klaxon. They stared in disbelief, speechless. And then they began to laugh. They rolled on the beach holding their sides, it hurt so much; sand sticking to their skin, tears pouring down their cheeks as the klaxon woman hooted like an owl.

Mickey touched the bruise as the bus pulled away. Kim had given him something to remember her by.

'By the time this fades, you won't hurt any more. I promise,' she'd said, lifting her mouth from his neck and giving him one last kiss.

58

Rose Bush

Alison is standing in a muddy hole, a spade in one hand and a rose bush in the other. She has already planted one bush, about two feet away. Sweat is dripping from her, trickling down her neck and soaking into her old vest and shorts. It's only ten a.m., but already the sun is stinking hot, and her patience is running out. When she's finished this she needs to get cracking. Hang out the washing, collect wood, walk Jess, sort out lunch, phone around to organise appointments and confirm lifts.

Beth is standing on the terrace, which she and Alison covered with a mosaic of fishes and hearts together a year or so ago, when they were able to share projects. Now she can only ask, offer instructions, thank, be grateful, be patient. A patient patient. There's so much that she can no longer do for herself. Like cook a meal, walk in the mountains, pick oranges, drive herself to the beach, plant a rose bush. And Alison knows she's grateful, but understands, too, that she grieves for her independence. And she realises Beth feels guilty about that.

But Beth knows a thing or two about roses, and she reckons Alison is about to plant them too close together. It's upsetting for Alison, too. She feels Beth's frustration at having to delegate every damn thing, but is pissed off at being told she's wrong. After all, she's not a fucking saint.

A friend arrives to take Beth to one of her appointments. She says bye to Alison, who is filling the hole up with the displaced earth, the rose bush still waiting, its roots in a bucket of water. As they drive through Turre, Beth asks her friend to slow down so she can check to see how much distance other people put between their roses. Finding that she was right gives her no satisfaction. As she tries to explain to Alison over lunch on the terrace, the bushes now planted further apart, all she feels is relief.

'This egg is just right,' Jo pronounced, like one of the Three Bears, dipping a toast soldier into the runny yolk.

'Mmm, mine too,' Hannah said. 'Bill, you're a genius. That expression "Can't even boil an egg" is all wrong. Mum always used to say that boiling an egg is one of the hardest things to get right.'

Bill, Hannah and Jo were sitting round the dining table having breakfast, their bags already packed and in the car.

Alison was still in the shower. They'd all turned in early last night. She'd slept well, more deeply than she could remember sleeping for a long time, and had woken up feeling great. The shower pounded between her shoulder blades, and she was aware of tension being released right through her; clearing from her neck, streaming down her spine and leaving her. It would be easier to leave the house than she had expected. There was nothing left to connect with, nothing that really mattered, apart from the plants in the garden. She thought about the rose bushes that had matured, completely filling the space, producing the roses that they'd thrown in the sea yesterday. Mum had been right about that, she thought. But tending to those now felt empty. The really important things – the mountains and the riverbed – they would still be here. Well, at least until the next round of development, she thought, and she could do nothing about that.

Last night she and Hannah had agreed it was time to put the house up for sale. It was what Beth would have wanted; not to pickle the place like a pair of Miss Havishams, but to turn the proceeds into something that could enhance their lives. That's what Beth would have done, and it was part of her legacy to them. She'd always been brave, moved on, carved out her own destiny. It was right they should follow her example; live in the spirit of her.

It had been easier to discuss than either of them had expected. In fact, it had been Hannah who broached the subject. They were on the terrace, watching the moon as it crept over the mountain, waning again, a day over full. Bill was inside, reading Jo a bedtime story at her insistence.

'Do you still feel Mum's presence here?' Hannah asked.

'No. Not now. Not like I thought I would. I love this place, but I wouldn't want to live here.'

'Me neither. I feel closer to her in the sea than here. Isn't that strange?'

'No, not at all; I feel the same.'

'So, should we carry on renting it out, do you think?'

Alison felt the old familiar pressure drop down on her like fog. She was tired of making the decisions, of having to take control. This time, she wasn't going to play.

'I don't know. What do you think?' she asked.

Hannah was silent for a while. Alison waited, watching as a transparent gecko scurried up the wall, listening to the crickets chirruping in the dusk. Hannah picked a jasmine flower from the tangle of green that spilled over the terrace, and breathed in its sweetness. Then she said it.

'I think that we should sell, if we both feel we can. Renting it means it'll still be here, tugging at us, and still needs to be resolved eventually. I think we should move on.'

Alison thought about this now as she turned the shower off and reached for a towel. The window in the bathroom looked out over the riverbed, and a cool breeze wafted in as she stood, wrapped in the towel, thinking this might be the last time she would stand here, looking at this view, feeling this breeze. She turned from the window to the mirror and studied her reflection, and decided that when she got home she was going to get her hair cut. Short.

59

Tearaway

The way his torso had been punctured with the thorns of prickly pear reminded Manuel Martínez of San Sebastián. Such a waste, he thought, checking the thermostat in the room before finishing up for the morning. The door downstairs slammed behind Carlos, who'd helped him prepare the body that lay on the table. Carlos had become a real clock-watcher now he'd finally got himself a girlfriend, Manuel thought as he cleared away the equipment. A plump young woman called Beatriz, who was already making his meals and talking about saving up for the future. Carlos had told Manuel that she insisted he took a long shower as soon as he got home, to cleanse the traces of death from him, she said. Manuel guessed she'd probably talk Carlos into getting himself a different job, something she wouldn't be so embarrassed to tell her friends about. Apart from the nuisance of having to train a new apprentice, he couldn't help thinking Carlos ought to be living a bit, having fun while he still was young and carefree. Kids today were in such a hurry to get lumbered with car loans and mortgages. But then, look at this young man. Look what happened to him.

There hadn't been any other vehicles involved, but a woman driving the other way had witnessed the accident and notified the Red Cross, who'd told Manuel that he was already dead when they reached him, halfway down the mountain on the road to Carboneras. It would have been instantaneous, they said. His neck had been broken when he hit the crash barrier, catapulted from the motorbike and pitched down the mountain. It was thanks to the prickly pear that he'd not ended up in the sea. The police had got his details from the driving licence and contacted his parents, who would be flying over from England this evening to identify him. That was something Manuel had never stopped finding distressing; the grief of parents who, in the natural scheme of things, ought to die first. Maybe that was the only true advantage of not having a family. None to grieve, none to grieve for you. To be spared the agonies as well as the ecstasies. Manuel certainly felt his temperament was better suited than a family man's to his job. He didn't return home transposing the different deaths he witnessed during his office hours onto his nearest and dearest, simply because there were none.

He recalled a documentary he'd seen about a man in America whose livelihood was clearing up after deaths. Shootings, overdoses, whatever; this man would clean it all up. He had, he'd boasted, found a niche market. The programme had ended with his marriage, and it hadn't seemed to Manuel that the couple were particularly fond of each other. In fact, the man's decision to wed appeared to be based on his desire to make sure there would be someone to clean up after he died. During the wedding vows, his mobile phone had rung. He'd excused himself to take the call, which had been a lucrative new job, a suicide. Manuel recalled the satisfaction on the groom's face as he organised the details, his bride in the background in her meringue dress, waiting under a flower-decked pagoda for him to resume his vows. Maybe Beatriz was right not to want an undertaker for a husband.

Manuel gathered up the few personal effects to give to the parents. As he put them in a box he searched for clues to who this young man had been. It was unusual to meet the deceased before he'd met the next of kin. In fact, this was the first time. He studied the driving licence: Michael Morris, date of birth 4 November 1979. How could a grown man have been born so recently? Nineteen seventy-nine was only yesterday. He was even younger than Carlos, but worlds apart; Manuel couldn't imagine Beatriz telling this lad to take a shower, or to save for the future. You don't drive a motorbike like that without being a bit of a tearaway. And then there were his tattoos. He had the most extraordinary one on his buttock; a skull with rabbit's ears. Carlos had called him over to take a look, sniggering.

In the wallet he discovered a single photo, a photo-booth picture, its edges torn. A pretty boy with long blond hair and an easy, confident smile. Manuel looked at the body again and back at the photo. It was difficult to see the likeness at first, but it was him, no doubt about it. Manuel bet he'd broken a few hearts; he looked like someone who had what they called 'animal magnetism' in the kind of books his mother used to read. He flipped the picture over. A length of printed black tape was stuck to the back. He read the letters punched into it, wondering who had written them.

'FLACA XXXXX'.

60

Sun

Jo held Hannah's hand during take-off, using her other hand to pinch her nostrils tight, like she did when she jumped into the swimming pool, and blowing until she felt her ears creak. She had a window seat again and, because it was daytime, when the plane lifted up she could watch as they swerved out over the sea, and she could almost count the lines of frilly waves.

There were loads of things she liked about Spain this time. She liked the noisy restaurants where there were lots of other children, and the big fans on the ceilings, and signs on the toilet doors to know which was which. She'd counted seven different lots of signs. There were some that she thought were a bit rude, with a little boy standing and weeing, and a little girl sitting on a potty. Some had ladies in flamenco dresses and men in cowboy hats, or men with pipes and ladies with lipsticks, or just trousers for men and skirts for ladies, which wasn't very good, because she wore both skirts and trousers. She liked the olives that had stones in that you had to spit out, and the serviettes and toothpicks on the tables. She'd put some toothpicks in her green box to take home, and some shells and pebbles, and a badge she'd found at Nanna's house that said 'Sixty Years Young', because that was how old Nanna was. She was sorry she hadn't seen Jess, but Mum had said they would think about getting a dog of their own. She'd said 'think' in that way that made Jo believe it might happen, but not if she kept going on about it. Jo knew her best chance would be to keep quiet about it for a while, but she crossed her fingers and wished and wished.

There were blue dragonflies in Spain, too. They were so beautiful; their wings looked like fairies' wings. And the crickets that sounded like people clapping a long way away, and see-through lizards that climbed up the walls but didn't scare her. She remembered the puddings in the restaurants, with cream they squirted from cans, like her dad's shaving foam that he squeezed onto her face once and made her look like Father Christmas. She couldn't wait to see her dad again. She wanted to tell him about the boats with names, and seeing *Mulan* at the cinema with Bill. She hoped she'd see Bill again soon, too; she really liked him; and Al, of course.

Two more hours and they'd be landing, Hannah thought, squeezing Jo's hand. They'd watched the stewardesses do their safety routine, pointing out the exits and demonstrating the life jackets: how to tie the ribbon in a bow, and top up the air and blow the whistle. The instructions were so innocuous, it was difficult to take them seriously, to imagine calamity. The emphasis seemed to be all wrong – taking off high heels, tying bows and blowing whistles. Everyone was far more concerned with the sale of perfumes, and the air hung with a thousand sampled scents that were sucked into the air filters and blown out again, mingling with stale farts in a stew of old, recycled atmosphere. Still, it was only two hours, and so far the journey had gone like clockwork, right from the drive to Murcia with Alison and Bill.

Even leaving the house for what might be the last time hadn't been the wrench she'd been anticipating. In fact, she felt light-headed. She looked out of the window, the brightness of the light making her feel irrationally happy. The clouds were illuminated like a church ceiling. They glowed with pure sunlight so you could almost expect to see angels resting on them. It was something that struck her afresh every time she flew; that, no matter what the weather below, the sun was still there. It was still just as bright, only sometimes it was hiding, behind these angelic-looking clouds.

61

Zimmer

Bill watched the baby buggies, golf clubs and Zimmer frames move in slow procession like a performance of the seven ages of man round the carousel at the baggage reclaim. Gatwick Airport had to be one of the most dismal places in the world, he thought, especially when returning and not leaving. As they'd landed, drizzle had spat on the thick oval windows, leaving forward slashes of grey, and suddenly they were in autumn. Short days and drizzle autumn.

The carousel chugged to a standstill and Bill sighed. He'd known this part of the journey to take longer than flights. Alison had gone to find them a trolley. It was always depressing to discover how few trolleys there were; as if they hadn't been expecting this many people to arrive. And it was even more depressing to see the ugly way people fought for them.

Just behind the black rubber flaps where the cases emerged, he could see someone in blue overalls hurling a case onto the pile. Bill thought of the scene in *The Wizard of Oz* when Toto exposes the wizard as a fraud, a frail old man hiding behind a curtain. A bell sounded and the cases began to move again.

Walking out into Arrivals, pushing their trolley towards the train terminus, Bill stared at the professional meeters of people. He read the signs with strange, misspelt names. Then he spotted a placard with red writing: 'Her Maj. Alison Vine'.

'Yoohoo!' Oi! Miss Vine! Taxi?'

'Sam!' Alison grinned, pushing through the obstacle race of

pissed-off-looking people and unwieldy trolleys. 'How did you know which flight we were on?'

'Aha! That'll be my psychic powers, and Jacques's phone number. Couldn't have you schlepping back on public transport when I have my trusty steed. Hi, Bill,' she said, as he caught up with them.

'Hi,' Bill said, not trusting himself to say more.

'Well, come on, I'm parked about three fucking miles away. Follow me.'

62

Rocket

'I hope there aren't any hedgehogs asleep under the bonfire,' Jo said.

'I'm sure they'll have checked,' Hannah said, unsure how exactly you'd check such a thing, and hoping Jo wasn't about to ask.

As the three of them walked along the muddy path towards the park, Jacques realised he liked Bonfire Night more than any other celebration in England. Maybe after spending the last few days without Jo and Hannah, his sense of community and completeness was heightened now they were home. Whatever the reason, it occurred to him that Bonfire Night was the only English celebration that felt communal. Nothing else had the same sense of sharing and belonging; of all doing the same thing at the same time. Guy Fawkes was just an excuse, a way of stopping it seeming so pagan. In his bones Jacques knew that it was really about the nights drawing in, appeasing the spirits before the onset of winter. That was how it felt, anyway, this gathering in darkness, mingling with crowds of shadowy people, and making fire. All around them was the hum of chatter, the noise of kids running and parents telling them to slow down, the faraway whiz of rockets and the crackly music being played over the public address system. The sky lit up intermittently, and an aeroplane cut through the night sky, temporarily garlanded in glittering light. The air smelled gloriously of damp leaf mulch and sulphur and baked potatoes.

'Can we light the sparklers?' Jo asked when they reached the display area's perimeter, joining the people who were already gathered waiting for the show to start.

Jacques smiled down at her. She was muffled up in a scarf and a woolly hat that practically covered her eyes. Despite it being a mild night for November, Hannah had worried the change of climate might have made her susceptible to colds. He knelt down and pulled her hat back.

'Sure,' he said, fishing in his carrier bag for them. He tore open the paper packet and pulled out three sparklers, giving them one each. He opened his Zippo and rubbed his thumb along the wheel, producing a fat blue flame. The three of them touched the tips of their sparklers together and waited for them to catch. They did so almost simultaneously, a flurry of crackling light illuminating their faces into a trinity; Mother, Father, Daughter.

Jo's face glowed from the heat of all her layers and shone with the reflection of the light. Her eyes were bright as she watched the sparks racing up the metal like a lit fuse in a *Tom and Jerry* cartoon. Jacques started to spin his sparkler in a wide loop, and so did Hannah. They whooped as they lassoed the air into circles of light, the afterglow fading into the next loop. Jo jiggled her sparkler in a zigzag like a dissolving graph. Their sparklers all gave out at the same moment, leaving the metal sticks charred a gritty grey and smelling smoky and tart. All around them, other families were spelling out their names in melting writing; making hearts and question marks like a mass of conductors interpreting a fantastic composition unique to each of them and common to all.

The display was about to start, and Jo asked Jacques to lift her up. He bent down and swung her up onto his shoulders, holding her skinny legs in their woolly tights while she shouted the countdown along with the rest of the crowd.

'Ten, nine, eight, seven, six, five, four, three, two, one!'

The team lighting the display moved around in the semi darkness like scene shifters on a stage, deftly lighting touchpapers and disappearing, making the sequence of catherine wheels and roman candles appear to ignite spontaneously. Explosions of whizzing glowworms hatched above them, rockets soared up into the night before fragmenting into fountains, bursting open, showering droplets of light. Hannah put her hand through the crook of Jacques's elbow and leaned against him as they all looked skyward, their faces bleached with intense light then dipped into the darkness over and over again.

This, thought Jacques, this second – with everyone simultaneously following the gorgeous light as it travels through the night sky; everyone saying 'Oooh' and 'Aaah' together, because there are no words that fit better, no better noises than those Oooh's and Aaah's. This acceptance of the moment, knowing how transient it is, that it exists only now and can be remembered only like the image blanched onto the retina of a closed eye – this is wonderful.

While they stood round the bonfire, feeling the intensity of its heat, watching the wood catch light and the wispy cinders floating up from the heart of the fire, Jacques made a decision.

After they'd returned home and got Jo to bed, he poured brandy into two bulbous glasses.

'I want you to promise me something,' he said to Hannah, passing her a glass.

'Sounds serious. What?'

She took the glass from him and swilled it round, cupping her hand beneath it to warm the brandy.

'If I die before you, I want you to organise for my ashes to be put in a firework.'

Hannah stared at him. 'You're joking, right?'

Jacques shook his head as he studied her face. 'No, I'm very serious.'

'Why?'

'It's what I want. It's how I want to be remembered by you and Jo.'

'Rocketing into the sky?'

'Yes. Going away in a second, disappearing in a ritual that you can enjoy, remember, and move on.'

Hannah looked into her glass, lifted it to her nose, smelling the pungent sweetness.

'Will you promise?'

'God, Jacques, there's no hurry, is there?'

Jacques smiled and shook his head again, kneeling in front of her and resting his arms on her thighs. 'No, no hurry at all, but I just know it's what I want, and I want to make sure you know what my wishes are.'

'What makes you think you'll die before me, anyway?'

'Nothing. But if I do . . .'

Hannah sipped the brandy. It warmed her throat. She could track it like a radar device as it travelled down into her stomach.

'I don't want to think about you dying, Jacques.'

'So promise me this, and then you can stop thinking about it,' he said, stroking her thighs, 'and we can get on with living.'

63

Brockwell

'I love being in the park after dark,' Alison said. She and Sam followed the crowds heading for the flat stretch of land between the lido and the café, where the firework display was each year. 'It feels so different. So illicit. It's like underage drinking, or smoking at school; the whole point is you're not supposed to.'

'I know. Like when you could legitimately spend the night together. I used to dream of what that would feel like. Nothing's ever as good when you can have it.' They passed a couple of guys selling fluorescent cords. 'Hey, the studio's having a party next Saturday. Dead pop stars.'

'Better than vicars and tarts, I guess. Who are you going as?'

'Haven't decided yet. I've a few ideas. The trick with fancy dress is to find a costume that's not only clever but also makes you look fantastic.'

'Can I invite Bill? I haven't seen him since Gatwick. I mean, he probably won't want to – you know what he's like – but I'd like to give him the option, if that's OK with you?'

'Sure. If he can handle it, I can.'

'OK, thanks. He was brilliant in Spain, Sam.'

'Was he? How?'

'Oh, just really supportive and sensitive and funny. Jo's besotted with him.'

Sam kicked a conker along the path. It bounced off the end of her boot and rolled onto the muddy grass.

'Well, anyway, there'll be enough people to cope with having an ex or two among them.' A rocket flew into the sky ahead of them, whistling as it ascended, followed by half a dozen more, and a cheer went up from the crowd 'Look, they've started without us.'

The abundance of the Brockwell Park display was always a good indicator of the state of Lambeth's funds. As the sky lit up in front of them, Alison couldn't help but notice the opulence of other, distant displays in neighbouring boroughs. Their wealthier cousins in Dulwich and Wandsworth were being treated to bigger, fancier, more sustained extravaganzas, which billowed silver and pink and green on the horizon. She felt cross with herself for not being able to focus entirely on the fireworks in front of her. It made her remember when she was little, being so occupied with what Hannah's present was that she missed out on the excitement of opening her own. She hated the idea that she might still be like that.

After the display, they made their way to the funfair. They walked around, ignoring invitations to throw balls, hook ducks or toss hoops.

Alison yawned. 'I don't think I'm in the right mood for a funfair.'

'Do you fancy going for a pint?' Sam asked.

Alison thought for a minute. 'Not really, no. I think I'm still done in from Spain. I fancy going home, having a bath and getting an early night.'

'Sure?'

'Yep, I'm sure.'

'OK. I'll walk back with you.'

When they reached the Hobgoblin, Alison gave Sam a kiss, and turned to cross the road.

'You're sure you're OK about me inviting Bill?' she asked.

The traffic lights turned to red and the cars slowed to a stop.

'I've already said, yes, I'm fine with it. But tell him the dressing-up bit isn't optional. If he turns up in mufti, he'll have Franco to deal with, so if he doesn't want to be forced into some Leigh Bowery creation, he has been warned.'

'OK, I'll tell him.'

64

Dead Pop Stars

The flash hit Alison as she arrived at the studios.

'Gotcha!' a man said, and when her eyes recovered from the assault she saw the photograph slipping out of the Polaroid camera. He tugged it loose, waving it in one hand as it developed. He looked at the image and then at her.

'Nice costume. Janis? Great. Come in.'

The double doors had been transformed to look like the pearly gates of heaven, all white and gold, with a painted surround of clouds and harp-playing cherubs. The man with the camera added Alison's photo to the ones already fixed to the wall. He was dressed in jeans and a black T-shirt, and he had a thick rope noose slung round his neck.

'Thanks,' she said, stepping inside. 'Ian Curtis?'

He looked down at his noose, twiddling the end of the rope. 'Yeah. I know it's a bit of a cop-out, but I didn't have much time. Only heard about it today.'

Inside, the corridor was decked out like a star's dressing room, with a row of mirrors surrounded by coloured light bulbs. All the ground floor studios were open, and music spilled from them as people milled in and out. Until now, Alison had only seen Sam's space. She'd been aware of the other artists, when she'd visited Sam, through their banging and sawing, their radios, and the smells of turpentine and sawdust. Although curious, she made her way towards the staircase to find Sam and to get a drink first. She glanced at her reflection in one of the mirrors, momentarily surprised to see her mane of frizzy hair, her eyes edged black with kohl. A man dressed as Buddy Holly in a sharp suit and glasses leaned against the wall, talking to a woman in a nun's habit. She had a cardboard cut-out guitar slung across her very round belly. They smiled when Alison squeezed through between them. The woman said, 'Janis; cool.' Alison smiled back politely.

The staircase had been draped in red velvet, festooned with crucifixes and illuminated with strings of tiny white lights. Alison reached the top, and tried to place the music coming from Sam's. It came to her as she entered the room: 'Love Will Tear Us Apart'.

Sam screamed when she saw her, and ran across to give her a hug. 'Marc! My first true love! Al, that's brilliant!'

Alison hugged her back. 'Thank you. Two people have called me Janis in the past five minutes.'

'Ah, pay no attention. I can tell; you look just like the poster I had over my bed and used to kiss every night. Your hair looks fantastic,' she said, touching a corkscrewed tress. 'Have you got a drink?'

'Not yet. Here, where should I stash these?' She offered Sam a carrier bag of cans, and took a step back. 'My God. Do a twirl.'

Sam wore black bondage trousers, a mini-kilt, a ripped T-shirt held together with safety pins, and a heavily studded black leather collar. On her slim neck, even the collar looked like a pretty choker. Her hair was gelled into blond spikes, and safety pins dangled from one of her ears. The delicate nose stud she normally wore was replaced with a silver sleeper attached to a chain that looped to a ring in her other ear.

"I told you I wasn't going to do authentic.'

'And you weren't lying. Technically, it's cheating.'

'Bollocks to that.'

'At least you've got the language to a T.'

'Come and have a tequila.'

A trestle table covered in black plastic and sprinkled with silver stars stretched along the far end of the studio. Bottles and glasses were lined up at one end, and plates of food were spread out at the other.

Sam poured tequila into two plastic cups and passed one to Alison. 'Cheers.'

They tipped back their heads, drinking them down in one.

'Everyone's gone to such an effort,' Alison said, taking in the room. 'There's a very pregnant nun downstairs.'

'Ah, that'll be Monica; she's one of mine.' Sam added Alison's beers to a plastic bin filled with ice and water. 'I photographed her first pregnancy and she's booked me to do this one next week. She's cutting it fine, if you ask me.'

'So who's she come as?'

'Don't you remember the Singing Nun? That Belgian one-hit wonder? I didn't imagine she'd take up the invitation, but her partner's at home babysitting while she has one last party. For her first portrait she smeared her stomach with chocolate; you must have seen it? She wants something raunchier this time, apparently.'

'Maybe in the nun's habit?'

'Hmm, possibly. Hang on, Al, I need to say hi to someone.'

Sam made her way over to the door, where she greeted the new arrivals. Alison opened a can of beer, looking around the studio. Sam had pinned her prints on the walls, large black-and-white close-ups; cropped details that kept the identities of the bellies a mystery. They looked impressive all together like that, prehistoric and epic. It was strange thinking of all those stomachs being flat once more; their lodgers now independent people with names and nappies, teeth and hair. Her eye returned to the door just as Bill arrived, and she waved to him. He saw her and came over, and Alison laughed when she got a closer look. His hair was sculpted into a quiff, and he'd attached sideburns along his jaw. He was wearing a white suit, the wide collar trimmed with rhinestone, and a gold medallion hung from his neck on a thick chain.

'You look amazing!' she said, kissing one of the sideburns.

'U-huh-huh. What d'you think?'

'I think you ain't nuthin but a hound dog.'

'Aw, don't be cruel.'

'OK, let's stop that before it starts. Where *did* you get the suit?'

'What the Butler Wore, Lower Marsh Street. I saw it and it spoke to me.'

He put his beers on the table, opened one and drank from the can.

'What did it say?' Alison asked.

'What did what say?'

'The suit, duh?'

'Oh. It said, "Buy me, Bill," and I did. Wasn't cheap, either.'

'Ah, but you can't put a price on quality like that.'

'No.'

Bill looked around, swaying slightly. The room was filling up now, and Alison watched as he casually scoured the crowd for Sam. She could tell when he spotted her, because his expression changed.

'She looks gorgeous, doesn't she?' she said. Bill nodded, not taking his eyes off her. He hadn't so much as commented on her outfit, Alison thought, which wasn't like him at all, but she forgave him. 'Oh, while I remember, I spoke to Hannah earlier,' she said. 'Jo asked her to say we're invited to her sponsored swim. By "we", I take it she means you. You've really got yourself a fan there.'

Bill smiled. 'When is it?'

'Next Sunday. You really don't have to come – you've done quite enough for us lot – but I did promise Jo I'd pass on the message.' Bill was only half listening to her, she could tell. She looked across the room. Sam had her back to them. She was with a guy who looked like Freddy Mercury, laughing at something he was saying. Alison touched Bill's arm. 'Do you want to have a wander? Come and be nosy with me.'

Bill put down his empty can and picked up a fresh one.

'OK, lead on,' he said, snapping back the ring pull, taking a mouthful of the foam that fizzed out, and following her through the crowd.

Downstairs was heaving with the post-pub arrivals. The air smelled of damp clothes and mothballs mixed with smoke and perfume. Alison heard some cheesy Hawaiian music, and poked her head round the door of the studio it was coming from. Lengths of bamboo were fixed to the walls, and fake windows were filled with Pacific Island vistas of blue surf and palm trees. Someone had carved three giant masks out of polystyrene and suspended them from the ceiling, each pair of eyes housing spotlights that spun round, pouring pools of green and blue light onto the crowded dance floor. Candles in glasses flickered on window ledges. Paper garlands hung from either side of a raised stage area, where a guy in tartan was in charge of the sound system. A woman dressed in a leopardskin bikini top and grass skirt was setting up what appeared to be poles for limbo dancing.

'It's the House of Bamboo,' Alison said to Bill, who was leaning over her shoulder.

'Hula hula,' he said, following her in, picking up a paper garland and swirling it round his head.

Alison realised Bill was much drunker than she was. He never normally danced at parties, but here he was, pushing his way through the crowd, thrusting his hips and swinging the garland around in the air. Alison looked on. She wasn't drunk enough to feel that uninhibited, not that Bill looked like he needed a partner. She thought she recognised some people, but it was hard to be sure with the costumes. There was a very slim man she thought she might know. He was dressed in a maxi skirt and a blouse with a Peter Pan collar, and she guessed he'd come as Karen Carpenter. She saw a John Lennon and at least two other guys with nooses. Looking to the centre of the room, she spotted Bill's white sleeve above the crowd, still spinning the garland. He appeared to be chatting to someone as he danced, but Alison couldn't make out who. The Betty Page woman started inviting people up onto the stage. The DJ put on some calypso, and within seconds people were filing into a line, hitching up skirts, and edging under the pole.

'What's happening?' Sam shouted in Alison's ear, handing her a fresh beer.

'Limbo dancing, look,' she replied. 'It's so un-English!' They both stared at the bizarre parade.

'No, look, it is English; they're queuing,' Sam said. 'Is that Mamma Cass, d'you think?'

'Possibly. Surely she won't get under there?'

They watched the woman gather up her caftan. She knelt down and crawled under. People laughed and cheered her anyway.

'And here comes Jimmy Hendrix,' Sam said, like a sports commentator.

The tall man with a large Afro and a bead necklace spread his legs apart, stretched out his arms and lowered his back, slowly making his way beneath the pole. As he made it out the other side, the crowd whistled and cheered, 'Yes! Go, Jimmy!'

Alison and Sam hadn't spotted who was behind him.

'Good lord, it's Bill!' Sam said.

The crowd began to cheer as Bill buttoned his jacket, shook his shoulders, pulled up his sleeves and prepared to lower himself down. Someone shouted, 'Go for it, Elvis!' He inched his way under. 'Watch your quiff!' someone else shouted. The crowd laughed, and then applauded him. Sam and Alison whistled and stamped their feet with the rest of the onlookers as he stood up and righted himself, jumping down from the stage and landing among the crowd.

'I thought he was going to stage-dive for one scary second,' Alison said, laughing.

She turned to Sam, who was shaking her head in disbelief. She was still clapping when he walked over to join them.

'My God, Bill, wonders never cease! Great costume, by the way.'

'I thank you,' Bill replied, bowing drunkenly. 'I need a drink. Any more for any more?' he asked, heading out of the door.

'Yeah, more beer, please,' Alison said. 'Didn't you see Bill when he arrived?' she asked.

'No. He looks . . . Well, he doesn't look like Bill, that's for sure.'

'Ah, the man has hidden depths.'

'Sam?' someone shouted from the door. 'Sam, that woman was asking for you.'

It was the Buddy Holly guy. He grabbed Sam by the arm.

'What woman?' she asked.

'The nun.'

'Who, Monica?'

'Yeah, the pregnant woman. She thinks she's started.'

'Oh, fucking hell. Fuck, fuck, fuck. Where is she?'

'Outside, getting some air, but she's shouting for you.'

'Shit, just my luck. Thank you, God.'

'Is there anything I can do?' Alison asked

'Yeah, find someone to help – anyone. I'll be outside.'

The limbo dancing had been replaced by karaoke, and Alison grabbed the mike to ask if there was a doctor in the house. After the initial laughter, it turned out they were in luck.

In what had originally been designated the chill-out room, Monica leaned against a life model's chaise longue, habit akimbo, and shouted obscenities. Ably assisted by Dusty Springfield, a midwife, and John Denver, a registered nurse, she pushed out a baby girl to the strains of a karaoke rendition of 'Young at Heart'.

'Fairy tales can come true./It can happen to you . . .'

65

Conkers

'Don't you mind at all?' Alison asked, sipping from her mug of steaming tea as they waited for their fry-ups.

'No. I'm delighted.'

Sam played with the stainless-steel sugar bowl, digging the teaspoon in, raising it and letting the white grains pour down. Behind her, the neon words glowed in reverse: 'espresso', 'cappuccino'. Drizzle splashed against the café windows, and a red bus moved slowly from left to right, blocking the view of the street. She was still wearing the remnants of her costume under her leather jacket, although she'd removed the chains and safety pins from her face. Alison was still in her glad rags, too, but they felt less glad and more rags.

The party had kept going till dawn. It had been a perfect time for a party; a final flourish before the nights drew in and the hibernating winter days began. But Alison had felt hopelessly sober.

After the tail lights of the ambulance had turned onto the street at the end of the track she'd walked back through the pearly gates and into the smoky corridor. There was nobody in Sam's studio; Sam had disappeared with someone after she'd dispatched Monica. The ghetto blaster had been turned off, although she could still hear the party going on downstairs. Searching among the empty cans and paper plates with cigarette butts stubbed out in the leftovers, she found a full bottle of wine. After she'd found a plastic cup and poured herself a drink, she looked at Sam's prints again. All those bellies throbbing with life that Sam had made quiet and smooth; all that Technicolor wide-screen surround-sound she'd tastefully rendered in monochrome. Alison could still see Monica squatting low, stretched beyond feasibility, the primordial noises emanating from her as the head of her baby, black hair matted in blood, squeezed out of her; slippery and purple and miraculous. Sam's photos gave no hint of the visceral messiness of it all. Alison made her way down the staircase; the red velvet and lights all looking elaborately pointless after the rush of searing flesh, the blood and mucus.

As she queued for the toilet, a woman in a white halter-neck dress pushed past. She was stunning. Alison noted the slim waist, the golden tan, the pretty ankles in high-heeled sandals, and the platinum-blond hair that looked fake but somehow right. And that was when she saw Bill standing in the corridor just ahead of her. She was relieved to see him, and was about to wave when she realised he was waiting for the woman in white. A jacket was draped over his arm and he held it out for her, kissing the back of her neck as she shrugged it on. Alison watched them walk towards the door, Bill swaying slightly, his arm round her shoulders to steady himself as they left the party. Alison saw the back of Bill's jacket: a heart embroidered in sequins. It read 'Love Me Tender'.

'You waiting to use it?' a woman behind her asked.

'Oh, sorry, yes. Thanks,' she said, locking the door behind her, feeling suddenly cold.

'Guess who's pulled?'

Alison had found Sam on the edge of the dance floor, laughing as a crowd moved in formation to some old Motown tune; a hybrid disco-cum-line-dance.

'Bill,' she replied.

'How did you know that?'

Sam shrugged. The dancers all shook their right hands, waggling their index fingers as if telling off an invisible person. They dipped simultaneously and turned ninety degrees. Sam slipped in next to the Freddy Mercury guy. He smiled at her as she fell into the routine.

When the booze supply dried up and the dance floor thinned out, people left in search of night buses and minicabs. Sam and Alison walked around West Norwood cemetery, climbing in by the library through a gap in the fence, and watching the sky grow pale above the stone angels and draped urns. The squirrels scampered over graves, collecting the fresh conkers that had fallen free of their casings and revealed themselves, shiny and polished as a Brownie's shoes.

Sitting on a bench that looked out over a derelict factory, Alison nibbled a blackberry, its sharpness waking her taste buds.

'How can you eat that?' Sam asked

'What's wrong with it?'

'Well, just think what it's been growing from.'

The tangle of blackberry runners clambered over the jumble of old headstones, obliterating inscriptions; crept up crosses, decorating them with the black fruit, much of it now dried up and past its best. There was something Beth used to say: if you don't eat blackberries before September, the devil will take them.

Alison nibbled another. 'The ground is fecund,' she said. 'I love that word. It's a perfect cycle. The dead live on as blackberries.'

'Jesus, spare me. Next thing you'll be breaking into "Where Have All the Flowers Gone?". I reckon I've had my fill of fecundity for one night.'

'I can't get the image of Monica out of my head. It was so . . . shocking.'

'I'm shocked, all right; I'm a couple of hundred down.'

They left the cemetery, passing a skip full of decomposing

wreaths. Fragments of words fashioned out of Oasis and ribbons poked through the dying flowers, spelling parts of loved ones' names like a cryptic crossword. It started to rain as they walked out through the main gates, which had just been unlocked, and onto the high street, peering into the shop windows. The estate agents displayed photographs of properties in little frames like they were artworks. Pastel flowers cascaded from a plinth in the window of the funeral directors.

The fry-up was just what they needed and they ate in silence, mopping up the baked beans, fried eggs and grilled tomatoes with the slices of white toast, then ordering cappuccinos. Sam pulled some Polaroids from her jacket. She flicked though them.

'Where did you get these?' Alison asked.

'Off the display. This one of you's quite good.'

Alison hardly recognised herself, flash-bleached and feather-framed. 'They were right: I do look like Janis.'

She glanced at the others as Sam passed them across the table, then picked one up. The white dress, white-blond hair, generous lips. She held the Polaroid by its edges, studying the face for clues.

'She's so young, and he can't even have known her.'

Sam let out a laugh. 'You can be funny sometimes.' Lighting a cigarette, she let the match burn down its length before dropping it into the glass ashtray. She exhaled a plume of smoke, leaned across and touched Alison's arm. 'Like you said before, you just can't guarantee what's round the corner.'

66

Steradent

Kim unhooked the towelling dressing gown from the back of the bedroom door and slipped it on, noticing its unfamiliar smell. In the hall, she tried to remember which door was the bathroom. After she'd peed, she looked at her reflection in the bathroom mirror. Her eyes were smudged black with last night's mascara. She tiptoed into the kitchen and turned on the tap until it ran cold. She found a glass in one cupboard and a packet of Solpadeine on a shelf. She dropped the two white discs into the glass of water. Her granddad used to have a glass like that for his teeth, she remembered, and round cakes of Steradent to soak them with. They'd been such an alarming sight the first time she came across them, as a little girl when she'd stayed overnight. So regular and big and pink; so not in the right place.

Outside, it was raining a fine drizzle. London suited drizzle, she thought, watching the grey pods of the Eye move slowly in a grey sky as she drank the fizzing water. A sediment of white remained in the glass like a tidemark. She placed the glass in the sink. Back in the bedroom, he was still sleeping soundly, his breathing heavy, his arm stretched across the empty space where she'd been. Kim picked her clothes from the floor, closed the door behind her and padded across the hall.

While she waited for the bath to fill, she explored the rest of the flat. As well as the kitchen, bedroom and living room, there was a small room that she took to be his office. Some photographs hung above the blue computer. She walked over to see if she could recognise him in any of them, but wasn't sure she would even if he was. The wall opposite was lined with bookshelves, and Kim ran her finger along the spines, catching random words until something grabbed her attention. She pulled it out and took it through to the bathroom. It was a hardbound catalogue of photographs. The picture on the cover intrigued her. She loved it immediately, but she didn't know why, because basically it wasn't of anything. It looked like the kind of photo you take accidentally when you're trying to suss out how the camera works, and when you get the set back from the chemist's, you chuck it. Like someone's shoe and a stretch of pavement, or half of a head, the eye red from the flash. This one was of a naked light bulb on a red gloss ceiling and the top edge of two walls. The frame of a door was just in shot on one wall, and on the other was a corner of that shitty poster, the one of all the astrological signs illustrated as sexual positions – Sagittarius doing it doggy; Cancer sixty-nine. The *Kama Sutra* done seventies-style. Just a tiny corner of it, though; exactly enough to be able to recognise it and go, 'Oh, it's that crappy poster.' A light bulb, some cables, red ceiling, red walls, poster, nothing. But, for some reason, great nothing.

The pages of the book still smelled new and Kim closed her eyes, pressing her nose into the pages, trying to find the right word. It was ink and oil and cereal packet and brown, but the exact word failed her. She lowered herself into the bath. Propping the book up on the toilet, she turned the pages at random, letting the images transport her to this strange place of axes on grilles, insides of ovens, sterile rooms and old men with guns. Then she lay back, looking up at the ceiling, and wondered what she was doing lying in the bath of a man she didn't know, somewhere in Waterloo.

It had been a mad night; the first party she'd been to since getting back to England, and a memorable one. God, hadn't there been an ambulance there at one point? And limbo dancing? That was what she missed about not going with a really good mate: there was no one to fill in the drunken blanks. She'd not even phoned Abi since she got back; too much had happened.

She'd gone with the crowd from the salon. She'd called in there earlier in the week to see whether there was any chance of picking up her apprenticeship where she'd left off. One of the stylists had a friend who was an artist. It was his studios' party, and they were all invited. They'd met at a pub beforehand, all done up in their costumes. Kim had gone as Marilyn Monroe. She didn't believe she had the bottle, but she'd borrowed one of the practice wigs from the salon and really tarted herself up; found a girly white dress with a full skirt – like the one Marilyn had worn standing over the air vent. It had felt amazing; the wig had just taken over, making her feel like someone else.

She picked up the clear bar of Pears soap and started to wash. They were already pretty drunk when they got the cab there, all the way out to West Norwood, the back of beyond. She remembered talking with this guy. They'd argued about whether Marilyn could be called a pop star, and she'd tried to remember all the words to 'Diamonds Are a Girl's Best Friend'. At some point, she'd realised that she couldn't find any of her crowd. She'd panicked, looking in all the rooms, wondering how she was going to get home. Then she stopped worrying and started to enjoy herself. She remembered dancing with him. The next thing she could recall was being in one of the studios with him, in the dark, lying on a lumpy velvet couch. Then getting a minicab, both hardly able to wait till they got inside his flat. He'd been really surprised when she'd pulled off the wig, but he'd started touching her head, then licking it. She sank under the water again to rinse the suds. Yes, she thought, it was good to be back in London.

Putting the stale, smoky clothes on, Kim fastened her jacket across the front of her dress, stuffed the wig in her bag, checked she had everything, and let herself out. She closed the door behind her, and breathed in the damp London air.

67

Silk, Satin, Muslin, Rags

The Eggleston catalogue lay open on his desk. Bill looked at the photograph. The old black man lay in the open casket; immaculately dressed in white shirt, black suit, black tie and white gloves. The casket was dripping white silk, or maybe it was satin; Bill didn't know what the difference was.

At school, when they had prunes for pudding, the girls used to chant a rhyme, 'Silk, satin, muslin, rags'. It was meant to predict what their wedding dress would be made of when they married their tinker, tailor, soldier, sailor, rich man, poor man, beggarman or thief. Considering there were four choices of fabric and eight of suitor, he'd never understood why it always surprised them which material corresponded to which man. It was so irrational: tinker and rich man would always be silk. But no one seemed to want to be told this, he remembered; they preferred to cling to the element of surprise, maybe as an incentive to eat the disgusting prunes.

Whether silk or satin, the casket was spectacular. The lid was lined with intricately pleated material ruched and tucked with precision, like an egg box for a thousand tiny eggs. The dead man's gloved hands were tucked under a quilt of shiny white, and a pure white pillow supported his head, cushioning the impeccable man against any knocks on his way to eternity. The casket reminded Bill of a jewellery box. Or a vagina. That was it, he thought; the man looked as if he was couched inside the folds of a giant white vagina, being born again.

He tried to work out whether there was any significance in her leaving this book out and open on this page, because he was certain it had been on the shelf when he left the flat yesterday. He returned to the kitchen, where the kettle was just coming to the boil, and poured water onto the coffee. The glass in the sink and the torn Solpadeine paper on the side were the only other clues she'd left, apart from the wet towel hung over the rail in the bathroom. There was no note, no phone number, no message in lipstick on the bathroom mirror – not that he'd really expected that, but he'd looked anyway. The only proof that he'd not imagined the whole event was the aching physical exhaustion he felt through to his kidneys, and the spent condoms, looking like he felt, and explaining the exhaustion.

The party certainly hadn't turned out the way he'd imagined, Bill thought as he drank his coffee, although what he'd imagined was pretty abstract. He'd been determined that if he was to go at all, it had to be with conviction. What he'd meant by that, apart from with half a bottle of cheap Spanish gin inside him, was unclear. Mainly, he'd wanted to prove something to himself, with Sam as his witness. Prove his existence. Prove he was three-dimensional, capable of living and breathing. A three-dimensional, living, breathing Elvis. He cringed as he remembered the Elvis bit. Christ, unless he was very much mistaken, he'd limbo danced. On a stage. Or was he making that bit up? He'd phone Alison in a while and sound her out. He wondered if Alison had seen him with Kim (that was her name, wasn't it?) and if Sam had. He wasn't sure whether he hoped they had, or not.

He tried to remember Kim. He'd been pretty drunk, but so must she have been. As he drained his cup, he suddenly recalled her shaved head. He'd forgotten that. When he tried to picture her, it was with the hair she'd had when he'd first seen her, but now he had to revise his memory. For some reason, the thought of her shaved head excited him. He closed his eyes and tried to coax back some more substantial details, but she reappeared in fragments, in little sound bites. Try as he might, he couldn't piece them together and make her whole. Try as he might, someone else kept getting in the way.

68

Dalí

'When did we agree to have this Dalí crap foisted on us?' Bill asked as they made their way past a cumbersome bronze of a female torso sliced in two, and a spindly-legged elephant with a pyramid on its back. 'It's so adolescent. I mean, we all have to go through our Dalí and Escher phases, but please God, we grow out of it.'

He and Alison were on the South Bank, picking their way through the crowds and the ubiquitous souvenir industry that had grown around the Eye. Ticket agents, hot-dog stands and, most recently, young men who squatted on the floor, fashioning words out of wire. Alison was at a loss why anyone would want to buy these, but guessed someone must. A man wearing a sandwich board depicting a red melting clock offered Bill a leaflet advertising the Dalí Museum. Bill glowered at him, and Alison giggled.

'Don't take it so personally. Look, the tide's out. Let's get to the other side of the Festival Hall; we can go down to the beach.'

They struggled through the bottleneck caused by the building work around Hungerford Bridge, and slipped through the gate that led down to the beach. It wasn't a real beach – the sand had been pumped in for the Festival of Britain half a century ago – but it always surprised Alison how white it still was under the Thames, and how frequently new bits of history washed up at their feet. The river continued to churn up the old clay pipes and worn glass from litter louts of centuries past. Few people came down here, which Alison could never understand. She was glad of it, though, because she and Bill had the patch all to themselves.

'So what time did you leave the party?' Bill asked.

'Oh, late. Very late. Later than you.'

Bill gave her a sideways look; she was grinning. 'You saw me leave?'

'Oh yes. And I saw who with.'

'I can't remember a whole lot about it. I was shitfaced by the time I arrived.'

'You don't say. She looked like a nice girl.'

'Yeah, I suppose she was. To be honest, it's all a bit vague.'

'Have you seen her since?'

'Are you kidding? Of course not.'

'Why "of course"?'

Bill made arcs in the sand with his shoe. 'Did I make a complete prick of myself?'

'When?'

'At the party.'

'No, 'course not. You were really funny. Anyway, do you honestly imagine everyone was watching you? Don't be so vain.'

'You sure I wasn't?'

'What?'

'A prick.'

'Shut up.'

69

Chicken Tiles

'Marc Bolan!' Hannah said as they walked along the Brighton promenade.

Hannah and Jo had met Alison at the station, and they made their way towards the pier, Jo on her scooter ahead of them.

'Who did Bill go as?'

'Elvis. You should have seen him, Hannah; he looked fantastic.'

'Which era Elvis?'

'Oh, I'd say early seventies. When did he do that version of "Are You Lonesome Tonight", and lose the plot?'

'Hmm, more mid, I think.'

'Well, sometime about then.'

'Do you remember where you were when Elvis died?'

'Yep. Where I was, what I was eating, what I was wearing, every last detail. And Marvin Gaye, and Bob Marley, of course.'

'Of course.'

'But Marc was my first big one. I was in the kitchen, making breakfast. I put the radio on and they announced it.' Alison could still see the details of the kitchen like a freeze-frame. The tiles that if you squinted had a pattern of chickens on them; the electric kettle with the red kick-switch, the beige toaster and the sliced white bread and the smell of toast. 'He was my first love,' she said.

'Ah, mine was Pete Duel. We were in the car on the M1 with Mum when we heard, do you remember? He'd shot himself.'

'Pete Duel was very cute. How did it go, the beginning of *Alias Smith and Jones?*'

'Oh, hang on. "Hannibal Hayes and Kid Curry, the two most successful outlaws in the history of the West. 'There's one thing we've got to get,"' Ben Murphy says. '"What's that?"' Duel asks.'

'"Out of this county!"' Alison finished, laughing.

'How is it I have total recall of that, but I can't remember what I went to Asda for until I'm home again?'

'I don't know. Don't you make shopping lists? I keep getting trolleys at Tesco's with people's old ones still attached; you know those trolleys, with the clipboard you can attach your list to?'

'No, but maybe I should. Shopping lists are about the only lists I don't make, and they'd actually be useful.'

'I've started to collect them. They read like little poems: "Greens, lemons, pots, loo rolls."'

'You are odd, Alison.'

'Well, it's not harming anybody, is it?'

'True. They can't touch you for it. Jo!' she shouted. 'Don't go so far ahead, please.'

Jo turned round and waited for them to catch up, her hair spilling out from under her pink safety helmet.

'We always used to have our hair washed before *Smith and Jones*,' Alison said. 'Maybe it's like those memory men: you attach each thing you want to remember to a real thing, like a body part. Maybe we attached *Smith and Jones* to hair-washing.'

'Hmm, but then we'd only remember it when we washed our hair. I just wish I could learn languages as easily as I can remember David Essex lyrics. Total recall there, even bloody album tracks.'

'Do you remember those plants we used to have?' Alison asked. 'We were given one each. They were like balls of fern, and when you put them in a saucer of water they opened out.'

'Oh yes, I do. God. I kept mine for years. I used to discover it in my drawer all dead-looking, but after a couple of hours' soak it would spring back to life. It stayed with me through loads of moves,

266

used to turn up after I'd forgotten all about it. I wonder when I eventually lost it? Where did we get them, do you remember?'

'They were a present, I think.'

'Odd present.'

'Yeah, but nice.'

'You two are so slow,' Jo said, scootering back to them. 'Come on. I want to get the table by the fish tank.' She raced off again.

'Well, that's promising,' Hannah said. 'She wouldn't touch fish after we got Polly and Molly. Now she not only eats fish, she eats it in the presence of their relations. Since Spain she's not been half so picky. I think it was Bill's influence. She'd probably eat anything he ate. With the exception of flan.'

Alison smiled. 'He's got a way with the girls. Did Jo ever twig about the incredible expanding Molly the Second?'

'I don't think so. What a long time ago that seems.'

When they got to the pier, they passed through the noisy amusement arcade and out into the open, where the sea breeze carried away smells of hot dogs and candyfloss, and whipped their hair across their faces. Their feet clattered on the slatted wooden planks, the sea visible beneath, churning and grey.

'Look, Mum, Al!' Jo shouted.

'Where is she?' Alison said.

'Hello-o!' she shouted, and they saw her.

She was behind an old-fashioned seaside painting; the face cut out for people to pose through. Jo's head popped out above a mermaid's body. The scale was all wrong, but she still made a lovely mermaid, Alison thought.

Waiting for their fish and chips, Jo pulled out a sheet of paper.

'Look how many people are sponsoring me tomorrow, Al,' she said, passing her the sheet.

'My goodness. You're going to raise a fortune.'

267

'Look, that's what Bill wrote when we were in Spain. He's said he'll give me ten pence a width. That's better than some of the others; they've just said a pound, no matter how many widths I do.'

'Pah! Where's the incentive in that? It wouldn't matter if you did one width or a hundred.'

'I know,' Jo said, laughing. 'Al, why couldn't Bill come with you to see me swim?'

'Because he's busy, poppet. Oh, but he did give me something to give you,' she remembered, 'and he told me to tell you good luck.' She dug into her bag and pulled out a package wrapped in thick red paper embossed with gold flowers. 'Here,' she said, passing it to Jo, 'I've no idea what it is, but he said he saw it and thought of you. Well, he said he thought of us all, but that it was for you, whatever that means.'

Jo took it and carefully unwrapped a Russian doll.

'Oh wow!' she said.

She held the base and twisted the head, disconnecting the doll at its midriff and revealing a smaller but otherwise identical doll within. She set to work, pulling them apart until she reached the solid wooden doll at its core, not much larger than a thimble. When the waitress came over, she had to put down the plates between the seven generations of yellow-scarved women, red-patterned dresses covering their skittle-shaped bodies. Seven sturdy wooden women, mothers of mothers of mothers, daughters of daughters of daughters, presiding over the food.

Kaleidoscope

'Twenty-five widths! I'm impressed.'

Jo beamed. She unfolded the worn piece of paper with her list of sponsors and pored over it like an accountant. 'That means Bill owes me twenty-five ten pences. How much is that?'

'Oooh, let's see,' Alison said, buttering toast. 'Ten twenty-fives, that's two pounds fifty.'

'That's much more than a pound.'

'Sure is.'

Hannah gave Jo the cutlery. 'OK, little mermaid, can you lay the table, please, then go and shout to your dad to get a move on. Brunch is about to be served.'

Jacques had volunteered to lifeguard for the swim and was upstairs, showering off the chlorine. He'd ended up as a piggyback service, ferrying the less good swimmers back and forth to bump up their totals.

Jo knelt on her chair, her damp hair falling in thick tresses down her back. She placed knives and forks in front of her and in front of the places to either side, and then leaned over to reach the other end of the table. She overstretched, and the knife clattered onto the floor.

'Knife on the floor, man at the door,' Hannah and Alison said in unison.

'Mmmm, that smells good.' Jacques said, rubbing his hands together. 'What? What's so funny?' he asked, looking at each of them in turn as they burst out laughing.

*   *   *

Before Alison caught the train home that afternoon, Hannah drove them all to the sea front. A flock of starlings swarmed in formation around the charred remains of the West Pier, creating complicated patterns in the chill November sky, separating and regrouping like beads in a kaleidoscope.

'How do they do that?' Alison asked. 'They're so precise. How do they know what to do?'

'I don't know. And then the next generation does the same thing, year after year. Maybe it's some genetic code.'

They crunched down the beach, Jacques and Jo running ahead. It was colder nearer the sea, and Alison pushed her hands deep into her pockets.

'Hannah, do you know if we were fed on demand?'

'You were, I wasn't. Mum tried to please her midwife with me, but you got all the Dr Spock wisdom. You got the benefit of my experience.'

'God, how come you know that?'

'I asked Mum. We talked about it when I had Jo.' Hannah looked over to Jo and Jacques, who were throwing pebbles into the waves. 'Of course, you can tell right away that she was fed on demand,' Hannah said. 'What Jo wants, Jo gets.'

Alison smiled. 'You'd never accuse her of being spoilt, though. Just, well, headstrong, I guess.'

'Don't say anything to her yet,' Hannah said, 'but we're thinking about getting a dog.'

'Oh?'

'Well, we've been looking into it, at any rate. We got this chart in a magazine, you wouldn't believe. It was so, I don't know, blunt. It lists all the different breeds according to size – how much walking they require, how much they bark, their average life expectancy. It was like reading a *Which?* report on what brand of washing machine to buy.'

'But you're thinking about it?'

'Yes. Jo would love one, and Jacques's into it, and I'm coming round to the idea. Well, you know I've always loved dogs. It would be a statement, like saying, we're here for a while; we're not going anywhere anytime soon.' She looked out to sea. 'I like the idea of that.'

Alison squatted down and picked up a smooth white pebble. 'Seeing Monica give birth . . .' she said, turning the stone in her hand.

'The Singing Nun?'

'Yes. It was so powerful, Hannah; it made me realise how brave you have to be.'

'To have kids?'

'Not just the birth, the whole thing. You have to leap into it; to trust that all will be well. Do you remember Mum saying, "Just remember, no one else wants an accident," when she was trying to persuade me to learn to drive?'

'Ha! I wish that was true.'

'But isn't that what you have to believe?'

'No. You have to learn to drive defensively, to anticipate any nutter who might be coming the other way.'

Strains of music caught on a breeze; the sentimental sound of a barrel organ reaching them, floating over the beach and mixing with the rasping of waves over pebbles. It came from a carousel up by the boardwalk. Alison recognised the tune.

'Oh, Mum loved this,' she said.

They stopped talking to listen. It ambled on, the plaintive song translated into something jolly by the insistent rinky-dink of the mechanical tempo.

Someone who'll watch over me . . .

Jo, Jacques, Hannah and Alison watched the merry-go-round horses moving by, up and down with a steady, majestic pace; so out of step with the modern world, fixed in time as they were fixed on their axles.

'I'm surprised this is still open. They pack it away for winter,' Hannah said.

Parents waved as their children floated past, clinging to the reins of their painted steeds. 'It folds up like a musical box, like that one they had at the beginning of *Camberwick Green*.'

When they slowed to a graceful halt, the riders clambered down and Jacques helped Jo onto the platform.

'Which one would you like?' he asked.

Jo had already decided.

'The one with the bow in her mane,' she said, pushing between the stationary horses, patting their fetlocks as she made her way to her chosen one.

Jacques helped her up, and then mounted the one next to hers, his knees bent like a jockey's. The music cranked up to speed and the carousel began to rotate. Hannah and Alison waved dutifully when Jo and Jacques bobbed past. Each horse had a name painted on its mane in old, elegant writing. Some had evidently been updated as a concession to time having passed. There was a Kylie next to a Gareth, and the ones Jo and Jacques rode were called Steven and Maureen. A couple of horses behind Jo's was one called Alison, and Alison felt a childish flutter of recognition, as if her name had been singled out at a school assembly. She smiled, looking to see what the horse next to hers was called.

'Ha ha, nice one, Mum,' she thought, reading the name inscribed on its mane.

It was as ludicrous as it was inevitable. 'Malcolm,' it read.

71

Frida

The studio walls were bare apart from a wide roll of white paper suspended from the ceiling and hanging down, creating a seamless backdrop. A spotlight was positioned at either side, the tangle of electric cables tucked out of sight. Sam's camera was set up in the centre of the studio on a tripod, facing a wooden chair in the centre of the empty space.

'You sure about this, Al?' Sam asked, frowning at the postcard Alison had given her.

'Absolutely positive.'

'OK. Let's do it.'

Alison had considered just about everything. She'd made lists. Heroes, heroines, legendary, mythical. Who? How? Why? She knew what she didn't want: not mermaids, not skaters or swimmers, Persephone or Artemis, Marc or Janis. Not in fancy dress, and not naked. Barefoot. Yes; barefoot. But what else? And then, on the train back from Brighton, she'd remembered the postcard.

She'd bought it at an exhibition years ago, and when she got home on Sunday she hunted through her shoeboxes of old pictures until she unearthed it. It was a painting of Frida Kahlo's called *Self-Portrait with Cropped Hair*. Kahlo was seated on a plain wooden chair, her long hair shorn and scattered in clumps around her. The man's suit she was wearing was far too large for her. It made her look abandoned as well as defiant. Like she'd cut off her nose to spite her face, as Beth would have said. Alison had flipped the card over and read the words on the reverse. Written in handwriting Alison didn't recognise, it was a translation of the Spanish inscription Kahlo had painted across the top of the picture: 'If you loved me, it was for my hair. Now that I have cut it off, you will no longer love me.' Attaching the postcard to the fridge door, she went to bed. That night she dreamed of Morning Glories.

Beth sits up as Alison puts a cup of tea on her bedside table, plumps her pillows and fetches a shawl to place around her shoulders.

'Good morning. How did you sleep?' Alison asks. She pulls open the curtains.

Outside in the garden, she can count seven Morning Glories on the vine that clambers up the tree by the window; seven fresh blooms the deepest, richest indigo, which have unfurled this morning. By midday, the edges of the petals will have become scorched pale, and by tonight they will have twisted shut, like seven closed umbrellas.

'Very well, thanks,' Beth says, sipping her tea. 'Slept right through. I had this dream, though; I dreamed you'd cut off your lovely hair.'

Alison sits on the edge of the bed, touches a loose strand of her hair which falls over her shoulder, and smiles.

'Well, thanks, Mum. That doesn't pressure me into keeping my hair long in the least.'

72

Tooth Fairy

Alison was on the phone to Hannah, who'd been reading her Jo's school curriculum.

'Listen to this: DT.'

'What's that?'

'Not sure. Design technology? "The children will work in small groups to create a model of a plague victim."'

'Fantastic! Has she started yet?'

'I think we'll hear about it when she does. Sweetheart, what's the matter?'

Alison could hear Jo wailing in the background. She kept quiet while Hannah transferred her attention.

'I've swallowed my tooth,' she heard Jo sob.

Alison listened in on the domestic scene that was taking place in real time, an hour's drive south, in a little house in Sussex. It was like an interactive radio play.

'Let me see . . . There's no blood . . . Oh my God, you have. It wasn't even loose. She has,' she added for Alison's benefit. Jo howled.

'Which one?' asked Alison

'Front bottom.'

'Front bottom?' said Alison, tittering.

Hannah chuckled. 'Here, talk to Ali.'

'Hi, Jo. How did that happen?'

Jo gulped for breath between sobs. 'I was eating my sa-a-andwich'

'What kind?'

'Cheese and pickle.'

'Well, that'll be it, then. Cheese and pickle sandwiches are the best for getting teeth out. They're famous for it.' Alison listened for Jo's reaction. Nothing. She tried again. 'Don't worry, Jo, the tooth fairy will still come.'

Jo wailed, 'No, she won't. I won't have anything to put under my pi-i-llow.'

'Of course she'll come – that's what tooth fairies do. They know. Even if you've lost it, or swallowed it, they still know; and they still leave something under your pillow. So don't you go worrying about that.'

Jo calmed down. Alison could hear her breathing heavily, weighing up the facts.

'Are you sure?'

'Absolutely. It happens all the time in their line of work. Now go and eat some more sandwich to make sure that tooth is nicely cushioned.'

Hannah came back on the phone. 'It wasn't even loose.'

'God, Hannah, a year ago you'd have been on your way to Casualty with her by now.'

'Yeah, well.'

They were both silent for a few seconds. It was a comfortable, sisterly silence which Alison realised she'd missed.

'I wonder how far down it's got?' she said.

'Oh, don't.'

'Gotta go. Bye, and don't forget to warn the tooth fairy, she's going to need her rubber gloves.'

'Ha ha. Bye.'

73

Barabarella's

It was one of those days that never quite make it to daylight; dim like a big room lit by a forty-watt bulb. The windows of Barbarella's were steamed up against the cold November. Capital Radio chirped through the speakers fitted into the white, polystyrene-tiled ceiling; 'I Love Your Smile' played as Alison sat on the beige plastic chair and watched the street. She had a table close to the door, and she kept her eyes on the people who walked past, on their way to and from Lower Marsh. She swilled the last of her coffee round the white cup, collecting the residue of froth and chocolate that clung to the edges, took a final mouthful and stood up to go and pay.

Back on the street, she wasn't sure what to do. A squat dog with a tail erect as a television aerial sniffed the plastic crates stacked outside the English Language School, cocked his leg and pissed on them before trotting into the market. A woman in a sari walked past, pushing a child in a buggy, another child following behind pulling a plastic tank by a length of string. Two Action Men sat in the tank, bumping their way along the pavement. Alison hadn't really got a plan, she'd just jumped on the 159 bus, pretending to herself that she didn't know where she was going, but unable to keep up the charade when she pressed the bell and jumped off. But it was too cold to hang around on the streets, and she didn't want to be spotted like this.

She walked towards the bus stop by the modern church on Kennington Road. The rain that had been threatening finally started to fall, and she fished in her bag for her umbrella. Standing outside the church, Alison read the poster fixed inside the window in the vestry: 'COME IN FOR A FAITH LIFT!' it proclaimed. Jesus, she thought. The rain fell harder. She felt like throwing a brick through the church's window with its complacent stained-glass evangelists.

Bill knew he was being illogical. He'd have to carry his shopping all the way back on the bus, and besides, there was an excellent market right outside his flat. He didn't know why he'd ended up here. He'd left his flat and taken a short cut under the bridge. When he reached the NCP car park, he saw a man and a young girl. She was maybe five and had white-blond hair down to her waist and the smallest pair of crutches Bill had ever seen. She hopped along on them, her right foot in plaster swinging like a pendulum, her hair bouncing with each hop forward, and Bill caught himself grinning. Walking through Archbishop's Park, he'd tried to work out why the sight of a young child on crutches had filled him with glee. Triumph over adversity, he concluded; it made him miss Alison.

The millennium path that ran parallel with Lambeth Palace Gardens had just been completed, and he read the plaques dedicated to famous Lambethans as he followed its course, feeling like a tourist in his own manor. Some he'd heard of, like John Tradescant, and Alfie the Town Crier, who was still doing the rounds; but others were news to him, like a man who'd bred leeches for the hospital, and the hundred-and-eight-year-old woman who'd been Queen of the Norwood gypsies. Reading their names Bill had felt a sense of belonging, an allegiance with Lambeth far stronger than his sense of being British or English. He'd walked out of the park, through the centuries-old walled passageway, and with his back to the Thames he ambled along the road. The smell of fresh pastries wafted from the bakery. He watched, drooling, as two men in overalls packed a van with croissants. That was when he'd jumped on a number 3 bus, thinking he'd drag Alison out to the Phoenix. He wasn't even sure if she was back from Brighton yet; and she didn't answer when he phoned. When it started to rain, he went to the Trinity for a lunchtime drink, settling himself in the corner with a pint of bitter and a bag of crisps, watching the other punters. It had been too depressing to hang around for a second pint, so he'd left, walking out along Trinity Gardens. The next thing he knew, he was in the startling light of Tesco's, feeling the avocados.

The bus finally arrived, and began its achingly slow progress back to Brixton. Alison cursed herself for not having bought anything at Lower Marsh market. She was behaving like a zombie. Now she'd have to go to Tesco's. Pushing her way through the crowd of people who were trying to get on the bus as she tried to get off, she headed up Acre Lane.

She wasn't sure if it was Bill. She hid behind the flower display, and watched him between the containers of spring bulbs.

It was against his principles, buying asparagus out of season, but Bill fancied some, even if it was imported from Peru. He delved to the back of the box, discreetly snapping off the woody stems, and placing the tender stalks in a plastic bag to be weighed at the checkout. It was one of those stupid acts of rebelliousness he fell prey to when he was out of sorts; and he was out of sorts.

Alison was in the aisle behind Bill's. She smiled when she saw what he was up to. She looked down at the exotic fruit on display in her aisle: papery Sharon fruit and star fruit, figs four for a pound, dates, paw paw. She saw just what she wanted, picked it from the shelf and walked up behind him, dropping it into his basket. Bill grinned when he saw it was her; she looked different. He looked in his basket. Two mangoes, their orange skin freckled green, nestled yin and yang in the cellophane-covered tray. Attached to the cellophane was a Day-Glo label. 'Eat Me, Keep Me,' he read.

74

Morning Glory

'If you want to call by, your portrait awaits, ma'am.'

Alison deleted Sam's message and rang her. 'How does it look? Are you pleased with it?' she asked.

'Aha, not telling. You'll have to come and see for yourself.'

'OK, I've just got to nip to the post office, and then I'll call round. See you in about half an hour.'

It was cold outside when Alison walked to Ferndale Road, and although only four it was already starting to get dark. The traffic moved slowly round the crane that raised two men up to the level of the lampposts along the High Street, securing the Christmas lights. So soon, Alison thought. There's still weeks to go, surely. She joined the snake of people queuing in the damp warmth of the post office. She placed her small parcel on the scales.

'First class, please,' she said.

'Get the kettle on, I'm parched,' Alison said into Sam's entryphone when it buzzed her in.

'Where are you?' she asked, opening the door to the living room. The lights were switched off; the Christmas lights on Electric Avenue twinkling through the window. 'Sam? Hello?' Alison shouted, feeling for the light switch.

It is a large print, about sixteen inches by twenty. By some magic that Alison doesn't understand, Sam has altered the background. What had in the studio been the plain white backdrop is now filled with a single, deep indigo bloom of Morning Glory. Stretched wide open, droplets of dew still on the petals, striations of paler, purple-blue drawing out from the deep, dark hollow of its centre to the delicate edge of the flower. And in front of it Alison, dressed in a black suit and seated on the wooden chair. Her legs slightly apart, her bare feet planted squarely on the floor, her toenails painted turquoise. Both arms raised, she holds a length of hair in one hand and a pair of scissors in the other. Her jacket is unbuttoned, and underneath she is naked, one bare breast exposed. Like an Amazon. All around her feet lie tresses of blond hair.

Alison smiles as she studies the photograph of herself staring unflinchingly into the camera's eye. She is reconciled; she likes the skin she is in, and it shows.

75

Inheritance

Jo picked up the package that was waiting on the table when she returned home from school. It wasn't her birthday, and it was still weeks till Christmas. But all the same, there it was. A small parcel about six inches by six inches by six inches, wrapped in brown paper and tied up with string, her name written clearly on the front in sepia ink: 'Miss Jo Vine'. At the top left, a little label in red: 'Fragile!'

Hannah watched Jo untie the knots, tear off the brown paper, and discover the small box inside. Lifting the lid, Jo peered in at the crumpled blue paper and pulled it free. After a few seconds' consideration she announced, 'I think it's a bit of a tree.'

She lifted the knotted fist of fern from the tissue paper. It fitted comfortably on her palm.

Hannah remembered immediately. Remembered herself and Alison both baffled at first, but then delighted by this ball of roots and wizened fern that opened; woke up and stretched, as if yawning after a long sleep.

She takes a saucer from the dresser and walks across to the sink. Switching on the tap, she says to Jo,

'Prepare yourself for a little miracle.'